AN INDISCREET SUITOR

"Margaret!" The earl captured her hands again. "For a generally sensible woman, you say the most extraordinarily foolish things!"

"Gi—I mean your lordship—" A blushing Miss Tolliver was finding it difficult to speak. "You forget yourself."

"Giles," he corrected her, kissing her fingers again and watching her face in enjoyment as she tried to pull her hands away. His hold remained firm.

"Your lordship—"

"Giles." He seemed to have a particular interest in the tip of her middle finger, rubbing his lips against it in a way that made the normally capable Miss Tolliver feel rather—well—incapable.

"Giles!" she said. "people in the room."

"Yes," he agreed approval and releasing them. "I have noticed th why they are still here!"

KIDNAP CONFUSION

KIDNAP CONFUSION

Judith Nelson

WARNER BOOKS

A Warner Communications Company

Warner Books, Inc.
666 Fifth Avenue
New York, N.Y. 10103

A Warner Communications Company

Printed in the United States of America

First Printing: September, 1987

10 9 8 7 6 5 4 3 2 1

Chapter
1

It was one of her brother Charles's infrequent missives that set Margaret Tolliver thinking. He had sent it to inform her that he was making some slight adjustment in his investment of her funds, and from long experience she knew that the letter was informational only; Charles did not require or want her opinion on what he planned to do.

Usually one to disagree with her brother in most matters, Margaret approved of his actions in this instance. She knew without doubt that he was as careful in the investment of her funds as he was in the investment of his own. And if, as Margaret suspected, that came less from familial affection and more from his tendency to look upon his sister's inheritance as his own, she was not unduly troubled. Charles had a profound dislike of dispensing with an unnecessary penny, and it made him a frugal agent in the long-term investment of her money.

If that were not the case, Miss Tolliver would have had no compunction about removing him as her agent; since he was such an expert manager of money, and since he was her only brother and moreover one of whom she was fond—although, she admitted fair-mindedly, it was much easier to be fond of Charles when she was in Yorkshire and he in London—she let him continue with the investment of her funds as he had done before she came of age.

At first Margaret scanned the letter rather absently, wondering how it was that she and her brother had both learned their penmanship from the same tutor, but Charles had never mastered a hand that could be described as more than a scrawl. Her interest sharpened, however, when she reached the next to the last paragraph in which he informed her that he would be traveling to Somerset a few days hence, to visit a friend, and would not be back in London for three weeks.

He gave his direction, but Miss Tolliver was not interested in that. What interested her was the information that he would be gone from the London house—information she digested as she folded the letter again and tapped it against the table.

For several weeks now, Miss Tolliver had been experiencing a feeling of ennui and a vague dissatisfaction with her life in Yorkshire—a life that usually pleased her greatly. It was Providence, she decided, that was sending Charles from London at a time when a trip there was just what she needed. She knew that now; Charles's letter made her realize that a chance to renew her acquaintance with those few persons among the *ton* whose opinions she valued, and to refurbish her wardrobe, see the capital's sights, and be part of the city's bustle would soon set her to rights, and make her happy to return in due time to her tranquil living. And if her return to Yorkshire coincided with her brother's planned return to London—well, she would call it Providence again and not a disinclination to spend time in her stuffy brother's presence.

Never one to argue with Providence when Providence happened to please her, Margaret smiled and began to make plans.

At supper that evening Miss Tolliver announced that she would be traveling south to spend several weeks in London. Her Aunt Henrietta, with whom she lived, was vaguely surprised—but Miss Tolliver knew that all of her aunt's reactions tended to be vague—but agreeable, declining Margaret's invitation to join her by remarking comfortably that she and Lazarus, her pet rooster, were more inclined to country life.

"Country worms are more tender than city worms, you

know,'' Aunt Henrietta told her niece wisely, ''and Lazaurus has a great fondness for them.''

Miss Tolliver, who did not know the merits of country wrigglers over their city brethren, but who was much too polite—and too little interested—to say so, merely smiled and nodded. Over time she had grown used to her aunt's unusual pet—especially after Henrietta had, by means unknown to Margaret, house-trained him—and to her aunt's predilection for starting the statement of many of her own ideas or partialities with ''Lazarus says . . .''

If Aunt Henrietta and Laz did not care to stir from home, they had Margaret's blessing. She was relieved to find that her aunt had received the news of her trip so agreeably, and turned her mind to other things.

So it was on the next day that Margaret informed her staff of her impending departure, and by Thursday morning she had nothing left to do but to pack those few of her belongings that she did not care to leave to her maid to handle, to kiss her aunt good-bye, and to be on her way.

It was during the last-minute packing that the most peculiar thing happened—peculiar at the time—and, when she thought about it later, even more peculiar.

Margaret had just placed her pearls in her valise, and was reaching for the ivory-backed comb and brush set that was a special gift from her late father when Lazaurus, who moments before was sitting quietly beside Aunt Henrietta on the bed as both of them watched Margaret pack, suddenly rose and jumped onto the valise, pecking at her pearls as if in an effort to pull them out again.

An astonished Miss Tolliver picked him up at once and placed him on the floor, admonishing him with a ''Lazarus, you silly bird! Whatever has gotten into you?''

The rooster, ignoring her words, ruffled his feathers and crowed loudly, making a great deal of noise in his throat and stretching and scratching in a way that she did not understand, but that seemed to affect her aunt greatly. Without ado Henrietta rose, lifted the valise, hurried with it to a cupboard, and stuffed it inside.

Miss Tolliver was even more astonished.

''Aunt Henrietta!'' she exclaimed. ''What are *you* doing?''

Her aunt gazed at her in surprise. "Why, I'm putting your valise away, my dear!"

"*What?*"

"I'm putting your valise away. Lazaurus does not think you should go."

"*What?*"

Miss Tolliver's voice rose in spite of her best efforts to control it, and Aunt Henrietta's surprise deepened.

"But Margaret," her aunt said reasonably, "Lazaurus just told you. And Lazaurus knows."

With a tolerant smile Miss Tolliver removed the valise from the cupboard and, holding it tightly, asked just what it was that Henrietta thought Lazaurus knew. Her aunt informed her it was not a thought, it was a certainty—Lazaurus was telling them that if Miss Tolliver took this trip, *something*—and, from Aunt Henrietta's tone, it was an obviously ominous something—untoward would occur.

"It's fate," Aunt Henrietta said simply. "It never does to tempt fate, Margaret. I'll help you unpack."

No, Miss Tolliver said, she would not.

With a great deal of firmness—and a disciplined grip on her laughter—she informed her aunt that she, Margaret Tolliver, considered herself mistress of her own fate, and that she was not going to cancel a trip to London on the advice of any bird—not even a bird with such high intelligence as her aunt's rooster.

"Chances are it was only a cramp in Laz's leg, anyway," she said with a smile, opening the valise slightly to drop in a bottle of her favorite scent, but not letting go her hold of it just in case the other woman should reach for it again.

Aunt Henrietta's headshake was grave. "Lazaurus knows," she repeated. "Fate is riding on this trip to London."

Miss Tolliver assured her she had her own fate well in hand, and with a quick kiss to her aunt's faded cheek, and an equally quick pat on the back for Laz, she went gaily out of the room and down the stairs, cloak over one arm, valise in the other. When she arrived in London without mishap, she tolerantly shook her head over her aunt's musings, and thought no more about it. Until later.

Fate, grinning widely, sat back and waited.

* * *

On the same day Margaret Tolliver felt she was taking charge of her own fate, fate was having a grand time meddling in the life of someone then unknown to her.

Standing in front of the mantlepiece, his collar growing tighter by the moment, Gillian Manfield was miserably aware of the loudness of his waistcoat. He could feel the hue grow in gaudy brilliance as his brother's eyes surveyed him, and casting wildly about for something to distract Giles, Gillian wondered what had ever possessed him to think the Willowdale library the most pleasant room in the house.

True, he and his younger brother Peter had spent many contented hours there by the fire, watching Giles and John maneuver across the polished chessboard the ivory pieces that were their grandfather's, their talk ranging from politics to war to the classics. It had seemed a warm room then, relaxed and inviting. But as Gillian surveyed it now, those memories were forgotten.

And as Gillian met Giles's interrogating gaze and glanced hurriedly away, it occurred to him that the library was filled—positively overflowing—with faults heretofore undisclosed to him.

The mantle clock, for one thing—it ticked much too loudly. Casting a covert look at his brother, Gillian was amazed that Giles could ignore it. For the first time, he wondered seriously about his brother's hearing.

And that portrait of Father, hanging above the fireplace— Gillian wondered if Giles recognized how accusingly the old man seemed to stare at his third son. Almost as accusingly as Giles . . .

Gillian gulped, and directed his glance to the windows. He thought it odd that such large, light spaces could cast such harsh shadows on his brother's already dark features. And the carpet, Gillian decided, was positively shabby! He wondered how Giles could prefer a worn antique from Persia to something bright and new of good English wool.

Gillian risked another glance at his brother and unconsciously tugged at his cravat, his eyes sliding hurriedly to the floor-to-ceiling bookcases as he wondered if the hundreds of books thereon had been dusted in years. It was a question that would have filled Mrs. Cross, their industrious house-keeper, with righteous indignation had she heard it.

It was when his gaze transferred to the ceiling that his mind was recalled by his elder brother and guardian.

"Well, Gillian?"

The tone was quiet, and quite calm, but Gillian, accustomed as he was to his brother's voice through long experience, heard the implacable note behind the simple words, and flushed.

"Well," he parroted, one booted toe unconsciously digging into the old carpet as he sought words to cast his latest indiscretion into a more appealing light. None came.

"Well," he repeated, his eyes rising to the other man's. "You see—" He stopped suddenly as he stared at his brother, and a note of indignation crept into his voice. "I must say, Giles, that I didn't expect to find you at Willowdale in the midst of the season!"

"No." Giles permitted himself a small smile as his intense gray eyes raked the young transgressor. "Nor did you expect to find John. Nor Peter—"

"Well, maybe Peter—" Eagerly Gillian entered upon that caveat, hoping it would divert his brother's thoughts. It did not.

Giles raised one languid hand and, in a bored voice, requested his brother to spare him a list of what he did not expect.

Hopes blighted, Gillian's face fell as Giles smiled again. "What I want to know, Gillian, is why Willowdale is now graced with your presence in what is—unless my lamentable memory fails me—the middle of the term?"

Really, Gillian told himself, he would have to speak to his tailor about these much-too-tight shirt collars, and he gave the offending article a tug, to Giles's unexpressed amusement.

"Oh, it isn't your memory that's at fault, Giles," Gillian responded, striving for cheerfulness. "It never is."

More feeling than he intended crept into the last sentence as Gillian recalled the times out of mind when Giles's memory had been painfully accurate, and as his thoughts were writ plain on his face, his eldest brother's lips curled again.

"But the fact is—well—" Gillian grinned placatingly at his brother. "The fact is, I've been rusticated, Giles. But only until the end of the term!"

"I see." Only Giles's iron will prevented his smiling at the happy insouciance of Gillian's "only until the end of the term." Gillian, relieved that the truth was out, looked much like a spaniel who expects to be kicked but hopes for a pat as he cocked his head to the right.

"I knew you would," Gillian burst out. "You're a great gun, Giles! Truly top of the trees—"

The "great gun" held up one strong hand, and when it had stopped his brother's impetuous words he turned it over to carefully regard the well-manicured nails before him. "And would there be a reason for this—ah—enforced return to the bosom of your family?"

The hopeful look died on Gillian's face and his gaze, too, seemed riveted on his brother's fingers.

"Well—" Gillian began, taking a hasty turn around the room before he came to stand once more before Giles's desk. A distracted hand pulled again at his high shirt collar and cravat, then moved upward to wreak havoc with his carefully arranged curls. It didn't seem fair to him, and his voice was aggrieved as he told Giles he thought it monstrously bad of all his brothers to be at their ancestral dwelling when he had expected them to be safely out of the way in London, and had thought he might just pop into Willowdale and stay there quietly until the term ended, with no one the wiser.

"I see."

Giles, sixth Earl of Manseford, was apparently satisfied with the state of his right hand, and turned his attention to his left before his eyes rose to his brother's face.

"Do you know, Gillian, I believe I must make you my compliments," he said. "The breadth of your optimism has previously been hidden from me. Do you mean to say that you honestly believed you could spend the rest of the term rusticating here and no one—not the dean, not the servants, not one of your numerous loose-tongued young friends— would tell me of it?"

Gillian's face fell further. All his energies had been devoted to reaching Willowdale without his brother's knowl-

edge; he hadn't thought beyond that. Now, staring across at
Giles, the enormity of his folly hit him. Sooner or later—
and usually sooner—Giles knew everything about his younger
brothers' lives. It was one of the most disagreeable things
about him. Gillian wondered if Giles knew *that* . . .

A quick glance up made him color and look hastily down
again. No doubt. Giles knew.

"I believe, Gillian, that you were about to tell me what
led to your rustication."

"Well, no," Gillian replied candidly. "I really wasn't. I
don't think you're going to enjoy this, Giles, and I don't
wish to distress you—"

Giles inclined his head gravely and thanked Gillian for his
consideration. "However," he said in the dry tone that
pricked the hair on the back of his brother's neck, "I shall
endeavor not to be completely unmanned by your disclosures."

Gillian regarded him closely. "You're bamming me, aren't
you, Giles?"

There was another grave shake of his brother's head and
an earnest request that he proceed. Sighing, Gillian sank
into a chair by the fire and plunged into his tale. His eyes
darted now and then to see what effect his words had on
Giles, but for the most part he fixed them firmly on the
fingers he was clasping and unclasping before him.

It would have cheered the young culprit considerably had
he known that in one instance, at least, he wronged the earl.
Giles *did* enjoy Gillian's story. He enjoyed it completely,
understood that once a pig wandered into Gillian's orbit it
was only a matter of time before disaster followed, and even
sympathized with the youthful spirits that, "a trifle above
par," as Gillian so delicately put it, hatched the merry
scheme. But none of that showed in his face as he listened
carefully to Gillian's involved explanation of how he and
some chums decided to put a pig to bed in the quarters of
one of the stuffiest nobs at Oxford.

"And then, of course, when we actually got into his
room, and just happened to see his nightshirt lying there—
well, it seemed a shame to put the pig to bed naked—"

A strangling sound from behind his brother's desk made
Gillian look up quickly to find Giles regarding him in

fascination. "Are you going to tell me—that you put the man's nightshirt—on the pig—" Try as he might, Giles could not make the words come out quite steadily and Gillian, mistaking the tremor for anger, blushed vividly and hung his head. Giles bit his lip and, when he had once again mastered his voice, bade his brother continue.

"Well, there isn't much else," Gillian said, busily regarding his clasping and unclasping fingers. "We left the window to Old Perkins's bedroom open so we could watch, and when we heard him coming, we bolted out that way— he has lodgings on the first floor, you must know—and I must say, Giles, that even if we probably shouldn't have done it—"

"*Probably* shouldn't have done it?" his brother repeated.

Gillian sighed. "All right. *Even though* we shouldn't have done it, I do wish you could have seen it, for it truly was a capital sight. As soon as Old Perkins opened the door, he startled the pig, and of course the animal squealed and jumped up, and seeing the open door headed for that, knocking Perky down as he passed through his legs. And if you've ever seen a pig racing across the commons in a nightshirt, with a nightcap falling over one eye, well, Giles—" The grin on his face disappeared as he saw his brother's raised eyebrows.

"And for this the Dean rusticated you until the end of the term?"

"Yes." Gillian sighed heavily. "Shabby of him, wasn't it?"

"My dear Gillian, it is a wonder to me you weren't sent down permanently. Of all the cork-brained schemes—"

Gillian, who had no turn for learning and who wouldn't mind being sent down permanently, said reasonably that the bagwig was laughing as loudly as anyone when he saw Old Perky chasing the pig for his nightshirt, and only sent Gillian down when the nob demanded that he do something...

He risked another glance at his brother's dark, impassive face, and waited in miserable silence for Giles to pass judgment. He did not have to wait long.

"I believe, Gillian," his brother said, the well-manicured fingers tapping together as they rested on his lean stomach,

"that I cannot concur with the Dean that it would be wise
for you to be separated from your studies for the remainder
of the term. In fact—" he held up one hand for silence as
Gillian tried to tell him that being separated from his studies
would not bother him at all—"I believe that it is important
now more than ever that you learn to apply yourself to those
topics for which you were sent to Oxford. And if I am not
mistaken—again, my most lamentable memory—you will
find, dear brother, that 'pigs' and 'annoying the nobs' are
not among them."

Giles appeared almost absentminded as his eyes swept his
head-hanging brother before continuing. "I am sure, Gillian,
that if we ask him nicely, John will be only too happy to
tutor you several hours each morning to keep you in form
for your return to school. That, coupled with what I am sure
is going to be your quite avid interest in the knowledge
found in this library—shall we say, an avid interest to be
pursued six afternoons each week—should put you in top
form. Don't you agree?"

His bored glance rested again on his younger brother,
whose mouth was opening and closing at an alarming rate as
he goggled at Giles. Gillian, who had planned to spend his
rustication riding and hunting, found many thoughts chasing
themselves around in his head, and gave vent to the chief
among them.

"John?" he repeated in horror, starting up out of his
chair. "*John? To lecture and scold past bearing—six days a
week? Confined to the library?* Really, Giles—"

His brother had risen also and now stood behind his desk,
one hand trifling with the papers that lay there as he gazed
down his nose at Gillian. Even in the midst of his anger,
Gillian could not help noticing how well the buff coat his
brother wore fit his frame, or how his elegant neck cloth
was so clearly tied with a mastery quite above that of the
more common gentry,, his brother included. Gillian sighed
enviously, and wondered again why Giles, usually the best
of brothers, would not share the secret to tying that elegant
cravat.

Giles, following his brother's gaze and knowing how that
young man's thoughts wandered, recalled him gently to the

topic with a dry "Really, Gillian. John is just what you need."

"Oh, no!" Hastily Gillian attempted to disabuse his brother of that misconception. "John is never what I need! He'll prose on forever, and he'll frown and he'll scold and he'll tell me that I shouldn't be putting pigs in nobs' beds—"

"Well . . ." Giles interrupted.

"Oh, I know I shouldn't!" Gillian burst out. "But when John says it, there's nothing I want to do more than go out and find another pig and another nob and do it again! Don't you understand, Giles?"

Giles understood perfectly but refused to say so. "John," he replied, each word deliberate, "is an excellent scholar, and definitely the most sensible of my brothers. You won't find John sitting in the rain, catching a chill, in the hopes of seeing if fish rise to the surface or dive deeper into the pond when the water comes down, as Peter does; nor will I find him betting on cockroaches"—here Gillian had the grace to blush—"or backing geese races in the park, as you have been known to do."

"Oh, well—I daresay—in my younger days . . ." Gillian began.

"Six weeks ago, Gillian?" Giles's mobile eyebrow lifted, and the sinner hung his head again.

"But *John*," Gillian moaned, and Giles frowned.

"If John agrees to help you, you may count yourself fortunate, Gillian. We will speak no more about it."

The thought that his next elder brother might not agree caused Gillian's face to brighten slightly before it fell, and he cast himself into a chair again. "Of course he'll agree," he said sulkily. "John always does what you say. We all do—"

Giles's brow lightened suddenly, and he smiled. "If that were the case, Gillian, I wish that sometime in the past twenty years it had occurred to me to tell you not to put pigs in other people's beds! Or in your own, for that matter!"

Gillian's grin was reluctant but, encouraged by Giles's smile, he suggested that it really wouldn't be so bad if he postponed his studies until the next term. "I'll tell you what," he offered, inspired, "I'll take young Peter in hand and endeavor to get his mind off his studies. You know you're always saying he needs to get out more, and—"

The earl agreed that it was true, and wondered aloud how he came to have one brother with no interest in books, and another who wished never to be without one. Gravely he thanked Gillian for the nobility of his proffered sacrifice, but declined to allow him to martyr himself in that way.

"Oh, it wouldn't be so terrible, Giles," Gillian began, but Giles interrupted.

"Yes, Gillian, it would. It would be very terrible indeed. Because next term, when the thought of doing something disgraceful pops into your head—as I have no doubt that it will—I fully expect the memory of the alternative form of study available to you to deter your more outrageous activities." With a nod he dismissed the young man in front of him, and a disgruntled Gillian made his way to the library door. He paused there, hand on the knob, to turn and stare at his eldest brother.

"I would just like to say, Giles," Gillian said with a reproachful dignity that sat awkwardly on his young shoulders, "that I expected better from you."

Giles raised his eyes from the papers on his desk, and smiled agreeably. "Certainly, Gillian. Say whatever you wish."

"Hmmph!" A disgusted Gillian slammed out the door and stomped down the hall. Had he stopped for a moment, he would have heard laughter echoing behind him as Giles gave himself up to the feelings that had for the last half hour been threatening to overcome him.

"A pig and Old Perkins," Giles gasped, sinking into the worn leather chair that had been his father's. "Sore temptation, indeed!"

Chapter

2

His temper not assuaged by that single slamming, an angry Gillian rushed pell-mell down the hall and through the mansion's front entrance, savagely pushing the large oaken doors closed behind him. His mood was in no way improved when those doors, too heavy and too well-hinged to partake of any intemperate action, swung shut with no more than a muffled thud.

Knowing himself extremely ill-used, Gillian strode toward the stables. Every feeling was offended, and all punishments meted out by the unfeeling Giles in past years crowded his mind. The problem, he told himself, completely forgetting the action that had led to the recent confrontation with his brother, was that Giles still considered him a child while he, Gillian, was more than ready to take his place alongside Giles as a leader of fashionable men. He knew that Giles at twenty already had established his place at the forefront of the *ton*, but now that Gillian had attained that age, Giles did not seem to consider it of any great moment.

That Giles had been a very different person from Gillian at twenty the younger man did not recognize; all his thoughts were focused on the infamy of his brother's actions, and the growing conviction that he must, somehow, convince the one he had always considered the best of all brothers that although his role as stern and guiding guardian might do very well for young Peter, Gillian's advanced age moved him far beyond it.

And if Giles really thought that Gillian was going to give his head to John for daily washing—well, neither Giles nor John had better assume that! It was foolish for Gillian to keep up with his studies, he told himself; very few of the people he wished to ape were known to have distinguished themselves at Oxford. In fact, when he put his mind to it, he could not think of one.

Oh yes, his brother John had distinguished himself, but Gillian could think of nothing more deadly dull than to pursue the career in politics so dear to John's heart. No, he was thinking about the sporting men in the world—the real men who knew how to drive to an inch, tossed off daffy with the denizens of the ring, and shot regularly at Manton's.

Visions of his eldest brother rose before his eyes, and he paused uneasily. In all fairness, he must admit that Giles has done well—the dons had even liked him. But it wasn't that Giles was a *scholar*—no, no, Gillian liked his brother too much to call him that . . .

Although not at the moment, he reminded himself, and his brow darkened. How *could* Giles? How could such a gentleman of the first order come so high-handed over a younger brother whose only wish was to imitate all the more daring of his adventures?

That his brother, learning from experience, might be trying to steer Gillian away from such adventures never occurred to him; his "Damme, it's not fair," came through gritted teeth as he reached out to break a branch off the nearest bush, and switched it angrily against the other shrubbery along the path.

"What's not fair?" a gentle voice inquired to his right and he stopped, startled, to meet the inquiring eyes of the youngest and certainly the least censorious of the late fifth Earl of Manseford's sons. Peter surveyed him closely, and his eyes grew sympathetic. "Really gave it to you, did he?" he asked, and Gillian sighed.

"He was bloody unreasonable," Gillian pronounced, joining Peter on the bench in the quiet alcove between the stables and mansion, and gazing gloomily out at the spacious gardens so loved by their late mother.

The bench had been a favorite resting spot of hers; Gillian

could vaguely remember finding her there after her early morning rides, or in the heat of the afternoon when she sat, stitchery in hand, directing the gardeners in whatever was her newest project. Peter had no such memory, for as the youngest of the four boys, he had been only one when their mother died. Yet ever since his brothers had mentioned in passing that the bench was once a prized location for the late Lady Manseford, Peter was often to be found there, his dreamy brow resting in one hand while with the other he turned the pages of whatever he was reading.

It never ceased to amaze Gillian that Peter, who despite his delicate constitution was an admirable brother, neither stuffy like John nor occasionally censorious like Giles, could be so bookish. In fact, John said half-grudgingly and half-proudly that young Peter would one day show them all the lead as a scholar. Gillian had been indignant on his younger brother's behalf the first time John said it, but when he realized Peter was coloring from pleasure and not anger, he had let it pass, tolerant of so odd an ambition in one to whom he was genuinely attached.

That Peter was not now at Eton was due to the severe bout with influenza he suffered shortly before term started, and not to any disinclination on his part to study. He had begged Giles to let him return to school despite his weakened condition but Giles, who remembered their gay and laughing mother with tenderness, and who saw much of her in this, her smallest and weakest son, would only say that he might study with a tutor when he was stronger, and return to school the second term, if he was completely well.

To that end Peter dutifully gulped the nasty potions left by the doctor who had treated him all his life, and studied daily with the Willowdale vicar. It was one of the pleasures of his existence when he could engage either Giles or John in a discussion of the works of Homer or Dante.

He never engaged Gillian in such discussions, of course; he was a sensitive child, and had long ago discovered that Gillian, so adept on the hunting field or in the boxing ring, or taking out a gun for a day's sport, was bored almost to tears by anything that would-be man-about-town referred to disparagingly as "using the old bone box." Peter knew that

to engage Gillian in any serious discussion would be a
struggle that would not produce any insight past the rudi-
mentary notions Peter had passed long ago.

Now it was with an air of quiet gravity that Peter closed
his book and eyed Gillian consideringly. "What did he
say?" he encouraged as Gillian sat, one hand disarranging
his hair and the other drawing slashes in the dirt with the
branch he'd so recently detached from the Willowdale
shrubbery.

"He said it's a wonder the bagwig didn't send me down
permanently," Gillian said indignantly. "And all because of
a little pig! Which isn't nearly the same as a dancing bear,
which Brandon wanted to use, but we couldn't find one..."
His voice trailed off, and his eyes were alight with enthusiasm as he turned toward his brother. "Wouldn't that have
been something, though? I mean, I can certainly understand
why one shouldn't use a dancing bear, because it would, I
would imagine, break the bed if one wasn't careful, but
still—"

Peter, older in many ways than this brother eight years his
senior, was quite young enough to appreciate the picture
conjured up by such words, and grinned back. "I wish I
could have seen it," he said with a sigh, and Gillian, moved
by the wistful note in his voice, forgot his own troubles long
enough to straighten up and clap him on the shoulder.

"You will someday," Gillian said in the bracing voice
that those who are never ill use when confronted by those
who often are. "One of these days, when you're up at
Oxford yourself, you'll cut some ripe old tricks. You'll
see."

Peter knew it would never be so, but the fact that Gillian
could think it pleased him, and he smiled. "I'll never be as
up to snuff as you, Gilly," he said, and his brother, agreeing
modestly to this tribute, forebore to remind him that now
that he had attained the advanced age of twenty, it was no
longer appropriate to refer to him by a childish nickname.

"Well..." Gillian adjusted his cravat and brushed a
speck of dust from his coat sleeve. "It ain't because you
ain't pluck to the backbone, old man. It's just that you don't
have the turn for it like I do. That's all."

Peter agreed with due solemnity and only a slight twinkle in his eye that he did not have Gillian's talent for getting into scrapes and then, seeing that Gillian was on the way to feeling quite sorry for him, turned the conversation by asking if Giles had had anything else to say.

Almost restored to his natural buoyancy before this reminder of his pressing problems plunged him to the depths again, Gillian's chin sank and he leaned forward to rest one arm on his knee while the other resumed making circles in the dirt with the branch he still held.

"He said I have to study with John." Both face and voice were morose as Gillian's eyes followed the branch back and forth.

"But that will be fun!" Peter was excited by the thought. "John knows so much—"

"It would be great fun for you," Gillian interrupted with a heavy frown as, straightening, he tossed the branch away and turned to face Peter, "but it's pure torture to me. And Giles knows it. He said if he punishes me severely enough, perhaps I'll remember it next time I'm up at Oxford and will have a care about cutting up such prime larks." He reflected a moment, and sighed again as his basic honesty made him admit that his eldest brother might be right. Then his indignation rose. "But I think condemning me to John is excessive!"

Peter, who saw much wisdom in Giles's decision, was moved by the long face before him, and put a hand on his brother's shoulder.

"Maybe it won't be so bad—" he offered.

Gillian shook his head mournfully, prophesizing that when he wanted to read the *Turf Guide*, John would badger him with *The Iliad*. "And probably in Greek!" he added, the horror in his face showing how deeply the thought affected him. "Lord, Peter—I can't understand it in English! And you can lay wagers that when I'm ready to depart for a prime prizefight, John will descend to drag me off to look at some moldy old ruin where somebody or other signed something or such."

His face assumed lines of deep mourning. "I tell you, Peter, it doesn't bear thinking of."

Peter, who could only think of it wistfully, politely refrained from saying so and patted Gillian's shoulder again. "Maybe Giles will reconsider."

Gillian grunted. "About the same time Old Perkins forgives me!"

Peter grinned, hoping for an answering smile on his brother's face. None came. After several moments surveying the dejected figure before him, Peter asked hesitantly if Gillian would like him to sit in when John held his enforced classes.

The thought made Gillian brighten briefly, for it occurred to him that once his two most scholarly brothers became engrossed in one of the subjects so dear to their hearts and so foreign to him, he would be speedily forgotten and could at the least allow his mind to wander. At the most he might be able to slip from the room when discussions grew particularly deep or heated. Then he thought of Giles, and sighed heavily.

"Giles probably wouldn't allow it," he said, scuffing one booted toe in the dirt. "And besides—most of the time I'd still have to listen to you!"

Peter accepted this stricture meekly, aware that the words had not come out quite as Gillian meant them.

"If this isn't just like Giles!" Gillian complained. "And besides—" He turned toward Peter and regarded him with a slightly furrowed brow. "What are you all doing at Willowdale, anyway? I thought you'd be in London for the season!"

"Not me!" The thought of a season in society appalled shy Peter, and Gillian nodded.

"Well, no, not you. I knew you'd be here. But I knew you wouldn't carry tales about my—ah—Little Misunderstanding—" Peter, who had a whimsical turn of mind, wondered if Little Misunderstanding was the pig's name, but said nothing, gratified by his brother's left-handed compliment to his loyalty.

"But it never occurred to me that Giles would be here," Gillian continued, turning over the question that still puzzled him. "Now if you were sick I'd expect it—" He broke off to peer closely at his brother. "You aren't sick, are you?"

Peter shook his head and said that he felt he was improving every day. Relieved of that worry, Gillian nodded and continued his cogitations.

"That's why I didn't repair to the London house, you know," he said conversationally. "There's nothing I would have liked better than to take a toddle on the town, but I was sure that was where Giles would be. And John! Of all people, I most wanted to avoid John . . ." He chewed on his lower lip as he tried to understand where his plans went astray.

"What are they doing here, anyway?" he demanded plaintively.

Peter shook his head, disclaiming hesitantly that he did not know. Immediately Gillian was alert, demanding to be told what his younger brother was hiding. Peter fired up instantly to say that he was not hiding anything, and it was several moments before he could be induced to tell Gillian anything at all, his disclosures coming only after Gillian begged pardon for even suggesting it, and assured his young brother that he knew he was a right 'un to be depended upon in all circumstances.

"Well . . ." Peter's brow wrinkled as he seriously considered whether he should proceed. "I'm not sure I should tell you, because it's something I overheard, and I don't perfectly understand it . . ."

His voice trailed off and Gillian, trying to forebear, could not contain his impatience. "Well?"

"I don't know if I should tell a confidence . . ."

"Now, Peter." It was Gillian's man-of-the-world voice, the one that ranged from avuncular to downright grandfatherly, and Peter grinned again. "It's not a confidence when it's not told to you as such. It would be one thing if someone confided in you and asked you not to tell; but when it's just something you overheard in passing . . . Dear boy, that's not a confidence. Really!"

"Are you sure?" Peter cocked his head to one side, and Gillian applied himself energetically to the task of convincing him. At last Peter conceded, reiterating that he wasn't sure what it was all about. He didn't understand it completely,

but several days earlier he had overheard John telling Giles
that no woman was worth being blue-deviled over forever.

"Giles said it was no such thing," Peter continued,
conscientiously. "In fact, he seemed quite amused that John
could think it was. He said he had planned to return to
Willowdale to see about some matters and to visit me long
before Vanessa left his protection. But John seemed skeptical, and when I later asked John who Vanessa was, he got
very red in the face, and told me that listening in where I
wasn't invited was much more in your line than mine,
so . . ."

The full import of his words hit Peter and he stopped,
red-faced, to look at his brother, but Gillian hadn't heard the
last part of his artless speech. Instead, that young man of
fashion was sitting bolt upright, one hand clasped to his
forehead and rumpling his hair with the other.

"Vanessa!" he exploded. "Of all the—well, well, well!"
Peter was regarding him inquiringly, and Gillian leaped
from the bench to stride back and forth before the younger
boy, his arms gesturing wildly in the air. "Do you mean that
Giles is so up in the bows because his latest ladybird found
herself another nest? Because if you do—"

Trying gravely to sort out the implications, Peter was
moved to interrupt. "No," he said slowly, "I think Giles is
punishing you because he thinks you shouldn't put pigs in a
nob's bed. I don't think it really has anything to do with this
lady . . ."

"Lady!" Gillian snorted the word, amused by Peter's
naïveté. "Ha! You wouldn't call her that if you'd heard some
of the tales I have . . ." He stopped suddenly as he became
aware of Peter's inquiring gaze, and coughed. "Well, no,
that's of no moment now . . ."

He threw himself down on the bench beside Peter and
continued to think out loud. "But I wonder . . . You don't
really think . . ." He found those inquiring eyes upon him
once more, and since Gillian did not want to explain the
entire situation in order to garner his younger brother's
opinion, he rose and took another hasty turn before planting
himself before Peter again. Gillian could not understand
why as rapacious a light-o'-love as the fair Vanessa would

leave the protection of as generous a benefactor as his brother, but if she had, and if, as John suggested, that was what was making Giles so testy, and it would—and indeed, it appeared that it very much would—complicate Gillian's life, he saw only one thing to do.

"We shall have to get her back," Gillian decided, and Peter stared at him in surprise.

"Get who back?"

"Vanessa, of course!" Gillian was quite as surprised as his brother.

"But—" Peter's mouth opened and closed several times. "She's not ours to get!" The protest ended almost on a squeak, and Gillian waved it aside.

"You can bet she's already regretting leaving Giles's protection," Gillian predicted confidently, and he was right. The lady deeply regretted it; but as Gillian's eldest brother could have told him, the leaving was not of Vanessa's choosing. The Earl of Manseford, usually the most easygoing and generous of benefactors, had a marked disinclination for sharing his mistress's favors, and when that lady's greed led her to cross the line to favor another gentleman also, Giles bade her a generous but quite final adieu. That he had no intention of explaining this, or any of his other affairs, to his brothers was also final—and to be regretted later.

Peter, far from seeing the brilliance of Gillian's pronouncement, seemed much inclined to argue, even going so far as to say that if Giles did appear a trifle distracted, Peter would lay it down to boredom much more than the missing Vanessa. Gillian stared aghast at his dubious brother.

"No, really, Peter!" Gillian protested. "You can't have considered! Giles always used to be the best of brothers—"

"He still is!" Peter interjected hotly; Gillian tactfully paid him no mind.

"—so if he suddenly cuts up stiff over a Trifling Prank" —here Peter was heard to murmur he thought the pig's name was Little Misunderstanding; Gillian ignored that, too—"there must be something bothering him. We know it's not money; he's as rich as a nabob. And it isn't you or John—you're too good and John is too stuffy to get into trouble. And Giles didn't know about me until today, so that's not the reason he left London in the middle of the season. Don't you see? It must be a woman. And if it is life without his actress that is making Giles as sulky as a bear, we have to get her back for him. To make his life happier. To make our lives easier. Don't you agree?''

Peter did not, and said so. Gillian ignored him as he continued, ''It shouldn't really be so hard. Giles isn't a bad-looking man—for his age. And he *is* rich.''

It occurred to neither of them that Giles, who one month earlier had celebrated his thirty-fourth birthday amidst the conviviality of friends who wished him many more by downing a great many glasses of Blue Ruin in his honor, and suggesting a round of boxing the watch just for old time's sake, would appreciate the ''for his age'' rider. Not even a whisper of the thought troubled them. Giles had stood as father to his brothers for so many years that they quite thought of him in that role; in truth, since Peter was three, Giles was the only guardian he had known.

Gillian had a better memory of their real father, but he, too, had long ago transferred his filial affection to the sibling left in charge by the late earl's untimely demise.

''I don't know...'' Peter continued to voice his objections, his head moving from side to side in expression of his doubts. ''From what Giles said, and the way he said it, I don't think it's the actress he is missing. I still think he's bored, and that's why he's here.''

''Bored!'' Astonishment gave way to disgust as Gillian stared at his younger brother. Gradually he drew himself up, and with all the worldly sophistication inherent in one who has seen twenty summers, gazed down his nose at Peter. ''You silly gudgeon! That's how much you know! Bored? A man who is a member of the Four Horse Club, shoots at Manton's, boxes at Jackson's, and is a member of Brooks's? A man anxious mamas look for at Almack's, a man positively courted by hostesses who beseech him to come to their musicales or card parties or drums?'' The picture he was drawing so appealed to Gillian that his eyes lighted, and his arms began to wave as he continued, almost to himself. ''Oh, I admit, the latter might wear on a man after a time—who wants to be sitting in someone's drawing room when you could be out at a really good mill?—but still—'' His eyes seemed to focus on Peter again, and he shook a finger at him admonishingly. "I'll tell you what it is, Peter! You're burying your head too much in those musty old books about the past! You don't understand us men-about-town today, let me tell you!"

A more hotheaded young man might have informed Gillian at that point that his self-promotion to "man-about-town" would be debated in many quarters—particularly those of their brother John—but Peter's sweetness of temper was inherited from the mother he did not know, and he forebore, only sighing as Gillian, who had long ago convinced himself, if not his listener, continued.

"No," Gillian said, "if Giles is at Willowdale in the middle of the season, there has to be another reason, and the reason has to be Vanessa. But it's not like Giles to nurse a broken heart over such a lightskirt, is it?"

He turned anxiously to Peter and that young man, unable to imagine Giles nursing a broken heart over any lightskirt at all, shook his head. Vigorously.

"So perhaps he really cared for her," Gillian continued, thinking out loud. His romantic nature flamed at the thought of his eldest brother in the throes of unrequited and quite ineligible love. "But that's absurd! Isn't that absurd, Peter?"

A goggling Peter agreed that it was absurd.

"So maybe his pride was pricked a bit," Gillian continued as he took another turn around the bench. His recent treatment at his brother's hands made him say with feeling that he really wouldn't consider that such a bad thing, but upon reflection he added that it couldn't go on. "After all," he said, "a stern Giles is hard enough to live with, but a blue-deviled Giles is impossible! I don't see anything for it, Peter! We'll have to find the actress and bring her here. From what I know of Giles and the ladies, once they're face-to-face, all will be forgiven."

"It will?" Peter fairly gasped the words and Gillian, looking down at him, could see the doubt written in his eyes.

"Of course!" Completely convinced himself, Gillian had

no trouble making a case for his brother. "They probably just had a quarrel—one of those lover's things—and she flounced out. Giles, of course, is too proud to go after her. Well, we can fix that!"

"We can?" Peter's weak echo captured his foreboding.

"Oh, yes!" The seeds of a plan took root in Gillian's brain, and his eyes sparkled. "We'll just have to go get her and bring her here!"

"We *will*?" The last word was a squeak, and Gillian looked at Peter in surprise. "I mean—" Peter floundered, playing nervously with the frayed edges of his book as he stared at the brother in front of him. "I mean—if they had a quarrel—I mean, Giles might not want her in his ancestral home—I mean—I mean—*what if she doesn't want to come?*"

Neither the question of whether Giles might like his brothers driving his lost lightskirt up to the family mansion, nor whether she might not wish to be reunited with the earl had occurred to Gillian, and since he had no answer for either, he waved them both aside. "Don't worry," he said in a tone meant to be reassuring, but which conveyed a little of his own apprehension at the unwelcome thought, "she'll want to come. And if she doesn't—why—we'll just have to kidnap her!"

"*Kidnap* her?" Peter gasped, sitting bolt upright as he stared at his brother in horror. "Well, really, Gilly!"

The use of his childhood nickname at that particular moment damped Gillian's plans slightly, but he made a quick recovery. "It will be romantic, once she is reunited with Giles," Gillian said, waving one hand in his best negligent man-of-the-world manner. "I wouldn't be at all surprised if she thanks us for it later."

"You wouldn't?" Peter wondered if his voice would ever lower again as, with eyes wide, he tried desperately to recall if there was any history of mental instability in the family.

"No." Gillian waved the negligent hand again. "Females love that sort of thing."

The number of females in Peter's acquaintance was admittedly small, but as he reviewed them in his mind, he could not discover one who would love it at all. In fact, those who did occur to him seemed much more likely to box a would-be kidnapper's ears. He tried to make some of that clear to Gillian, but his brother only dropped a reassuring hand on Peter's shoulders and gave the thin form he found there a squeeze.

"Your problem, Peter my boy, is that you have a great deal yet to learn about women," Gillian said.

Peter sighed, knowing it was true. But he couldn't help wondering if there might not yet be a thing or two still missing from Gillian's education, as well.

Chapter
3

Peter had great hopes that something would soon divert Gillian's thoughts, but in such hopes he indulged his optimism too far. No word of a mill reached Gillian's ears, and no idea of taking out a gun or pole for an afternoon of hunting or fishing occurred in Gillian's mind, so that young man was left at his leisure to weave plans for what he was coming to think of as his Grand Scheme.

Few Grand Schemes are simple, and how he was to accomplish his goal occupied Gillian's mind for the rest of the day and into the evening. He was lost in a brown study when he joined his brothers for supper, sitting so silently through the meal and ignoring both his plate and his brother John's homily on the folly of Gillian's youth so thoroughly that Giles's mobile eyebrows rose, and he stared intently at his second youngest brother. A glance at Peter, fidgeting slightly as he looked from Giles to Gillian and back again, confirmed Giles's suspicions that it was more than the enforced retreat from Oxford that troubled Gillian's mind, and he was moved at last to call his brother to book, inquiring mildly if Gillian had anything to say to John's forceful description of his character and manners.

"What?" Suddenly aware that Giles had repeated his name several times, Gillian noticed that all his brothers were staring at him, and he dropped the fork he'd held suspended in air for the past several minutes as he looked wildly around. "What?" he repeated.

"I was wondering if you'd care to respond to what John has been saying," Giles prompted.

"Should I?" Both tone and glance were cautious as Gillian looked from one elder brother to the other.

John frowned heavily. "One would almost think you hadn't been attending to a word I said, Gillian."

Giles gave a slight smile. "One could almost be certain of it."

"Well . . ." Gillian looked hopefully toward Peter, seeking enlightenment. "What do you think of what John has been saying, Peter?" he asked.

Peter shook his head and answered in his soft voice, "I think he has been saying some terrible things about you."

"Oh!" Gillian straightened and stared in surprise at John. "Well, I must say . . . I think that's terribly shabby of you! And I'm glad I *wasn't* attending. Because it's certainly no concern of yours what I do, *Johnny*."

The use of his nursery name was certain provocation and John, whose face grew more austere with each of Gillian's words, stiffened alarmingly at the end, remarking in his most repressive tones that it must always be the concern of one family member when another runs amok.

"Not amok," Peter protested, distressed.

John shook his head and corrected him. "Amok," he said firmly. "And I will thank you—" his full glance, and a very quelling glance it was, was directed toward Gillian— "to refrain from childish retaliation, and to have some respect for your elders and your betters."

"Well!" Gillian's abstraction was completely gone and he girded for battle, his eyes sparkling with anger, his color heightened. "Of all the arrogant, pompous, stiff-necked . . . You may be older than me, *Johnny*, but you really can't take credit for that; it was up to mother and father; but when it comes to my betters, you certainly aren't—"

Both men were leaning forward, and the lapels of Gillian's coat seemed in imminent peril of taking a bath in the gravy on his plate when Giles's voice interrupted them.

"I wonder," the earl said softly, "if I am the only one here who is conscious of the difference between conduct befitting a gentleman's dining room and that found in the city's back alleys.''

Peter gulped, and watched in fascination as Gillian's and John's heads swiveled toward their eldest brother. John, whose color was almost as high as Gillian's, clamped his lips together and picked up his wineglass, tossing off the burgundy found there before stiffly begging pardon, and adding as if he could not stop himself, ''But that young jackanapes makes me so angry—''

''Well, he started it!'' Gillian fired up.

Giles interrupted both, addressing himself to Peter. ''I wonder,'' he said in the deceptively mild tone that sent chills down his youngest two brothers' backs and made John shift slightly in his chair, ''what on earth possesses them to think I am in any way interested in self-justifications?''

Gillian and John had no answer to make, and Giles seemed to expect none. He smiled encouragingly at Peter and picked up his fork to continue his meal. When the momentary silence had lengthened into minutes, Giles asked what Peter and the vicar were studying at present, and Peter's stammered reply that it was the works of Homer made Giles cast back in his mind for some of the nuggets gleaned in his own readings of the poet. This encouragement soon had Peter pelting him with questions, and at length John, who could not resist adding his own weighty wisdom to any scholarly discussion, forgot his stiffness and was drawn into the conversation. Gillian, listening resentfully to what might as well have been a foreign tongue, ate sulkily and entertained himself with visions of the day when both Giles and John would find themselves on the sharp end of Gillian's tongue, with no ready comebacks or sarcastic repartée. He told himself that if he were Giles, he would take a very dim view of a second oldest brother prosing on forever to a third oldest brother, and he—if he were the earl—would tell John to mind his own business and be quick about it.

That thought draped a wistful smile across his face and Peter, watching Gillian out of the corner of his eye, shifted uneasily. From long association Peter knew that Gillian did not entertain many ideas, but those he did have he clung to with remarkable tenacity. John said it was because Gillian had so few ideas, and that left so much room for those that did plant themselves in his brain to grow, but then, Peter thought fairly, John *would* say that. Although thoroughly devoted to each other past and future, in any present John and Gillian could not scrape through more than half an hour together without rubbing each other quite wrong. Peter wondered why that was, and sighed heavily.

He looked up to find Giles eyeing him with a slight smile and, when John's attention was diverted, Giles winked. It was ever so slightly, but he winked. Peter smiled back, and felt the better for it.

There was little question, Peter thought reflectively a week later as he sat on horseback in a small grove of trees, feeling the mist turn into rain and watching the day's gray turn to slate as the hour grew later, that he would find himself in this situation. His eyes were fixed on his brother Gillian's dark bulk before him, and off to his side he could hear their lifetime friend and long-time groom, Jem, sighing heavily. Both Peter and Jem had been drawn into Gillian's schemes since they were barely breeched; there had been little doubt that it would happen this time, too.

It wasn't that Peter hadn't tried to avoid their present situation. When Gillian came to him, eyes alight, to outline The Grand Scheme, Peter had been first stunned and then indignant that his brother meant to draw not only Peter but also their hapless servant into what Peter could not help but think of—with a great shudder—as a sordidly clandestine affair. He protested when Gillian said he planned to send Jem to London to discover where the fair Vanessa was, and if she had any travel plans in the near future.

"It isn't that I wouldn't *like* to go myself," Gillian assured him, misunderstanding Peter's protest, "but with Giles so up in the boughs at the moment, I don't think this is the time for me to be nipping off to the city. Do you?"

His "do you?" was so hopeful that Peter, in assuring him that it would not do at all, could not then make him understand why it would not do to send Jem, either. Gillian only looked at him blankly, and said that if he could not go,

of course Jem must, because Giles was sure to notice if
Peter was absent for a few days...

Peter, who had no intention of popping off to London,
gazed at him in amazement, and was frustrated to find his
argument that the earl would not like to find either his
brothers or his servants off spying on actresses—or anyone
else—falling on deaf ears. Gillian, whose mind was on
other things, said absently that neither of them had any
intention of telling Giles about it, so there was nothing to
worry about. When Peter represented to him that Giles had a
way of finding out such things, a flicker of uneasiness
crossed Gillian's face, but he waved it aside with an airy
"Well, Giles isn't totally omniscient, you know!"

Peter, who kept his own counsel, wasn't so sure...

And so now they sat, as they had sat all day, waiting for a
coach carrying the fair Vanessa to pass them on the Great
North Road. Gillian had been ecstatic when Jem returned
from the city, only slightly the worse for wear from his first
great venture alone, beyond the influence of the earl's head
groom, to report that after much nosing about, and lavish
dispersal of the coins Gillian had so thoughtfully provided
him with, he had discovered that the actress was to leave the
city on Thursday next and travel by the Great North Road
toward York.

What's more, Jem informed them proudly, he had, as
Gillian had straightly instructed him, discovered at which
house the actress's coach was likely to hire outriders, and
had gone there straightaway to bribe said outriders into
being late with their defense of the coach if, say, three
masked ruffians should accost it next Thursday. Such action
had been judged necessary after Peter raised the sticky
question of what they would do if those escorting Vanessa
did not understand they were kidnapping her with the best
of motives, and decided to fire at them.

It had taken Gillian much thought and considerable hair
pulling to find an answer to that one, and Peter had almost
believed they would be saved by this seemingly insurmount-
able problem. But when his brother bounded to his feet with
the words "bribe them!" on his lips, Peter sighed, exchanged commiserating glances with Jem, and said nothing.

The only thing that still caused Gillian concern about those accompanying Vanessa was the unwelcome information that Jem had stopped short of bribing the coachman.

Jem's long-term acquaintance with the redoubtable Mr. Peeks, who had been in the fifth earl's service and was growing old in the sixth's, bordered on such awe that the very thought of even approaching such an august personage with a dishonest scheme made his ears ring with the boxing he was sure they would receive. Nothing Gillian could say, not even the thousandth assurance that not all coachmen were as honest or as upright—or as big—as Mr. Peeks, could move Jem from his stand. In the end Gillian shrugged philosophically and assured Jem and Peter that the coachman would be so busy with the horses that he would have no time to reach for a gun; the more he said it, the more he believed it himself.

And so, beyond wishing aloud once or twice a day that Jem had brought himself to offer the unknown driver a bribe, he thought no more about it.

And now, Peter thought, as he sneezed and sighed, here they sat, with Gillian still sure that his Grand Scheme would work, supremely unaware that Jem and Peter had considered it doomed from the beginning. Peter hoped that Giles wouldn't be too angry when he found out that Gillian hadn't been in the library all day, as instructed before John and Giles rode out with word they'd return late evening. That thought made him sigh again.

In one thing Peter was wrong; Gillian was still not confident that his scheme would work. In fact, he had entertained grave doubts for the last hour, and the increasing damp and Peter's sneeze merely confirmed that somehow— by means unknown to him—the plan had gone awry.

The first check to his enthusiasm had come hours earlier when, fresh for their adventure, they'd mistaken the coach of an octogenarian for that of the actress. The elderly gentleman, instead of showing the proper fright and concern of one whose coach has just been stopped by masked ruffians, waved his cane at them and advised them to come on, shouting he'd show them a little of the home brewed.

Gillian's bow and explanation that it was a misunderstanding—they were looking for another coach—made the
old man crow, "A misunderstanding, is it? You're right, it's
a misunderstanding, you miserable highwayman! No doubt
you're looking for easier pickings, you cowards! That's
what you are—cowards, all of you! Coachman, drive on!
Drive on, I say!"

With a resigned wave of his hand Gillian sent the stunned
coachman on his way, listening in gloomy silence as the old
gentleman, gleeful in victory, hurled insults at them until his
coach was lost to sight by a curve in the road.

Peter had wanted to go home then, followed by the ready
Jem, but Gillian assured them it couldn't happen again, and
they had, with a great deal of heavy sighing and painful
glances of resignation, settled in to wait. Their ears perked
at the sound of each coach, only to find that it was the mail,
or the stage, or a carriage with a crest that they knew could
belong to no actress. Jem's suggestion that she might be
riding in a gentleman's crested coach drew Gillian's scorn,
but now, as dusk turned to darkness, he wondered woefully
if Jem was right and they had missed her.

Then, too, as Gillian sat miserably huddled in the frieze
coat Jem had borrowed for him, he was beginning to have
second thoughts about the brilliance of his scheme.

Back at Willowdale, with the sun shining brightly and the
ever-present optimism of youth, it seemed such a simple
thing to abduct a woman from the King's road and bestow
her upon an older brother who, eternally grateful, would
realize once and for all that Gillian was more of a man to be
reckoned with than Giles had ever thought.

But now, sitting in the rain and hearing young Peter
sneeze behind him—how he hoped Peter wouldn't take cold;
he couldn't forgive himself if that happened, and he was
pretty sure Giles wouldn't forgive him, either—he was given
to doubt.

What if, the unwelcome thought presented itself—not that
it was likely, but what if—Giles didn't want the woman
back, as Peter had so stoutly asserted when Gillian first
broached the subject to him? Not that Peter knew anything

about women and the ways of the world, he assured himself hurriedly, but just suppose . . .

Or suppose the woman didn't want to come. Suppose she really did hold Giles in aversion. He couldn't force her to stay with his brother, no matter how it would alleviate his own problems. No, that wouldn't be right . . .

And another thing, he told himself glumly, ten to one she wouldn't even appear. Perhaps Jem's information was all wrong. Perhaps she had changed her plans.

The muffler wound round his head to prevent his being recognized—another donation from Jem's shadowy friends— was scratchy, and as it grew damper the smell of sweat and onions, strong enough when the muffler was dry, grew almost overpowering. Gillian tried not to breathe too deeply.

Yet heavy as the mufflers were, they could not disguise another sneeze from Peter, and Gillian was about to turn and say they might as well go home when the sound of horses' hooves, traveling at a steady pace, reached his ears.

"This has got to be it, men!" he whispered, feeling rather than seeing Peter and Jem also prick up their ears. "Now remember, just ride at them and brandish your pistols, and we'll have it done in no time!"

Gillian had decided earlier that he was the only one who could be trusted to fire, and had thoughtfully removed the ammunition from his brother's and Jem's pistols. His plan was to ride down on the carriage from the front, creating a commotion and startling the coachman so that he would draw up. When he moved cautiously out of the trees, the failing light showed there was no crest on the carriage door, a piece of good luck that so delighted him that he neglected to note what Jem saw after his employer began his ferocious charge, Peter thundering gamely behind him. There were no outriders.

"Mister Gillian!" Jem cried, spurring his horse after them. "Mister Gillian!"

Gillian did not hear the frantic call, so intent was he on his task; nor did Peter, whose hat had slipped down over his eyes and ears, and who was busy trying to keep his horse moving while he strove to remove the hat's blinding influence. In that he succeeded too well, for the hat flew off, displaying his golden curls.

The first part of Gillian's plan worked brilliantly. The sight of three horsemen galloping down upon them did indeed cause the coachman to draw his horses up and to sit gaping at them before he realized the full attack. Then, shouting "Highwaymen!" he thrust the reins into the hands of the slack-jawed groom goggling beside him, snatched the old-fashioned blunderbuss that individual held in a nerveless grasp, and let fly.

The sound startled the lady in the coach, and she was about to stick her head out to inquire what was happening when she heard an indignant young voice shout, "Here, I say! You could hurt someone with that thing!"

Gillian swerved around toward Jem, who came panting up behind him. "I thought you paid these people off—" he began angrily, and had not yet started to assimilate Jem's hurried warning that there were no outriders, only a coachman and groom, and this must be the wrong coach, when the man with the blunderbuss let fly again, and Gillian felt a thud and violent stinging in his right shoulder. As he slid to the ground before the horrified eyes of his brother and Jem, one thought remained uppermost in his mind.

"I told you," he whispered. "Should have...bribed...the coachman..."

Chapter

4

The occupant of the carriage was recovering from the shock of gunfire at such closes range when the carriage door was wrenched open and a pale young face, its eyes large with horror, peered in.

"Miss Vanessa!" the boy gasped. "You must help! It's Gillian—my brother! He's—he's—"

The face disappeared as quickly as it had appeared, and when Miss Margaret Tolliver stepped down from her coach it was to see, in the fast vanishing light, that the owner of the frightened face was even now kneeling over a still figure in the road. Another young man—almost a boy himself—stood nearby, staring in stupefaction at the still figure. The reins of three horses hung loosely over his arm.

Miss Tolliver's brother's coachman, busy on the box, was reloading his old gun with enthusiasm, the stories he could spin of this night already forming in his mind. He had just pointed the gun gleefully at the kneeling figure when Miss Tolliver commanded him sharply to put up. He gazed down at her in astonishment.

"But Miss—" he gasped. "Highwaymen—"

One mobile eyebrow quirked as Miss Tolliver gazed up at him. "Highwaymen?" she repeated, her voice scoffing the word as she gazed at the scared young faces turned toward her. "Children dressed up for play, more like."

She moved toward the huddled trio in the road and knelt beside the youngest member, watching his anxious if inexpert efforts to staunch the flow of blood from his unconscious brother's shoulder. In a few moments, Margaret took matters into her far more capable hands, asking if the young man kneeling and the other standing had handkerchiefs that she could use to pad the wound before binding it up. Peter's hand dived into his pocket and pulled out a large, white linen square, which he quickly handed to her. After several moments of searching, Jem produced a bedraggled specimen that she declined with a polite word and only the tiniest quirk of the lip. With a sigh she turned slightly and a ripping sound was heard as one of her petticoats gave its ruffle for the nursing cause.

"Now, Miss—" By this time the coachman had clamped his jaws together and climbed down from his perch, leaving the reins in the hands of the hapless groom he castigated as a regular jackstraw. He advanced upon them, incensed, talking all the time. "Miss Tolliver, whatever be you about, helping those nasty varmints after they tried to hold us up? Think you, do, and come away from there this instant. What would your brother say if he could see you?"

"A great deal, probably," the lady replied. Her voice was dry. "But I wish, Johns, that you would rid yourself of this disagreeable habit of thinking I would care at all what my brother says."

Drawing himself up, the coachman was about to launch into a catalog of what the absent Sir Charles Tolliver expected of those who drove his sister about, and how those who did not live up to Sir Charles's expectations could expect to suffer, but his speech was cut short by the boy kneeling in front of him.

"Miss—Tolliver?" Peter said dazedly, and Margaret glanced up from her work to smile at him.

"Yes," she said, extending a hand. "Margaret Tolliver. And you?"

Peter made an automatic and really quite credible bow, for one kneeling in the road, and stammered his name even as he continued to stare at her, forgetting he held her hand until, with a twinkling eye, she told him gently that if he were quite done with it, she would like it back. Then he startled and blushed, dropping said appendage as if it were

hot, and spoke again. "But—" he said, "you . . . you—"
There seemed to be a large lump in his throat, and he had to
swallow twice before his words emerged around it. "Aren't
you Vanessa, the actress?"

"Actress?" The coachman harumphed the word loudly
into the night, and Peter turned to stare at him before his
eyes, aghast at their mistake, returned to the woman before
him.

"My dear boy," Miss Tolliver said, her amusement
evident, "do I *look* like an actress?"

It was not a question that had occurred to him before, so
for the first time Peter surveyed her carefully. Under her hat
he glimpsed a lock of light brown hair, and blue eyes and a
mouth that even now brimmed with laughter. She was
dressed neatly, and with propriety, and although Peter was
not an expert on female garb, something told him the cut of
her garments and the tone of her voice and the way she
carried herself bespoke very much the lady.

"Oh, no," he groaned, glancing down at Gillian still
lying quietly in the road. "What have we done? Oh no, oh
no, oh no!"

He rubbed his forehead hard, as if to clear it of the vision
in front of him, and Miss Tolliver felt her ever-ready sense
of humor threaten to overtake her as she continued her
handiwork on the unconscious Gillian.

"But—" Peter seemed to feel an explanation was necessary as he looked from her to Gillian to Jem to the frowning
coachman and back to Miss Tolliver again, but he didn't
know where to start. "But you're supposed to be—I mean,
we thought—we've been waiting all day to—"

Peter was searching for the right words but Jem, thinking
him lost in his sentences, came helpfully to his rescue.
"We've been waiting to kidnap the actress," Jem explained
soberly, nodding at Miss Tolliver as if it were an everyday
occurrence.

Miss Tolliver was visibly startled, and stared at the boys
in front of her. "Kidnap?" she gasped, wondering if her
first impression was wrong.

"Kidnappers!" The coachman fairly stumbled over the

word, then turned on the run to retrieve his gun from the coach.

"No, no, not really!" Peter was appalled by the turn of events, and tried to correct them. "You don't understand!"

Jem, finding his help had not been appreciated, tried to excuse himself with "But that's what Mr. Gillian said—"

"I know," Peter assured him, clearly harassed. "Only it wasn't really kidnapping! It was more like . . . borrowing. For my brother!" The last was said to Miss Tolliver, who regarded him in bemusement. She looked doubtfully down at the still figure in the road, and Peter's confusion grew. "No, no!" he said. "Not that brother. My other brother!"

This time her glance, more doubtful still, turned toward Jem. It took him several moments to assimilate its meaning, but when he did so he informed her so earnestly and with such force that not only was he not a brother, he also wouldn't have an actress, no ma'am, no way, no matter what anybody—including Mr. Gillian, who he'd lay down his life for—said. Now completely mystified, Miss Tolliver's glance returned to Peter's face.

"For my eldest brother!" Peter said desperately. "The Earl of Manseford."

Miss Tolliver started, and her perplexity grew. Although not acquainted with the earl, she knew of him, and what she knew did not correspond with what was being told her. "Your eldest brother—the Earl of Manseford—sends you out to kidnap *actresses*?" Try as she might, she could not keep her voice from rising on the last word, and Peter shook his head hopelessly.

"No," he said. "No, he doesn't. He doesn't even know— and I think he'll be most angry when he finds out. I can't explain it all now. But please, Miss Tolliver—my brother, Gillian. Is he going to be—I mean, he's not going to—"

Her bandaging now completed, Miss Tolliver turned herself to what she considered the next most important task, that of soothing the worried brow before her. "I take it the poor unfortunate now lying at our feet is your brother Gillian," she said as she rose, and Peter's mute nod confirmed her suspicion.

"Well, no," she said, smiling down at him, "he most

assuredly is not going to die. At least, not if we stop chitchatting here and get him out of this drizzly damp and into someplace warm where he can be seen by a doctor. I've bound the wound for now, which will considerably slow his loss of blood, but the ball in his shoulder must come out, and the bleeding must be stopped completely. Tell me, is your home near here?"

Peter's headshake was mournful. "Almost twenty miles," he whispered, and Miss Tolliver suffered a slight check. She had hoped for better but, after frowning over the information, she said with great composure that that was too far to carry the injured Gillian in his condition, so they must find a closer shelter. Jem and Peter gazed toward her expectantly, and she realized with a rueful shake of her head that in the last several minutes she had become not their victim but their hope. With a wry inward smile she thought of how only an hour earlier she had been bored, and thinking of her dinner.

Well, this was a bit more than she had hoped for when she wished for something to ease her boredom, she thought. Aloud she said, "I believe we passed a small inn several miles back; I think it would be best if we took him there, and had the doctor sent for immediately. Johns, you must help us get this young man in the carriage, and—"

She got no further for Coachman Johns, who had been regarding her with a fulminating eye, was outraged by the very suggestion. "Miss Tolliver!" he cried. "You cannot mean that you are going to help these—these—"

Inwardly she wondered why her brother hired servants as tiresome as he was himself, but outwardly she produced her best smile. "Now Johns," she said. "It was all a mistake!"

But that, Johns told her, he would not and could not allow it to be. He informed them all that he didn't care what anyone said of earls or such, it was a mighty havey cavey business when earls sent their brothers out to hold up honest coaches—or to abduct actresses, for that matter—not that he believed it for a minute, not he . . .

Miss Tolliver let him talk on as she directed Jem to take Gillian's shoulders, and she and Peter each held an arm.

Johns, still scolding, reached for the unconscious man's feet, and carried him to the coach.

"And another thing," the coachman said as he watched Miss Tolliver arrange Gillian's head more comfortably on the coach seat, "Don't be thinking I'm going to take you to that tavern we passed several miles back because it ain't seemly, nor no fit place for a lady, and if you think I'm going to do what Sir Charles wouldn't like, you're wrong!"

There was a dangerous gleam in the lady's eye as she said, "I have told you once, Johns, that I wish you would rid yourself of this notion that I am ruled by my brother. I do not wish to tell you again."

Johns's shoulders went back and his jaw clamped tight, and Miss Tolliver, moved by the small moan issuing from Gillian's lips as he shifted slightly on the carriage seat, tried to forestall the coming argument by taking the offensive. "And if you have a better idea of where we might take this poor young man, I would be happy to hear it," she said with some asperity. "If not—"

To her surprise, Johns did have a better idea, and he was only too happy to say so. He did, he told her austerely, have a cousin who ran a small inn about two miles off the main road only a mile north of them. And although it wasn't the type of place she was used to, he said with a sniff, it was at least clean, and not filled to overflowing with the cutthroats he was sure inhabited the tavern she had suggested they apply to for help.

Miss Tolliver told him at once that his was a fine idea, and they were all in his debt, which he so heartily agreed with that he grew quite mollified, and when she suggested he climb back onto the coachbox and drive them to said inn immediately, he did so with only a minimum amount of grumbling and dark predictions. Quickly she adjured Peter to climb into the coach and prop his brother up as best he could; she told Jem to follow the carriage with the boys' horses; then she herself stepped into the carriage and collapsed back against the cushions to contemplate what the evening had brought her.

Chapter
5

To the nervous Peter, half-kneeling beside his brother in an attempt to keep Gillian from sliding off the seat, the trip to the inn was interminable. Even after Miss Tolliver put her head out to order the coachman to "spring 'em," they continued to move at a far from clipping rate, the coachman having his own very precise idea of what speed it was proper for Sir Charles's sister to travel the King's roads.

Miss Tolliver, biting her lip in vexation, smiled at Peter and apologized. "I really am sorry," she told him. "Usually I travel with my own servants, but while in London my coachman fell ill, and since it was important that I return home immediately, my brother made me the loan of his. The groom is his, too. Johns is a good man, basically, but he is totally deaf to anything I say that he doesn't want to hear. Please don't worry. We'll be at the inn shortly, for all his lack of cooperation."

Peter forced a smile and nodded, his eyes traveling to Gillian's face as the unconscious brother moaned. Peter looked back at Miss Tolliver for confirmation.

"You're sure that Gillian w-w-will..." The words betrayed a shiver in his voice, and Miss Tolliver peered sharply through the dusky interior of the coach in an effort to see his face. When she reached out a hand to feel his forehead she found it hot and dry, despite his soaked raiment, and she whisked up the lap rug at her feet and threw it around his

41

shoulders, saying half-scoldingly, but with real concern, "My dear, you're ill yourself! Why didn't you tell me?"

Peter gave a shivery shrug, trying to disclaim. "It's nothing," he said, wondering why Gillian seemed blurry. "The merest cold . . . I've had the influenza . . ."

There was a buzzing in his head, and he tried to think around it. "But you, ma'am," he continued, "you said you have to go home immediately, and we are detaining you. Perhaps after you have taken us to the inn you can continue your journey. We don't wish to be a burden to you . . ."

Concentrating on the words and not his voice, Peter was unaware of the muffled accents in which his speech emerged. Miss Tolliver heard them, and her concern increased. Once again she stuck her head out the window and ordered Coachman Johns to "spring 'em!"

This time there was an added note in her voice that made him increase the pace—albeit slightly—and she settled back against the cushions, telling Peter soothingly that there was really nothing that required her immediate attention at home; in fact, the only thing that had made her wish to leave London immediately was being in her brother's company several days while Sir Charles sat grumpily home with the gout.

That drew a muffled chuckle from Peter, interrupted by a sharp cough, and as he leaned his head onto the cushion, he told her drowsily that his eldest brother was a great gun, not at all given to gout, and . . . and . . .

His voice drifted off, and Miss Tolliver reached out to feel his forehead again, frowning heavily as she did so.

Her brother had darkly predicted that her precipitous behavior would end her in a bumblebath. That was not unusual; Sir Charles regularly predicted that her actions would lead her into trouble. But this time—through no fault of her own, Miss Tolliver told herself, if you ignored Johns's grumblings that a wise lady would have driven on—it appeared that Charles might be right. At least, a little bit right.

If she wasn't to be troubled actually, she foresaw several days of inconvenience and sighed. Miss Tolliver felt she had been more than a little inconvenienced lately.

At twenty-eight, Margaret Tolliver was a soft-spoken, quick-witted woman who knew that in the eyes of her family and London society, she long ago had been consigned to the shelf. It was not a thought that troubled her unduly, and for most of the year she resided near York with her vague Aunt Henrietta, who kept a pet rooster named Laz. His true name was Lazaurus, because, as Aunt Henrietta was want to tell anyone who would listen, she had, if not raised him from the dead, brought him back from as near to it as a rooster can get without crossing over when, as a young chick, he had followed a string of ducklings bravely into a pond only to discover, too late, that chickens do not swim.

Henrietta, who saw it happen and liked his style, saved him from his watery grave and called him Lazaurus until her sister Delphinia enlisted the rector's aid in declaring the naming of the rooster sacrilege. The ensuing battle—which Miss Tolliver liked to think of fondly as the Sisters' Holy War—ended only when Margaret, tired of the claims and counterclaims to her attention made on behalf of the chicken, suggested that in public he be called Laz, and in private Henrietta could call him whatever she wished—perhaps even adding an extra vowel in the rooster's name so that no one would think his christening a biblical reference. Her Aunt Delphinia had not thought it enough of a compromise— Aunt Delphinia's idea of a compromise being that everyone agreed with her and did things her way—while her Aunt Henrietta had acquiesced with a sniff and a murmured "If I remember, dear; you know how absentminded I am . . . ," and Miss Tolliver knew without a doubt that all bursts of absentmindedness would come in Aunt Delphinia's presence. She also knew her Aunt Delphinia knew it too, and was relieved when that dame gathered up her belongings and went to live with her long-suffering son and his equally long-suffering family.

Miss Tolliver's recent trip to London and the reason she was on the road when these absurd children stopped her carriage was the result of one of her rare bouts with boredom and one of her equally rare whims to update her wardrobe and visit those few friends she still enjoyed among the *ton*—people with whom she could laugh and talk freely without being asked "Whatever do you mean, Margaret?" or censured as a bluestocking. That, plus the information that her brother was to be from town, visiting friends in the country, had made her pack her trunks, kiss her aunt good-bye, and head south.

It was with real dismay that she found Charles ensconced in his library upon her arrival in London, and the discovery that it was gout that had canceled his plans to visit friends filled her with foreboding. Yet she was already there, and she reasoned optimistically that they might contrive to rub along pretty well together for a week or two if she were out a great deal and Charles amused himself with his favorite sickroom pastime of running his staff from one floor to the next in search of an item he could not do without until it was presented to him, at which time he had no further need of it, and sent them off looking for another.

Such was not to be. Although Charles encouraged her with great fortitude not to think of him at all, but to go on her own merry way, enjoying herself while he stayed home and suffered, he made it apparent that each time she walked through the front door she stabbed him in the heart with the knowledge that his sister—his only sister, too—was immune to his hour of pain.

The evening she stayed home with the noble hope of taking his mind off his troubles had done Charles no good, either, for not only did Margaret have the temerity to best him in a game of chess, but also her suggestion that they play piquet for a pound a point truly shocked him. His shock was increased when, to show her a lesson, he agreed to the bet and lost heavily.

His censorious comment that cardplaying was not a skill befitting a lady made her laugh, and when he inquired stiffly who had taught her to play, she laughed again and told him it was their father "oh, years ago, when he was convalescing, and needed a partner."

"Father was not always a good influence on you, I fear," Charles began in the austere tone that would have made their late father itch to box his ears. Then another thought occurred to him. "Do you mean," he demanded, "that you haven't—that you haven't played since Father died—"

Usually quick-witted, Miss Tolliver was slow this time to catch his meaning, and said reflectively that it had been several years before their father's death that they had played their last hand. Charles fairly goggled at her, mentally computing that their father was dead three years, and several years before that would mean they had last played . . .

"And you *beat* me?" he demanded.

Miss Tolliver always forgot that one of her besetting sins—as many of her older relations were quick to tell her, the females baldly and the gentlemen in more indirect ways—was that she never learned to pander to the male ego, whether that of her relations or other men. Her Aunt Delphinia said it was a much worse sin than being dowryless on the marriage mart.

So when Charles, who considered himself a fair cardplayer, sat staring at her with his eyes wide and his usually ruddy color heightened, Miss Tolliver did not even consider telling him it was luck. She smiled quite engagingly and said, "But dear Charles, you know you cannot play!"

Charles, who knew nothing of the sort, stiffened and glared at her. "I beg your pardon?"

Miss Tolliver's eyes twinkled, inviting him to share the joke. "Charles, really—it was Father who taught me, and you know you never could beat Father—"

"Father was a man, adept at the game," Charles said huffily. "You, on the other hand, are a woman—and the luckiest woman I ever met."

Miss Tolliver rose, slightly bumping the stool on which Sir Charles's afflicted foot was resting. Neither brother nor sister could swear it was an accident.

"My dear Charles," she said, bending to kiss his cheek before retiring for the night, "if I were the luckiest woman you ever met, *surely* I wouldn't have been blessed with a brother as chuckleheaded as you!"

"Chuckleheaded!" He was sputtering the word as she moved softly across the floor. "A fine way to talk to the head of the family! Do you know what your trouble is, Margaret Marie? I'll tell you what your trouble is—"

The soft click of the door behind her made it impossible for Miss Tolliver to hear what Charles considered her trouble as she moved down the hall, and she smiled softly as she walked up the stairs to her room. That she had seriously irked him was apparent by his use of her full name. Yet she was fairly confident that he would have forgotten it tomorrow because Charles, although trying in the extreme, had too good an opinion of himself to permit his carrying a grudge against someone blessed only with a female mind— and a sister's female mind, at that. He was always only too happy to tell anyone who would listen his ponderous and detailed opinions on the natural superiority of men.

Charles had been like that since they were children, and Margaret had no doubts that his view of her as his little sister had not changed drastically since he was nine and she three. She wondered why he clung to such shadows of who they had been so obstinately, when their father had set quite another example by encouraging her to go her own way— "within the bounds of what's allowed, Maggie; always within the bounds," he used to tell her—and had helped her find the bounds when she was likely to stray over them. Upon her father's death three years earlier, she had felt as if she'd lost her best friend, and having never met a man she considered his equal, she had left off looking after a time.

None of this was known to anyone but herself, of course, and certainly not to Charles. So when she met him at the breakfast table the next morning it was with the expectation of finding him somewhat sulky, but recovered from the worst of his anger. In that expectation she reckoned without his gout.

Charles had, as he told her with much sighing and heroically almost-stifled groans, spent a terrible night. The gout that confined him to bed and chair had kept him awake half the night, and when Charles, usually the heaviest of sleepers, was awake, he also was inclined to brood. Her recent victory at the card table gave him plenty to brood about, and dwelling darkly on that incident led him to many others in which he felt his sister had played a less than admirable role. Although he might, as he told his Aunt Delphinia, as a good Christian forgive, Charles was never one to forget, and he kept a very long list of grievances ready in his head to pull out whenever he was ready. And he was ready now.

Thus it was that over the teacups Charles proposed another game of piquet. He pointed out that the morning was damp and Margaret would not care to go out, never minding that it was her custom in the country to walk each day, rain or shine. He also told her that it would give him a chance to redeem his money and his reputation.

Her light, "But Charles, you have no reputation with me!" did not make him laugh as it would have their father; instead, his heavy frown appeared. Miss Tolliver considered telling Charles that she had another engagement, but a thoughtful study of his face told her she would be postponing, not ending, the issue. So with a sigh and a "You really shouldn't tempt fate so, Charles," she assented, and they were soon ensconced in the library.

In the first hand, the cards fell heavily to Sir Charles's favor, and Miss Tolliver indulged the hope that her brother would play better than usual. She knew it would greatly improve his temper to rise a winner.

But in the second hand, the cards fell evenly, and it was superior skill that took the trick. Charles went down the loser, with each hand putting him deeper in the hole, and his brow growing blacker with each tally. When luncheon was announced, he waved it away, and Miss Tolliver's protest that all their activity had made her hungry was met with a muttered "In a moment, in a moment," as he shuffled the cards to deal.

By three o'clock, Margaret absolutely refused to play one moment more, and he huffily bowed, declaring that he would deliver her winnings to her forthwith.

"Oh, don't be ridiculous, Charles!" Miss Tolliver cried. "I don't want your money!"

He was torn between relief at her last words, for Sir Charles was seriously fond of his cash and had problems parting with it, and offense at her first words, which labeled him "ridiculous." Knowing that a gentleman always pays his debts—even if only to a sister—he hobbled painfully toward the desk where he kept his strongbox (the pain made

more exquisite by the purpose of his trip), and after much
fumbling about and fuming, extracted a roll of ready. He
tossed it to Miss Tolliver who caught it without thinking,
and, with real loathing, he shouted, "There! I hope you're
satisfied!"

"Oh, really, Charles—" Caught between amusement at
his indignation and consternation that he should take what
she considered a mere game so seriously, Miss Tolliver put
the money on the small table at which they had both so
recently sat. Her brother hauled himself up and, with the aid
of his cane, lunged forward until he held the notes again,
and pushed them into her resisting hands.

"No," he said, knowing he acted unfairly and glad no
one but his sister was there to see it. "No, take it. You
know a gentleman always pays his debts, even to someone
who shouldn't have won his money in the first place—"

"Now, Charles," she said soothingly, "I tried not to
win your money. I told you we shouldn't play."

The fact that she was right exacerbated him further. "Oh,
yes," he shouted, glaring across at her, for although Sir
Charles far outweighed his sister, he had never surpassed
her in height—another point which, now that he thought
about it, tried him sorely—"Take the high tone. Pretend
that you won because of superior skill and not confounded
luck. Pretend that this—this—this debacle—is not to be laid
at your door. Pretend—"

"Debacle?" Miss Tolliver interrupted, one eyebrow raised.
"Oh, really, Charles!"

"Don't you 'oh, really, Charles,' me, Margaret Marie!"
he started. "I say debacle and I mean debacle—"

She yawned, incensing him further. "Really, Charles,"
she said in a voice often used with children, "you are being
foolish beyond permission! The only debacle here is the one
you're making by acting like a complete idiot, turning what
should be a pleasant little card game into a major battle!"

"Idiot!" Charles's body stiffened, and he banged his cane
on the floor. It felt so good that he banged it again. "A
pleasant little card game! Indeed! As if it could be pleasant
for a man of my caliber to be bested by a female—and not
just any female, my sister—"

He stabbed the cane toward the floor again for emphasis, but his aim was not good, and in a moment he was collapsed into a chair, holding his wrapped foot and swearing heartily.

"Oh, Charles!" Miss Tolliver laughed—regrettably, she laughed—even as she started forward to help him.

"Keep away from me," he snarled, hugging his foot with one hand as, with the other, he tried to break the offending cane on the table next to him. The table, unused to such treatment, turned over, sending cards and books skittering in all directions. This only frustrated Sir Charles further, and one glance at his sister's laughing face was enough to set the seal on this ignominious day.

"It's all your fault," he charged, pointing the still unbroken cane at her. "My life was ordered—tranquil—until you arrived, and now look at it. Look at it!" For emphasis he reached toward another of the small tables that littered the library, and sent the papers lying there flying, too. One of them landed at Miss Tolliver's feet and she bent to retrieve it, smiling as she did so.

"Really, Charles," she said, "your tantrums haven't changed much since you were twelve; it's just that now you have more things to throw! Do be reasonable. I know your foot troubles you, but that is no reason to take it out on your poor library. Or on me, for that matter."

They were, perhaps, not the best choices of words for a man so far gone down the tantrum path, with little chance of graceful return, and at them Sir Charles stiffened again.

"It is not my foot that troubles me, Margaret Marie," he said with a glare. "It is you. You and your refusal to learn your place and to curb that too-free tongue—"

Margaret rose from collecting papers on the floor, and for once the good humor was gone from her face. "I believe, Charles," she said, her voice low, her back straight, "that you owe me an apology."

Later he might think so, too, but for now Sir Charles was too wrought up to back down. "Apology!" he sputtered. "Well, I never!"

"I know you've never, Charles," she said in that same low voice, "but you should. And since it is my presence that you say so troubles you here, I shall remove it immediately. Good day."

Without another word she turned and walked from the library, pausing at the door only long enough to sneer coldly at him when he told her she'd forgotten her winnings. Entering the hall in a cold rage, she commanded the butler to have her coach sent round immediately, and upon being reminded that her coachman was indisposed, she had no compunction in saying that her brother had very kindly offered her the use of his coachman, since a matter of some urgency required her to leave for home immediately.

The butler, harboring his own doubts as to whether Sir Charles would wish to see his sister set off for home at such a late hour, volunteered to just step into the library and confer with him on the matter. Miss Tolliver said affably that she thought it a very good idea, adding as he set off that he should, of course, be ready to duck at a moment's notice, Sir Charles being in one of his rare takings where he was likely to hurl at least his snuffbox and very probably something larger at anyone who interrupted his solitude.

"Or," she added reflectively, watching the struggle on the face in front of her, "had the temerity to doubt his sister's word . . ."

Digesting both the first and second warnings, the butler paused in midstep and with a grace usually reserved for the ballet, turned to execute a bow that made clear the depth of his understanding. Wooden-faced, he suggested that she might like to step into the morning room to write her brother a note while the carriage was brought round and the maid assigned to her in London—Miss Tolliver having thoughtfully given her own abigail a holiday—flew round to pack.

Miss Tolliver assented, telling him to tell the maid that all she required was her nightclothes and two changes; her other clothing could be sent later. Not by so much as a quiver did the butler betray his understanding of how unusual was the situation; he merely bowed again and ushered her into the morning room, where he withdrew after making sure she had pen and paper.

Her note was brief and to the point.

"Dear Charles," she wrote, *"since, with the best will in the world, we cannot seem to rub along tolerably well together, I have gone home, telling your servants that you offered me the use of your coachman. I shall return the good fellow to you shortly, so don't bite anyone's nose off for doing what I assured them were your orders.*

> *Your loving (although not particularly at the moment) sister,*
> *Margaret*

Had she known it at the time, Miss Tolliver's brother's coachman would return to Sir Charles much sooner than she liked.

Chapter
6

Pandemonium was the word that thereafter came to Miss Tolliver's mind when asked to describe the first hours at the small inn to which Johns drove his employer's sister and her ill charges.

At the first sound of the coach the innkeeper emerged from his establishment, bowing and scraping, only to be brought up short by the sight of a woman descending from the coach, ignoring the groom's proffered arm as she turned to half-support a youngster who seemed inclined to faint as he looked hazily about him. And if that were not peculiar enough, she informed the landlord briskly that he must immediately carry a wounded and unconscious young man, still in the carriage, into his inn and summon a doctor.

It wasn't, as he guiltily pointed out to his spouse later, that he didn't believe the lady was a lady, exactly—it was just that, when he asked himself what sort of a lady arrives unescorted and unattended by an abigail, with two sick young men in her carriage and another looby trailing along behind, leading two horses and talking wildly of kidnappings that he knew they never should have started upon, no they shouldn't, while the innkeeper's wife's cousin Johns sat huffing and puffing on the coachbox, exhorting the woman to get back into the carriage, adun do, while he summoned the constable—well, he said, it had fair thrown him for a ringer, it had, and he hadn't known what to think. His wife, shaking her head and pursing her lips in that look that always made him bethink himself of something to do in the taproom, said sadly that his problem was he had nought to think with, nought at all, and it was a good thing he had her to do his thinking for him. Which she did, and which she had when Miss Tolliver first arrived.

Which was a good thing, for Miss Tolliver had found herself nonplussed when her pleasant "How do you do? I take it you are Johns's cousin" to the landlord was met with every evidence of loathing, both men bitterly denying kinship as the landlord made it clear that although one might love a woman, he was in no way required to love her relations, no way at all.

Luckily at that moment the woman the landlord did love appeared on the scene and, being as quick as her husband was slow, understood at a glance what was needed. She dropped Miss Tolliver a curtsey, then began at once to bully her husband and cousin into carrying the injured Gillian up the stairs and into bed. Peter trailed feverishly behind.

Miss Tolliver was left to instruct her brother's groom to stable the horses, and to send the open-mouthed Jem to the village in search of a doctor. In impressing the urgency of his mission upon Jem, Miss Tolliver suggested that he might like to make use of her name in leaving a message for the doctor. It was on his frantic ride into the village that he decided if one name was good, two would be better, and of his own volition upon finding the doctor away from home left the message that the Earl of Manseford and a Miss Tolliver required the doctor's services at the inn.

The doctor's housekeeper blessed herself and promised to deliver the message immediately upon the doctor's return, inquiring delicately if the lord's and lady's servants might be able to attend to their needs until the doctor arrived. Jem's innocent reply that he was the only one of my lord's servants present, while the lady had only a borrowed coachman and groom made her bless herself again, and upon his departure grab up her cloak and hurry next door to discuss with her neighbor, Mrs. Rackett, the strange ways of the quality. Such strange ways were the talk of the village by morning.

Meanwhile, Jem, pleased with his success in impressing

the housekeeper by the dropping of "my lor's" name,
returned to the inn to find an anxious Miss Tolliver awaiting
his return. She fell back in dismay at his news, her eyes
opening wide as she stared at him.

"But—" she began, as he stood before her wet and
dripping in the small private parlor to which John's cousin
had escorted her after seeing Peter and Gillian disposed of in
two bedrooms upstairs. "But—he has to come! We can't
wait several hours! That bullet must come out of your Mr.
Gillian's shoulder immediately, while I very much fear the
younger Mr. Manfield has taken a terrible chill!"

Jem, never a hand in a crisis, goggled at her, and said
fervently that he wished Mr. Gillian was awake to advise
them, since he was alert to every trick, was Mr. Gillian.

Miss Tolliver's dry comment that he had not been alert to
them all sailed over Jem's head, leaving the young groom
inclined to argue.

"Now Mr. Gillian could take a ball out of Mr. Peter's
shoulder, if it were Mr. Peter who was shot," Jem informed
her, "because Mr. Gillian once took a ball out of my
leg—"

Momentarily diverted in spite of herself, Miss Tolliver
asked how he had gotten a ball in his leg, her eyes twinkling
as she wondered aloud if it had been in another kidnapping
try.

A blushing Jem assured her hurriedly that it was no such
thing. Mr. Gillian had put the ball there when they were
hunting—quite by accident, of course—and so had thought
it only right that he take it out again, posthaste. And he had
done it, too, Jem told her proudly—not that it had done
much more than broken the skin, but still . . .

Miss Tolliver was regarding him in astonishment, and his
words trailed off as he looked first at her, and then nervously around to see what could be making her stare so.

"But—" Miss Tolliver started, "didn't you—*mind*?"

Oh, no, Jem assured her, he had not. At least, not much.
That is to say, he had not liked it, because it hurt like—
begging her pardon—the devil, and he might have minded if
Mr. Gillian had done it on purpose, but that he hadn't done,
Mr. Gillian not holding with shooting people in general, and

not his friends in particular, and Jem and Mr. Gillian had been friends ever since they were first breeched together . . .

His long and convoluted explanation showed every sign of continuing, so Miss Tolliver cut it short with a "Yes, yes, I can clearly see that your Mr. Gillian is a paragon—"

But that Jem would not allow. "No," he told her gravely, "he's not a paragon—although I'm not quite sure what that is, but I know it ain't Mr. Gillian—it's only that he's—he's just—just—" He frowned with the effort to find the right words. "He's just Mr. Gillian!"

Miss Tolliver smiled, touched by his loyalty to his friend. "Yes," she agreed, "I can see that he is. And I, too, wish he were not lying unconscious upstairs, for if he were not, perhaps this whole ridiculous thing might never have happened!"

Jem could not argue with that statement and stood quietly for a moment as the lady before him stared into the fire, thinking hard. Trying to think of what they should do next, she asked Jem if he was aware of another doctor in the neighborhood. Jem said he was not, but volunteered to go in search of the landlord to find out. Miss Tolliver thanked him, and said he would find her upstairs with the invalids when he was ready to make his report.

There was a warm and crackling fire in the room where Gillian lay, and Miss Tolliver noted how it cast long shadows across the slanted ceiling as she quietly slipped through the door and looked across at the silent figure beneath the blue and gold coverlet. From time to time one of Gillian's hands plucked unconsciously at the quilt, and Mrs. Murphy, sitting beside the wounded man, patted the restless hand as she rose to approach Miss Tolliver. Her voice was low as, with a quick glance toward her patient, she asked if the doctor had arrived.

Miss Tolliver shook her head, explaining that Jem had found the doctor from home. Her uneasiness increased as Mrs. Murphy's lips tightened.

"Isn't that just like a man?" the innkeeper's wife burst out, running a hand down the ample folds of her apron in her harassed state. "Never there when you need them, underfoot when you do not! Doctors and tapmen and husbands and cousins—and I dare say earls and dukes too, no matter that some of them has learning, and some of them has manners, and some of them has brains (a little)—deep down they're really all the same. And happen not a ha'pence of rumgumption between 'em. All the same!''

Mrs. Murphy seemed predisposed to dwell on the shortcomings of men, and Miss Tolliver's lips twitched as she wondered what the innkeeper had done to put his loving spouse in such a flutter. She did not have to wonder long.

"For instance," Mrs. Murphy said, "I told my man, 'we could take the ball out of the young sir's shoulder, you and I,' for many's the one I've taken out of the gentlemen—'' She heard herself suddenly, and colored brightly under Miss Tolliver's eyes, remarking self-consciously that they didn't really have doings with the free traders, especially after their move in from the coast, but there had been times when, compelled through Christian charity, she'd taken a ball from the shoulder of some poor unfortunate who was unwise enough to step in the way of an exciseman's bullet. But that was when her sister Clara was about, for Clara wasn't squeamish like these he-men.

Miss Tolliver murmured sympathetically in favor of the absent Clara, and asked what Mr. Murphy had said to his wife's proposal. The dark frown descended on Mrs. Murphy's round face again.

"What did he say?" she repeated. "What did he say? The big looby! He says—just as foolish as you please—'but Martha, there would be blood, and you know I cannot abide blood' for all the world as if it was his blood he'd have to be looking at! Now I could see how a person might be queered by the sight of his own blood, but when it's someone else's—well, all it wants is a little resolution, isn't it? But he doesn't have any resolution, does Mr. Murphy, for all his size. He's got the strength of an ox, and the brain to match, and so I told him, I did. Yes, I did!'' Mrs. Murphy's head nodded vigorously, her chins trembling with her fervor, and Miss Tolliver, watching the indignant face before her, had no trouble believing she'd said all she said, and more.

Gravely she asked if Mrs. Murphy felt it important that

the ball be removed immediately, and was met by another passionate nod. Miss Tolliver sighed, and said that since she was not given to fainting at the sight of blood, she would volunteer her services, if only Mrs. Murphy would tell her what to do.

Mrs. Murphy gave her shoulder a motherly pat and said that she had known from the beginning that Miss Tolliver was a good lass, whatever her cousin Johns might say—a reference that made Miss Tolliver's eyes twinkle—but the truth was, Mrs. Murphy's sister Clara was a big, strapping wench, able to pin a man to the bed if he was inclined to cast about while the ball was taken from his shoulder, while Miss Tolliver . . .

Miss Tolliver understood the delicately trailing sentence, and sighed. She agreed with Mrs. Murphy that with the best will in the world she would still be unable to pin Gillian to the bed should he decide to roll about, but after a moment's thought she volunteered to enlist Jem for that task. Then she asked in what other way she could help.

Mrs. Murphy patted her shoulder again, and told her handsomely that she could hold the basin. Accepting this lowly position with downcast eyes, Miss Tolliver promised to return as soon as she checked on their second patient. Mrs. Murphy, a martial light in her eye, promised to set her husband to finding the lint and bandages she would need, as well as the knife and basilicum powder. At mention of a knife Miss Tolliver suggested politely that it be held in the fire to cleanse it, and Mrs. Murphy replied just as politely that that would indeed be done. Thereafter, Miss Tolliver retired to the other bedroom, the ladies tolerably well pleased with each other.

In Peter's room, however, Miss Tolliver found no such helpful nurse. And although a fire burned brightly in this chamber's fireplace also, there was no feeling of warm goodwill, perhaps because of Coachman Johns, who sat glowering and muttering darkly that the lad tossing and turning under the blankets piled upon him was likely to slip his wind before morning, and then whatever would Sir Charles say?

"Oh, Johns," Miss Tolliver cried, hurrying forward,

"Don't say so! Is he really that bad?" In a moment she had adjusted the candle that burned by the bed so that she could better see the boy's face. True, he was flushed and muttering incoherently, but she was not as quick as the coachman to take such a dim view of his situation. Any young man just recovering from the influenza who had spent the day in the rain might find himself in the same situation, she thought, and reached for the cloth in the cool basin of water on the table beside them. With it she wiped his hot forehead and hands, lending less than half an ear to Johns's continuing litany behind her as he adjured her to leave the boys to their fate and either return to London or journey on, "for I don't know what Sir Charles will say, miss, that I don't, nor do I wish to."

About to answer that she had a very good idea what her brother would say, but did not care, Miss Tolliver's attention was diverted as Peter opened his eyes briefly, trying to focus on the face in front of him. He stared at her frowningly for several moments, searching with vague memory until he at last felt he had her identity. "Mama?" he murmured.

Miss Tolliver, her hand suddenly stilled, returned his doubtful smile with one of her own as the boy sighed and closed his eyes. For the time, at least, he was quieter.

"Well!" Johns exploded behind her, "I never! Calling you his 'mama,' the little—"

"Oh, Johns, really!" Miss Tolliver returned, shifting slightly so that she faced him. "The boy is not in his right mind. You might call for your own mother if you were in his state. One only wonders if she would come."

Not quite sure what to make of her last statement, Johns perceived another argument and warned her portentously that she bore the risk of infection if she were to stay, and she should with all due speed move away from the nasty little varmint and out of the inn before she took the illness and was carried off by an inflammation of the lungs, "for what Sir Charles would say then, I'm sure I don't know—"

As the coachman began his favorite litany, Miss Tolliver rose and slowly viewed him from head to toe. His words trailed off before her gaze, and instinctively he ducked his head, thinking there was something of the old Sir's look about her, and the old Sir had been something when he was in a taking, that he had . . .

Several seconds passed before Miss Tolliver said in a cool voice of authority that might well have been her father's, "I have told you several times, Johns, that I wish you would rid yourself of this notion that I am in any way concerned with what my brother thinks, says, or does. I am also—and this should *not* surprise you—even less interested in *your* opinion of my actions. I should think that if you had even one shred of Christian kindness in you, it would make you aware of our duty to help these boys. Since you do not, I believe I can well dispense with your services. You and that poor groom of my brother's whom you are always bullying may return to London immediately. Please instruct my own coachman to come for me when he is able. You may take my carriage, and he may bring it back. Now go."

But Johns, goggling at her, seemed rooted to the spot as the full import of her words hit him.

"But Miss Tolliver!" he gasped, trying to both justify himself while placating her, for he had a pretty good idea of what Sir Charles would say to a coachman who abandoned his sister, and he did not wish to hear it. "Miss Tolliver, I beg of you!" Earnestly he assured her that it was only his sense of duty to her family that made it incumbent for him to persuade her to remove as soon as possible from this establishment. The lady yawned. He told her that nothing could induce him to leave her unattended at the inn in this hour of danger.

She asked him roundly what a danger he thought two sick boys posed her, adding that she was not unattended while Mrs. Murphy was present.

Snatching at his cousin's name, he suggested that Mrs. Murphy could easily look after the boys alone, for all her bossy and forward ways, she had a good heart, did his cousin . . .

Miss Tolliver told him she was glad someone in his family had a good heart, and the look in her fine eyes made him cringe. But, she added, she could not dream of imposing on Mrs. Murphy to that extent, and she turned a deaf ear to his almost tearful entreaty that it would not be an imposition.

"Besides," he said, voicing the argument chief in his mind after all other avenues had been exhausted, "I don't know what Sir Charles will say when he learns I've left his only sister alone with the two young men who tried to kidnap her—"

He got no further as Miss Tolliver smiled—no, positively beamed—at him. "Why, Johns," she said silkily, taking his arm and leading him, resisting, toward the door, "—just think—you're to have the opportunity to find out!"

With that she fairly thrust him from the room, paying no heed to his redoubled arguments. Mrs. Murphy, about to reenter Gillian's room from the hall, nodded calmly as Miss Tolliver informed her that her cousin was leaving, and a silent message passed between the women. Taking a firm hold on his arm, Mrs. Murphy led Johns toward the stairs; Miss Tolliver shut the door behind them, and quickly heard the perturbed coachman's voice fading away. She returned to Peter's bedside feeling very grateful for Mrs. Murphy.

Chapter
7

When Jem arrived to tell Miss Tolliver there was no other doctor available to wait upon Mister Gillian and Mister Peter, he was met with the pleasing intelligence that in the absence of such a helpful member of the medical profession, he—Jem—was to take part in the upcoming surgery. His wide eyes and the involuntary step back he took at her words told Miss Tolliver he was not overjoyed at the prospect, and his stammered profession that he would willingly lay his life down for Mister Gillian, but he was unable to see that Mr. Gillian lay down—quietly—during the removal of the ball from his shoulder left her regarding him in vexation.

"But Jem," she protested, "surely you're not afraid you can't handle a wounded man who has lost blood and might toss about a bit—"

Jem drew himself up to his full height and told her with a dignity that sat oddly on his bedraggled shoulders that he could handle Mister Gillian wounded, drunk, or stone sober; he certainly wasn't one to shrink from a struggle.

"No, miss," he said, gazing down at the cap he was twisting uneasily in his hands, his eyes avoiding the ominous preparations by the bed where even now Mrs. Murphy was laying out bandages and lint and a wicked-looking knife glinted in the firelight. "It's not that Mister Gillian can best me in a wrestle—at least, not without a fine fight! It's just that—that—"

Miss Tolliver looked toward Mrs. Murphy, who nodded sapiently.

"He's afraid of the sight of blood, miss," Mrs. Murphy said, pursing her lips as she looked him up and down. "A big, brawny lad like that! Just another lummox like that man of mine."

"What?" Miss Tolliver turned her full attention back to Jem, who shifted uneasily from one foot to the other, his color rising with Mrs. Murphy's words.

"Oh, surely not!" Miss Tolliver's rallying tone suggested that Jem could at any moment counter these charges impugning his courage, but he did not do so. Instead, he was heard to mumble to the floor that while he wasn't afraid of the sight of blood, exactly, there was something about it that made him want to cast up his accounts immediately.

"And that wouldn't be a good thing to do, would it, miss?" he asked, gazing hangdogged into Miss Tolliver's bemused face.

She had, perforce, to agreed that it would not be a good thing, and Jem watched anxiously as she cradled her chin in her hand and thought deeply. Mrs. Murphy, standing by the bed tapping her foot and frowning ferociously at the unhappy young man, muttered darkly that if they were to ask her which was the weaker sex—which no one would, of course, not at all—well, it wouldn't be women she was saying, no sir. It wasn't the women turning coat this night. Resigned to letting Jem go with no more than the sharp edge of her tongue, she turned her attention to Miss Tolliver, who was made of sterner stuff.

"You know, Jem," Miss Tolliver said, smiling brightly in a way that would have instantly warned Sir Charles that she was out to change his mind about something, "one of the most exciting things about life is that it allows us to face new challenges daily, and to meet our fears and conquer them."

Jem was not a quick study, but a lifetime with a sister of his own made him greet her words suspiciously. "Miss?" he questioned, taking a step backward. That put him nearer the bed, and since that was the direction in which Miss

Tolliver wanted him to move, she followed, watching in satisfaction as he stepped back again.

"What I'm saying, Jem," she told him in the same encouraging tone, her smile growing brighter each moment, "is that tonight you have the opportunity to meet one of your fears and conquer it. You have the opportunity to help a friend—one of your best friends, one you tell me you would lay down your life for—"

Jem shook his head obstinately and stepped back again. "I'd die for Mister Gillian, miss, and that's the truth. But dying for someone and watching him bleed is two different things, and the latter I won't do."

"But you will, Jem," Miss Tolliver assured him, her smile now a positive beam. "You will, because you must. And we will hear no more about it. Now grasp his shoulder like a good boy, and quit your nonsense."

Perhaps it was the way she uttered the last sentence; perhaps it was something he had heard from his own sister since birth and responded to reflexively; but when Jem turned with some idea of escape to find that he was, instead, standing at the edge of Gillian's bed and looking down at his young master, he did what he was told. In a moment Mrs. Murphy had laid bare the wound, which bled sluggishly as she probed it. Gillian moaned unconsciously, and Jem joined him.

"Courage," Miss Tolliver commanded, picking up the bandages and basin and joining Mrs. Murphy on the other side of the bed as that good lady set competently to work. "I am to hold the basin, and you are to hold the patient."

Sweat appeared on Jem's forehead, and he stared at her wildly.

"Now, Jem," Miss Tolliver commanded, holding his eyes. "Don't look down. Look at me. Thinking of something else. Count, Jem. Count!"

"Count?" he repeated blankly.

Mrs. Murphy did not look up as she entered the conversation to say, "He can't count, miss. Look at him. A regular slowtop."

Thus distracted, the "slowtop" let his eyes drift toward

the surgeon and her patient, and his face, which had been so red a moment before, turned chalk white.

"Jem!" Miss Tolliver commanded, watching him. "Jem! Look back at me! I'm sorry I said count. It's something I do in times of trauma and I thought—maybe I could teach you—"

Begging her pardon, and carefully avoiding looking down, Jem suggested that it might not be the best of times for him to learn to count.

"Quite right." Miss Tolliver agreed promptly with an encouraging smile. "That is a very wise decision on your part. This is not the time at all. Your realizing that proves how well you are doing, Jem. Doesn't it show how well he is doing, Mrs. Murphy?"

The question was a mistake, for when Miss Tolliver directed her gaze toward Mrs. Murphy, Jem did likewise, just as the landlady's skillfully wielded knife drove home for the bullet, and fresh blood spurted from the wound. Gillian's body protested, and Jem felt blood ooze through his fingers as he lost his hold on his unconscious friend and reached for it again.

"Hold him, Jem!" Miss Tolliver cried, also grabbing the restless patient. "Hold him! And look up, Jem! Look up, and—and—and *sing*!"

"*Sing?*" The suggestion so startled Miss Tolliver's audience that for a moment Jem was distracted from the twisting of his stomach, and Mrs. Murphy from her task of busily dusting basilicum powder over Gillian's wound.

"Why, miss," Mrs. Murphy protested, "All you have to do is look at him to know he can't sing! A big lummox like that—"

Her disparagement ended in open-mouthed amazement as Jem, casting frantically about for something to take his mind off the red fluid he could feel on his fingers, threw his head back and burst into the only song that entered his mind.

Thus it was that Gillian Manfield had the bullet in his shoulder removed and his wound competently bound by an innkeeper's wife who learned her medicine nursing the smugglers who plied their trade along the coast; a maiden lady he had only recently tried to abduct; and his frantic, faithful groom, singing at the top of his lungs a song so bawdy that Miss Tolliver knew without a doubt that her brother would have blushed to hear it.

The lady herself remained remarkably unmoved.

When Jem awakened in his position on the floor—it was unfortunate, Miss Tolliver informed him kindly, that he had happened to look down just as Mrs. Murphy picked up the basin containing the bloodied towels and water—it was to find Miss Tolliver kneeling beside him while the landlord cradled his head and held a glass of brandy to his lips, and the landlord's wife stood at his feet shaking her head and muttering "lummoxes, lummoxes, every last one of them!" Jem noticed in her a striking resemblance to his sister.

Coloring and scrambling hastily to his feet, Jem was grateful for the landlord's grasp on his arm when the quick movement sent his head spinning. "I must have fallen," he stammered, and Miss Tolliver agreed gravely that he had. Mrs. Murphy was not so kind.

"Fallen!" The redoubtable landlady harrumphed. "Oh, yes, my brave buck, that you did. Right after you fainted dead away at Miss Tolliver's feet. Knocking against her like that, it's a wonder you didn't push her over, you big lump!"

Jem looked from the landlady to Miss Tolliver in embarrassment, and the latter assured him in a grave tone at odds with her dancing eyes that she had been in no danger of toppling. Solicitously she asked if he had been injured in his fai—er—fall.

A self-conscious shake of his head was the only answer as he shrugged off the landlord's sustaining hand, his eyes anxious as he looked toward the bed where Gillian lay, his head moving fretfully on the pillow. He asked if Mister Gillian was going to be all right, and Mrs. Murphy snapped that if he was, it was no thanks to his weak-kneed friend. That Miss Tolliver would not allow, however; she told the miserably blushing Jem that he had performed his part admirably, even going so far as to point out that he had not, as he feared, cast up his accounts.

This observation so cheered the young groom that only

one worry remained, and it was with a sheepish face and a slight stammer that he voiced his concern that Mister Gillian and Mister Peter never learn of his—ah—fall. His voice had no sooner trailed off than Miss Tolliver assured him that it would never be known—in fact, it was forgotten already.

His painful gaze of entreaty toward Mrs. Murphy made that good lady hmmph and announce to the ceiling that she certainly was not one to be carrying tales, and nor—her severe gaze transferred to her mate—was her husband, seeing as how it could just as well have been him there on the floor . . .

Said husband shifted uncomfortably and, bethinking himself of a task left uncompleted below stairs, bore young Jem off to the taproom, there to recoup his strength as the landlord liberally poured his ale and shook his head repeatedly, with many sighs, over the puzzle known as Woman. It was in the taproom that Miss Tolliver eventually found them, commiserating heartily with each other over their vaguely expressed but deeply felt ills.

Both straightened and ducked their heads at sight of her, the landlord glad he had no other customers present to see the lady in these common surroundings, for it was not the thing, not the thing at all. Hurrying forward, he suggested that she might be more comfortable in the small private dining room reserved for those few of his clients who could afford it, but Miss Tolliver merely smiled and said no, thank you, she and Jem needed to talk, and their present surroundings would do nicely.

Recalling their last talk and its outcome, Jem blanched slightly and swallowed a big portion of his ale before taking a hesitant step forward.

"Yes, miss?" he asked, hoping mightily that whatever she required of him would in no way involve blood.

His thoughts were apparent in his face, and Miss Tolliver schooled her expression to inform him kindly that there was one last favor he must do his ill friends, and that was to go at once to the Earl of Manseford, and inform him of the accident befallen his brothers.

Once again the color drained from his face as Jem, assimilating her words, gaped at her. In the excitement of the evening, he had forgotten that the earl knew nothing about their adventures, and would very likely be extremely—even intensely—interested in them. Nor had it occurred to him that in the absence of Mister Gillian and Master Peter—both of them being indisposed and unable to apprise the earl of their conduct—the task of informing his lordship would fall to the young groom whom, Jem felt fairly certain, the earl would feel should have told him of their scheme immediately it was hatched. It also occurred to Jem that Mister Gillian and Master Peter—to say nothing of Jem himself—would much rather the earl knew nothing of the night's encounter, and swallowing mightily, he tried to make Miss Tolliver aware of that fact. She regarded him with tolerant amusement, and a certain amount of sympathy, but could not agree that the earl should be left in the dark.

"And while I'm sure that you are right, Jem, and hearing of his brother's injuries will distress his lordship, I think it would be even more distressing for him not to know of their whereabouts for several days, don't you?"

Put that way, Jem had to reluctantly agree that it was unlikely the earl would not notice the disappearance of his two youngest brothers from their ancestral home, no matter—as he hopefully pointed out to Miss Tolliver, only to be met by a sympathetic shake of her head—how big the house might be. And in the end, having casted frantically about in his mind for someone else to be the bearer of bad tidings and having thought of no one, he sighed heavily and said that he would ride at once for Willowdale.

Trying to relieve some of the worry on his face, Miss Tolliver teased gently that at least he would not have to face blood again.

A gloomy Jem shook his head. "I don't know, miss," he said, his movements slow as he pulled on his greatcoat and reached for his hat. His thoughts were on the earl's punishing right—a right he had often seen in the practice ring at Willowdale. "I just hope it won't be mine!"

The doctor had come and gone, merely shaking his head over the strange tale the landlord told of how his honest inn was turned from a quiet country house to a gentry hospital

in the last few hours. He approved Mrs. Murphy's handiwork and left some laudanum for both Gillian and Peter,
promising to return in the morning with a mixture he
thought might help his youngest patient's fever. He said he
felt the greatest alarm for the younger boy, but agreed with
Miss Tolliver that any youngster recovering from influenza
who subjected himself to the rain and the strain of the day
was likely to end up just as Peter had.

"That's the way it is with some of these young ones," he
said gruffly, his brows beetling as he talked with her. "All
nerves and no stamina. No sense, either. Should have been
home by a fire on a day like this."

Miss Tolliver agreed, but absently, and the doctor fixed
her with one of his keen looks as he inquired about her
connection to the young men. She replied with composure
that she was a chance stranger who happened along when
they needed help, and he seemed satisfied with the answer,
but his intense gaze did not abate as he said he understood
there to be an earl staying at the inn, too.

Mrs. Murphy, also present for the conversation, blessed
herself and said there was no earl staying in her house, and
never had been. It was something she seemed to feel she
should be congratulated upon, and the doctor considered her
for a long moment before returning his gaze to Miss
Tolliver. She told him that his two young patients were the
brothers of an earl, and that the gentleman might be expected
shortly, to assume their care. Mrs. Murphy threw up her
hands and with a disgusted "Men!" stomped from the room
to inspect her larder for what she was sure would be an
excessive demand upon it.

Watching her go, the doctor gave a grunt of dour satisfaction. "It's as I thought," he said. "My housekeeper can
dress a joint of meat as neatly as you please, but when it
comes to getting messages straight . . . She swore to me the
young man who came requesting my presence here said I
was to wait upon an earl and a lady. An unaccompanied
lady."

"Oh." Miss Tolliver knew the implications of such a
rumor as well as the doctor, and she met his interrogating
gaze with a calm she did not quite feel. "Well. I honestly

can't say if that was the message she received, for the groom sent to fetch you, while I'm sure a young man of many excellent qualities, cannot be considered a coherent conversationalist by any stretch of the imagination . . .'' She sighed, her eyes hopeful. ''I hope we can rely on your housekeeper's discretion?''

''Discretion?'' The doctor shook his head, in real if silent pity. ''My dear young woman, she has none!''

''Oh.'' Miss Tolliver did not need her brother's coachman present to hear, ''I wonder what Sir Charles will say'' reverberating in her head, and she frowned. Trying to help, the doctor told her he would set straight in a hurry anyone who asked him about the rumor. Slightly cheered, Miss Tolliver could not know that the doctor's way of ''setting someone straight'' was to scowl ferociously and tell him to mind his own business, which usually set tongues wagging even harder.

Determined not to worry over what she could not prevent, Miss Tolliver promised to follow the doctor's nursing directions to the letter, bade him good-bye, and made her way back to young Peter's room, there to wait for whatever the night might yet bring.

Chapter
8

The doctor had been gone no more than an hour when the sounds of horses rode fast and furiously were heard in the innyard, followed almost immediately by the voice of someone obviously used to command calling for an ostler. Miss Tolliver, pausing for a moment in her efforts to make Peter more comfortable, listened carefully.

"It is my opinion," she told the sleeping boy with a smile, "that your brother has arrived!"

She finished her duties quickly and settled in a chair in the corner of the room, out of the fire and candlelight, to await with her customary composure—and a great deal of interest—the coming developments. She did not have to wait long.

No sooner had the noise died in the courtyard than it was taken up in the inn, and the sound of boots, taking the stairs two at a time, was heard outside Peter's door. There was a pause on the landing as two male voices conferred, then she heard one pair of feet move off toward Gillian's room as another came toward the door behind which she and Peter waited. In a moment the door was thrust open and a man stood in the doorway, his boots muddied and his expression forbidding as he surveyed the room.

Before his eyes reached Miss Tolliver they landed on Peter, tossing uncomfortably in the bed, and he moved quickly forward, concern replacing the anger in his face.

Miss Tolliver, deciding she liked the second expression

much better, rose and walked toward him, extending her hand. "How do you do?" she asked, smiling pleasantly up into his startled face. "I take it you are—er—'my brother, the earl'?"

Automatically he took her extended hand and bowed over it, saying politely as he straightened that he was indeed the Earl of Manseford.

"And who the devil—" the heavy frown descended again "—begging your pardon—are you?"

Something in his clear irritation at the situation in which he found himself, coupled with the day she had herself experienced, made the question extremely funny to Miss Tolliver, and, forgetting her family's constant chiding that she must at all costs contain her unreasonable lapses into levity, she put one wrist to her forehead, raised her eyes heavenward, and in the style of the most expressive tragic heroines to ever trod the boards, drooped slightly to sigh, "I—alack—am the poor unfortunate female kidnapped—most against my will, my nerves will never recover!—by your brothers!"

"The devil!" The earl said, not bothering this time to beg her pardon as he glared at her. "Then that faradiddle Jem told us—"

He was interrupted as an indignant John burst into the room, outrage apparent in face and figure.

"Giles!" John cried. "There's a woman in Gillian's room who called me a lummox and ordered me out because she said I was upsetting her patient! Of all the—"

"Oh, is your brother awake then?" Miss Tolliver asked. Two pairs of male eyes turned toward her, and she explained that Gillian was unconscious when brought to the inn. Her explanation continued as she told them kindly that lords to landlords, men were all the same to their hostess, Mrs. Murphy—"without a ha'pence of rumgumption between them," she added conscientiously.

Their reactions to her disclosures could not have pleased her more, for the expression of blankest astonishment on one face and of narrowed examination on the other nearly sent her into whoops. She smiled—positively grinned—at them as they surveyed the medium-built woman whose once-neat dress was now spotted with bits of Gillian's blood, whose light brown hair straggled to escape its confinement at the back of her neck, and whose forehead contained a positive smudge from her efforts to make the fire in Peter's bedroom burn more evenly.

John bowed stiffly, fishing for her name. "Miss—?"

"Tolliver," she supplied, beaming at him. He looked to his brother for enlightenment.

"The woman," the earl said dryly, "that our three idiots kidnapped in place of the fair Vanessa. Jem had not merely lost his mind when he told us that garbled story."

"What?" The word exploded out of John, and he stared from Miss Tolliver to the earl in disbelief. "You must be joking! Even such a corker as Gillian can tell a diamond of the first order from—" The infelicity of his remarks occurred to him and he colored brightly. Miss Tolliver finished the sentence for him.

"—from a lump of coal, my lord? Oh!" She placed her hand to her forehead again, raising her eyes to heaven. "I am undone. So mortifying. So mortified. Oh. Oh. Oh." Fishing for her handkerchief, she found she had lost it, and was forced to bury her face in her hands instead. The effect worked just as well, for a disordered John hurried forward, his face horrified.

"My dear Miss Tolliver!" he said, one hand moving distractedly through his hair as he stopped just short of her, not quite certain what to do. "I am so very sorry—so inconsiderate of me—my wretched tongue—indeed I did not mean—I would never—it is just that—"

Miss Tolliver was enjoying herself immensely when the earl's languid and very dry voice cut through his brother's disjointed remonstrations.

"I am not so sure," the earl said, "that Gillian did not kidnap an actress after all."

"What?" John turned toward him, then started when Miss Tolliver raised a laughing face to them, the laugh disappearing only when Peter moaned slightly and called for his brother again. Instantly she was at his bedside, bending over to smile into his hazy eyes and reaching for the laudanum as she remarked, "And here you are, Peter! Just the man you've been asking for! Your brother Giles!"

The earl was right behind her and she handed him the glass, watching in approval as, John at his shoulder, Giles raised his youngest brother's head and tipped the medicine down his throat, smiling gently at the drawn face before him.

"I am afraid," Peter ventured in muffled tones as Giles settled himself on the bed, drawing one of the restless young hands into his own, "that we are in a bit of a scrape."

The earl agreed it was true.

"Is Gillian all right?" Peter asked, and upon being told that his brother would mend quickly, turned his head so that his blurry vision encompassed Miss Tolliver, standing behind his elder brothers, almost in the shadows.

"And you, ma'am?" he asked with grave courtesy, "are you all right?"

"Right as a trivet," she assured him, stepping forward, not noticing the sharp glance the earl directed at her cheerful face as she smiled down at his youngest brother.

"She's awfully nice," Peter informed them as he drifted off again, still holding Giles's hand. "I wish she *were* that Vanessa . . ."

The silence in the room grew until the earl, removing his hand from Peter's slack grasp, rose, slipped his brother's arm under the coverlet, and directed a level glance toward Miss Tolliver.

"I believe," he said, "that it would be wise for you to tell me all that has transpired today. From the beginning. We have only Jem's account, which is so wild as to border on the incomprehensible, and although I shall certainly have a thorough reckoning from Gillian in time, I would appreciate knowing as much as you can tell me. Now."

The way he said "now" sounded a great deal like an order to Miss Tolliver, and she was not a lady who liked being ordered. His kindness to his youngest brother had done much to establish him in her esteem, however, so she overlooked the autocratic tone for the moment as she described, as simply as she could, what the three young

Willowdale residents had done to amuse themselves that day.

Her apology for the stupidity of her brother's coachman was waved aside by John, who said he would certainly expect his own coachman to behave in the same manner, were he carrying a defenseless female. He meant it well, for his younger brothers' behavior so shocked a man of his temperament that he was overwhelmingly grateful to find that the lady did not plan to make a scandal the type of which he most deplored—in fact, she had told them the least said, the soonest forgotten—but Miss Tolliver fired up at once, informing him that she was far from defenseless. It was only the earl's timely intervention that saved his open-mouthed brother from being wholly bested in the coming argument.

The earl said dampingly that the coachman had acted as he thought he ought, and he wished that they would do him the courtesy of doing the same—a statement that made both regard him with either relief or hostility, depending upon their position in the argument. After a severe struggle with her tongue, Miss Tolliver continued, skirting lightly over her own part in the night's drama.

Well able to read between the lines, the earl was aware of what might have happened to his foolish young brothers had no one with a kind heart and cool head been there to help them. He had much to be grateful for, and he said so, but Miss Tolliver refused to be thanked, laughing as she told them it was more of an adventure than had ever before come her way, and if Peter and Gillian took no serious hurt from it, she certainly was not one to dwell on the night's events.

"Adventure!" John fairly barked the word, regarding her as sternly as when he had first discovered she was roasting him. "You're as bad as they are! Adventure indeed! It goes beyond all bearing—"

Miss Tolliver regarded him fixedly for several moments, until his words trailed off and he took a hasty turn around the room, coming to stand again behind his elder brother.

"You know," she said, nodding tolerantly at the late earl's second son, "I believe you will like my brother. It is just as well." She sighed as she smiled at them. "Charles's coachman left here in high dudgeon and is on his way back to London to tell my brother of what you can be sure they will characterize as my abominable behavior. Unless I am very much mistaken, it will bring Charles here posthaste tomorrow.''

Her voice was apologetic as she continued. "He has the gout. His presence is a fate I would not wish on anyone.''

Forgetting his own often withering indictments of his two youngest brothers, John said austerely that that was no way to speak of one's brother. The earl, however, smiled in understanding and said he would be most pleased to meet Sir Charles.

"Will you?" Miss Tolliver's eyes opened in considerable surprise. "How very odd! But then, I have had cause to wonder about the mental stability of your family...''

"I say!" The words were John's; the earl refused to be drawn, merely favoring Miss Tolliver with the glint of a smile before his gaze returned to Peter once again.

"Well," Giles said, "your tale makes me think the situation is not quite as bad as it could be.''

About to agree, Miss Tolliver bethought herself of one more thing, and sighed.

"Oh yes," she said, "there is one more thing—a ridiculous thing, really!—hardly worth mentioning! But I imagine it best that you know about it." Both men regarded her courteously, and to her annoyance she felt the color rising in her cheeks.

"It really is too ridiculous for words," she assured them. "But there! You know how people are!''

Neither would admit to such knowledge, and Miss Tolliver, feeling uncharacteristically harassed, plunged on.

"The thing is," she said, smiling brightly in a way meant to show how ridiculous she, herself, considered this one last thing, "somehow your groom—that is—when the message was left for the doctor to come—" She took a deep breath, and the words tumbled over each other in her haste to say them and be done. "Well, the long and the short of it is, there are people in the village nearby who believe that you and I, your lordship, are staying at this inn alone.''

Chapter
9

"What?" The word exploded in unison from the brothers, and for the first time Miss Tolliver felt real dismay at her situation. She had not had time to consider it while Gillian lay bleeding, and while Peter was tossing and turning dependent on her alone; when the doctor told her of the rumor sure to be circulating in the village, she had compartmentalized the knowledge, telling herself that it was not so very bad after all. But now, faced with two members of the *ton*, and knowing full well the price exacted for irregular behavior by her society, the full enormity of it swept over her.

"Well, don't shout at me!" she replied with some asperity. "It was your groom who left the impression! And as for that, if you'd keep a better eye on your wards, they wouldn't be out trying to kidnap an actress for you." That thought made her regard the earl with some severity. "And it seems to me that if you want any kidnapping done, you ought to do it yourself, and not corrupt young boys."

The earl's brows snapped together as he informed her that he had not sent his brothers to do any kidnapping, and he had no need to do so. John, eager to back him up, added, "Lord, no, not with all the women throwing themselves at Giles—why, he could have his pick of any lightskirt or any lady." He stopped to find his brother regarding him in annoyance, and Miss Tolliver with a return of her good humor.

76

"You are not helping, John," Giles said.

"Oh, but you are," Miss Tolliver assured him with great affability. "Now that you have made it clear that your brother need only snap his fingers to have women flocking to him—"

"I never—" John began, uneasy under Giles's frosty eye, but Miss Tolliver continued around his words.

"—I quite understand that it has all been a silly misunderstanding, and that our present situation is in no way your brother's fault; in fact, when I think about it, it is no doubt mine, for if I had not the temerity to venture out upon the King's road, my carriage would never have been there to tempt your brothers to stop it—"

"I didn't mean—" John began again.

"And embroil me in this affair."

"Not an affair," John protested feebly, and Miss Tolliver, cursing herself for the slip, agreed soberly that it was a poor choice of words. Because the earl's second brother seemed inclined to believe her to be serious, she relented slightly.

"Oh, please!" she said. "Don't look so. No doubt we'll laugh about it in the morning."

"Laugh?" John was honestly shocked, his expression putting Miss Tolliver forcibly in mind of her own brother. "Laugh, to have my brother put in this compromising position—?"

Miss Tolliver, who rather felt her position to be every bit as compromised as the earl's—perhaps more—bit her lip, and tried to smile. "No, no," she said. "You don't understand! It is such a small village—who is to know? I could leave right now, if you'd like, except that—well, I sent my brother's coachman off with my carriage, but I'm sure there is something for hire somewhere near here, and—well—" She cast a fleeting glance toward young Peter, lying with one hand thrown out across the covers. "I do think your brothers are in need of some careful nursing tonight, and unless you two are good at it—"

She eyed them hopefully as the brothers exchanged glances; with the best will in the world, neither could claim any competence in nursing.

"Perhaps," the earl said stiffly, angry to be caught in this

potential scandal of his brothers' making. "you would do us
the favor of remaining with my brothers until our old nurse
can be fetched from Willowdale. At that time I will be
happy to send you on to your destination in my own
carriage."

"Oh! Well! As for that—my brother will, as I've told
you, probably be here tomorrow with either my own or his
coach. And if he is not, I will merely need a ride to the
nearest posting inn. There is no need for you to convey me
home."

But this the earl would not allow; he said his coach was
entirely at her service. Feeling neither the inclination nor the
need to argue as the day's fatigue began to grow on her,
Miss Tolliver smiled pacifyingly. "There!" she said. "Things
have not turned out so badly after all!"

The earl and his brother exchanged slight smiles. It
certainly seemed so at the time.

An hour later, John was dispatched back to Willowdale
with orders to bring Nurse and any of the potions and
notions she could think of to make the invalids more
comfortable in the morning, and Miss Tolliver and the earl
settled down to their night of patient watching. Mrs. Murphy retired for a few hours' sleep, telling Miss Tolliver she
would spell her with the young gentleman in the early
morning hours.

At first Miss Tolliver took the watch in Gillian's room,
that young gentleman not quite up to facing his eldest
brother and guardian yet. He drifted in and out of sleep,
asking her a question each time he awakened. He was much
surprised to find that she was not the fair Vanessa—"it
wasn't that you looked like the beautiful actress," he
assured her, not noticing the twinkle that brought to her eye,
a twinkle hidden behind a deceptively meek face—it was
that he had been so sure they were stopping the actress's
coach.

He was much shocked to hear of Peter's condition, and
Miss Tolliver tried to minimize the news as best she could,
touched by the overwhelming guilt displayed on his face.

The news that his brother the earl was present made

Gillian's pale face even paler, and although he allowed that Giles was just what Peter needed at this time, he thought rather glumly that his brother's presence would do nothing to improve his own health. The information that John was gone made him brighten slightly, but his face fell again when he heard that John was expected back with Nurse in the morning. Miss Tolliver nodded consolingly.

"I know," she said. "I have a brother just like him."

A weak grin touched Gillian's lips. "It isn't that he's a bad sort, you know. It's just that he's so damnably—begging your pardon—*righteous*."

Miss Tolliver nodded again. "*Just* like him. You have my condolences."

Gillian drifted off again, and she was left to think. That Charles would have much to say about her present circumstances she knew, and her one hope was that Mister John Manfield and the old nurse would arrive and send her on her way before Charles joined them at the inn. That would spare her the mortification of having her brother try to come high-handed over the earl—an action she was sure would earn him a heavy setdown, and one that she was curiously unwilling to see—and it would also mean that when Charles did have his say with her, as he would no doubt do, it would be in the privacy of her home. She did not want the scene enacted in front of the Earl of Manseford—or anyone else, she told herself fiercely—nor did she wish to give the earl the satisfaction of hearing her brother tell her what was so apparent in the earl's own face and posture—that her actions, although well-intentioned, could, at least by some persons, be called ill considered and forward. She remembered the grim lines around the earl's mouth when he realized she was traveling without her maid, and bit her lip. A fine one he was, with his female-kidnapping brothers, to talk about propriety!

Such thoughts were interrupted by the earl himself, who came softly into the room to ask if she would join him at Peter's bedside. Disturbed by the grave expression on his face, she rose quickly. Once in the hall he bowed stiffly and said he very much feared Peter's condition was worsening.

"Oh, the poor boy!" Miss Tolliver said in swift sympathy, and turned toward the second bedroom. The earl opened the door, then followed her to where Peter lay tossing and turning, muttering incoherently as he tried unsuccessfully to find a cool spot on his pillow. He was doing his best to rid himself of the blankets, and Miss Tolliver hastened forward at once to tuck them in about him, saying in a kind but firm voice that no matter how hot he felt, he must lie quietly under the blankets, and not try to kick them off. Although he did not open his eyes or appear to hear, Peter left off fretting at the covers, and contented himself with hunting for that cooler spot on the pillow. The earl stood looking helplessly on until Miss Tolliver requested his help in raising his brother so she could turn the pillow, at which he moved swiftly forward. He watched without comment as her capable hands plumped and smoothed, and reached for the cool cloth beside the bed as he laid Peter down again. She wiped the boy's face and hands with the cloth before rinsing it out again and placing it on his forehead, all the time murmuring the soothing sounds that seemed to come naturally to her.

"Now, my lord," she said, her voice soft as she held one of Peter's hands, patting it consolingly, "I think that if you would pour a little of that laudanum into that glass, we might try to pour it down your brother's throat, and then I believe he would sleep easier. Sleep will help him tremendously, you know."

The earl nodded, tight-lipped, and did as he was told, coming around to the other side of the bed and raising his brother to grasp him firmly against his shoulder. He held the glass to Peter's lips and when Peter opened them slightly in protest, tipped the contents of the glass quickly down his throat, causing his brother to protest incoherently.

The earl met Miss Tolliver's eyes as he said, "I hope that is the way to do it. I've always found the fastest way over hard ground the best."

She agreed warmly, and continued to pat Peter's hand as the earl laid him down again. For a moment Peter opened bleary eyes, directed toward her, and managed another of those wavering smiles before drifting off again. The earl, watching, surveyed her critically.

"My brother seems to like you," he said.

Miss Tolliver, still holding the young boy's hand, answered absently, "He thinks I'm his mother." She turned inquiring eyes toward the earl. "I take it she is dead."

He nodded. "For a very long time."

"Ah. Poor boys."

He noted the plural in her last sentence but said nothing.

It was Miss Tolliver's suggestion, and the earl did not demur, that she spend the rest of the night with Peter, while the earl stayed with the wounded Gillian. Thus it was that that young man, awakening from one of his forays into sleep, was appalled to find his guardian posted in the chair beside him, the earl's long legs stretched out before him as he regarded his brother consideringly.

"Giles!" Gillian gasped.

His brother smiled slightly. "I am pleased to see, Gillian, that your wound has not impaired your mind. What there is of it . . ."

Gillian groaned, and closed his eyes. "I suppose this means I shall have to study with John forever . . ." he muttered, focusing on the first thought that entered his head before he opened his eyes again.

"Oh, at least that long," his brother assured him. "Maybe longer . . ."

Gillian shook his head, his voice rueful. "I really am sorry, Giles. Truly I am. Especially about Peter." His anxiety was apparent. "How is he?"

Like Miss Tolliver, the earl had no desire to add to Gillian's present burden, and assured him that Peter was resting.

"I made quite a mull of it, didn't I?" Gillian ventured.

The earl agreed that he had. "Compared to putting pigs in a nob's bed, this new scheme is far more serious. If I had to choose between the two, I believe I would have gone out and found you a pig!"

Gillian's face was glum. "I think," he said, "that if I were you, I would put me on the first boat for America."

Giles shook his head. "I do not believe," he said carefully, "that even our former colonies deserve that."

Gillian's face relaxed a little. "Then you don't hate me, Giles?"

The earl said he did not and, so assured, Gillian drifted off again, smiling.

Chapter
10

Morning brought good counsel for both the weary watchers. When Mrs. Murphy tiptoed into Gillian's room an hour before dawn, it was to find the patient resting comfortably, and his lordship dozing—albeit uncomfortably—before the fading fire. She "tsked, tsked" at him for his negligence as she energetically put the flames to right again, warning him in an austere whisper that it wouldn't do for the young sir, so recently weakened by a loss of blood, to take a chill now, would it?

Gillian, brought awake by her energetic application of the poker and several pieces of wood, smiled as he heard his normally autocratic brother agree with becoming meekness that it would not do. The smile disappeared in a moment, however, when Giles raised his voice and said, "We certainly wouldn't want that, would we, Gillian? It might interfere with your studies!"

Gillian turned his head in astonishment to stare at his brother. "You knew I was awake!"

Giles smiled slightly. "I know everything about you, Gillian. Always. I wish you would remember that and save us these—experiences—in future."

"Peter said—" Gillian began in astonishment, then caught his words up as his brother's smile grew. He was about to inquire just how Giles did it when Mrs. Murphy interrupted to say that since he was awake and all, she would just fetch up a basin of water to give him a proper little wash and shave, a suggestion that so overset him as he stared at her in amazement that all thoughts of his brother's omniscience vanished.

"You?" Gillian asked, startled and unsure he had heard right.

"Well, of course," the good lady responded, "and who else?"

"But—" Gillian looked in vain for help from his brother. "But—but—you're a woman!"

"Aye," Mrs. Murphy stood with her hands folded over her apron, agreeing with him.

"I can't have a woman bathing and shaving me!"

"Oh?" She inquired politely if he knew it was a woman who first brought him into the world; she asked if he'd had a nurse, her tone so reminiscent of that awesome and often bullying creature—who, Gillian remembered, was to descend on them shortly and reduce him to the age of three again in as many minutes—and she asked him just who he thought had been digging in his shoulder and no doubt saving his life the night before.

Gillian's eyes opened wide. "You—" he sputtered, his good hand moving to his bandaged shoulder. "You—" He looked for confirmation to Giles, who smiled more broadly. "I thought there was a doctor!"

"Oh, sure, now," Mrs. Murphy scoffed. "There was a doctor. But he came after all the work was done—just like some other men I could name—and only said it was a good job and he'd be back this morning. To collect his fee, I'll be bound. Ha!"

The thought seemed to so affect the landlady that she turned and stomped from the room, murmuring darkly to herself.

"Giles!" Gillian beseeched his grinning brother, who seemed prepared to follow her. The earl looked down at him.

"I'll be back," Giles promised, "after I've looked in on Peter. And because I am your guardian and suppose it is among my duties to keep you from dying of mortification at your tender age, I'll even undertake the washing and shaving. But there is the chance, dear brother, that you will soon wish yourself in that redoubtable woman's hands! The work of valet has never before come my way."

The grateful Gillian, his cheerfulness restored by his brother's promise, told Giles to wish Peter a good morning, and to say Gillian would be in to see him by and by, a statement Giles vetoed with the order that Gillian was to stay in bed for the day, and they would talk about his getting up only after the doctor's visit. About the cavil, Gillian saw the glint in Giles's eyes and, realizing that he could still renege on his promise to keep the awesome Mrs. Murphy at bay, subsided.

Once on the landing, the earl's smile vanished, and his eyes grew anxious as he moved toward his youngest brother's room. The door to it stood open, and Mrs. Murphy's voice came to his ears as he entered.

"I knew *you* wouldn't be sleeping, miss, not like some I could name who are set on to watch after their suffering kin, and then nod off like they haven't a care—no, I said to myself, you'll not find that the case with the lady—"

The lady, who was listening with half an ear as she smoothed the bed covers over the now quiet Peter, straightened, and saw the earl watching her from the doorway.

"—you can depend on the lady, I said to myself, not like some others I could name—" Mrs. Murphy rattled on, and the twinkle in Miss Tolliver's blue eyes was met by an answering one in the gray eyes meeting her own.

"Quite right, Mrs. Murphy," Miss Tolliver said, her mouth set primly. "It is so shockingly hard to get good help these days!"

"Wretch!" The word was spoken softly, and it surprised his lordship who had meant to maintain an air of polite formality with the lady in question. It made Miss Tolliver laugh, but Mrs. Murphy rose from her position beside a brightly burning fire to regard him with grave sternness.

"Ah, now," she said, shaking her head at him, "that's no way to be speaking to the lady who probably saved your brother's life, and you in the other room there, enjoying yourself and having yourself a little nap—''

The earl considered telling her with great acidity that the small chairs in her establishment made enjoying oneself nearly impossible for a man of his height, and that he thought the crick in his neck might be permanent, but Miss Tolliver intervened, her dancing eyes once again at variance with her prim face.

"Now, now, Mrs. Murphy," she said, "his lordship can do no more than his best, and we can't expect everyone to meet our high standards . . ." Her voice trailed off as the earl moved forward and Mrs. Murphy, shaking her head in full agreement as she eyed him severely, said she would be off, then, to see about breakfast for them all, and about the other young man's bath.

True to his word, Giles told her pleasantly that he would relieve her of the bathing and shaving chores, a statement that both pleased her and left her uneasy.

"Are you sure you can do it, now?" she questioned, her hands on her hips as she stood back to stare up into his face.

The earl assured her that he had been both bathing and shaving for some time and would endeavor to put his practice to good use. A gurgle rose in Miss Tolliver's throat, behind him; but Mrs. Murphy, after subjecting him to several more long seconds of inspection, agreed at last that he could at least make himself useful as long as he was here. Then she walked out, leaving a bemused lord and a laughing lady staring after her. When his lordship turned toward Miss Tolliver, the twinkle was back in his eye.

"I do not think the innkeeper's wife rates my presence highly," he said.

"Oh no," she was able to assure him, her eyes brimming with laughter at her soon-to-be-expressed thought, "for she was telling me only this morning that they once had a twelve-fingered man from one of the traveling fairs here for a night, and she rates your presence *far* above his!" She seemed to consider for a moment, then amended the sentence. "Or at least, slightly higher."

"I hope that doesn't mean I shall find half the countryside standing in the courtyard waiting to catch a glimpse of me," he said pleasantly as he walked forward to look down at the sleeping Peter, one hand going out to feel the boy's forehead. His eyes sought Miss Tolliver's for confirmation.

"He's better, isn't he?" the earl asked hopefully.

She smiled as she nodded. "The high fever seemed to abate toward morning. He seems much better."

"I thank you." Gratitude mixed with relief in his face, and Miss Tolliver shook her head with a smile.

"Truly," she said, "there is no need. I like your brothers; they're delightful children—although you mustn't tell Gillian I called him a child!"

The earl assured her he would not, and seemed about to say more when Peter stirred and opened sleepy eyes. "Giles?" he questioned, and as the earl sat down on the bed beside him, Miss Tolliver slipped through the doorway in search of her bags and her room, feeling a change of clothes and a good washing would help restore her flagging spirits. To that end she sought out Mrs. Murphy, who bustled her into the inn's back bedchamber, and suggested that she might like to lie down for an hour or two. Miss Tolliver declined the offer, but after she had washed and exchanged her soiled gown for one of mint green, its high waist set off by a forest green ribbon that matched the ruffled hem, and had once again done up her hair, she found the idea of a brief nap—just a few moments to rest her eyes—so entreating, that she lay down on the bed for a moment. It was with a start that she awoke several hours later, confused by her surroundings and the sound of coach wheels in the innyard.

For a moment she lay staring in puzzlement at the ceiling; then it all came back to her, and she hurried to the window, hoping that the coach she'd heard belonged to the earl's brother and not her own. To her disappointment she could not see the vehicle that had stopped in the yard in front of the house, so she hurried from the room and down the stairs just as the earl, who was partaking of a late breakfast in the private parlor, strolled into the hall expecting the arrival of John and the old nurse.

They collided at the bottom of the stairs, and the earl's arms automatically enclosed Miss Tolliver to prevent her falling. "So sorry," both murmured, abashed, just as the coach's occupant walked through the door. His startled "I say!" made them turn and part so quickly that Miss Tolliver had to grasp the bannister to keep from almost falling again. The gentleman who stood before them in a drab driving coat sporting a boutonniere the size of a small nosegay was unknown to her, but it was apparent the earl found him no stranger.

"Chuffy!" Giles seemed thunderstruck as he stared at the newcomer, but his amazement was nothing compared to that of the Honorable Charleton—Chuffy to his friends—Marletonthorpe. In fact, that gentleman seemed to be able to do little more than stand and goggle, his jaw opening and closing as he stared first from the earl to Miss Tolliver and back again. Instinctively Giles stepped forward to block his view of the lady, and his brow darkened. "What the devil are you doing here?" he asked irately.

At that, the Honorable Charleton found his voice.

"Live here, old boy," he said apologetically. "Well, not here but nearby. In the district, that is."

Giles, who remembered now that Marletonthorpe Manor was in the area, said with petulance that that fact did not explain his friend's appearance at the inn.

"But it does, old boy!" the other man assured him, his head moving up and down in a vigorous motion that put Miss Tolliver in mind of a horse. "Truly it does. Heard the rumor rumbling through the village this morning about this earl and a lady putting up at—uh—" He seemed to lose himself in his sentence and his face grew red as Miss Tolliver peered around the earl to eye him consideringly.

"Go on." The earl's voice was barely audible, but there was a note in it that made both Marletonthorpe and Miss Tolliver flinch.

"Well, the thing is," the unhappy visitor said, "—the thing is, I said to Harry, you can bet it's all a hum, Harry, because Giles is a high stickler, he is, and you know he wouldn't be staying at an inn with an unchaperoned lady— or even one of his ladybirds, for that matter . . ."

His voice trailed off again as his eyes met Miss Tolliver's, but after a brief struggle he went manfully on. "So I said, 'Harry, I'm just going to pop over to that inn and lay this all to rest before anyone further maligns my good friend Giles...'"

This time he seemed unable to continue, as the earl, with a slow expulsion of breath, said, "Are you telling me that Harry is in the area also? That both of you—in the middle of the season—have retired to the country?"

Chuffy nodded his head sadly, his expression making it apparent that he regretted their meeting as much as the earl. "Had to, old boy," he apologized. "I had business here. Harry's pockets are to let. All to pieces. Thinks if he stays around long enough, I'll drop my blunt just to be rid of him." The gentleman considered for a moment, then nodded. "Probably right, too. Awfully hard to countenance, is old Harry."

The earl sighed again. "I suppose it would be too much to hope that you might drive away and forget you ever saw us?"

The Honorable Charleton appeared even unhappier. "Be happy to, Giles. Really happy. Want to oblige you. But—thing is... never could keep a secret from old Harry. Or from anyone else, for that matter."

Miss Tolliver, feeling her world tilt, was thrown even further off kilter by his lordship's next words, so at odds with his tightening mouth and the disgust apparent in his eyes.

"Then you, Chuffy, are just the man I want," the earl said, his voice even in spite of his anger at the circumstances in which he found himself, "for there is no secret in the fact that I am about to take a bride." He turned to Miss Tolliver, and with a slight bow, said, "My dear, I would like to present to you the Honorable Charleton Marletonthorpe. Chuffy, this is my affianced wife, Miss Margaret Tolliver."

So great was Chuffy's astonishment that he did not notice that Miss Tolliver's was far greater. She stood stock still, her mouth an *O* and her eyes wide as she stared at the earl. Her cheeks, bright red only a moment before, drained of color. "You—you—" she started, but her accusation was cut short by the sound of another carriage pulling swiftly into the innyard.

"And there," the earl said, his words cutting across hers as he reached for her hand and gripped it hard, drawing her fingers through the crook of his elbow, "unless I very much miss my guess, is your chaperone, my dear—back from a morning drive."

Chapter
11

The earl more pulled than led Miss Tolliver from the hallway into the yard, and they were followed closely by a bemused Chuffy Marletonthorpe, whose mouth hung slightly ajar until the earl reminded him in the dryest of dry tones to shut it. This Marletonthorpe did, opening it again to say in strangled tones, "*Betrothed*?" The thought obviously horrified him. Miss Tolliver shared his sentiments exactly.

"No, no," she started, "there has been a mistake—*ouch!*"

She stared up at the earl in indignation, for his sharp pinch to her fingers made her break off her sentence in surprise.

"Yes, yes, my dear," he soothed, his tone at odds with the angry warning in his eyes, "I know we didn't plan to make it known until later. Bereavement in the family..." the earl explained to Chuffy, and Miss Tolliver thought bloodthirstily of the person she would like to suggest should die. She was not allowed to dwell on the thought, however, and her color heightened as Lord Marletonthorpe, always punctilious in such matters, expressed his condolences. Her disjointed response was thankfully cut short by the fast and furious arrival of another coach in the innyard, just as John, apparently harassed and not a little apologetic, was helping an elderly lady from the first carriage. Her dress, and the way the earl said "the devil!" at the elderly lady's appearance, suggested that she was not the expected nurse. Miss

Tolliver, seeing the earl's brows snap together, sighed heavily and awaited further developments.

They came quickly. The earl stepped toward the first coach, dragging Miss Tolliver with him. John, seeing their approach, turned to his brother with a "This wasn't my idea, Giles, believe me! Grandmama arrived this morning just as Nurse and I were ready to leave, and nothing would do but for her to come along. I tried to discourage her. Truly I did!"

He seemed to have little hope that his excuses would be listened to, and he was right. Giles afforded him only a curt nod, and the little lady to his left only crinkled up her nose at his explanation as she craned her neck up at the eldest of her grandsons.

"Well, sir?" she challenged him, her head to one side as her sharp brown eyes met his cold gray ones.

"Grandmama," Giles replied, bending to place a quick kiss on her cheek before straightening again. "I did not know we were expecting you."

The words might have been considered a setdown by some, but the old lady grinned heartily at his frown. "Weren't," she replied briefly. When he did not immediately reply, she said in the most affable tones imaginable, "Knew you would be delighted to see me, of course. Always are."

The earl bowed. "We are, of course, always pleased to have you with us. But at present we find ourselves not easily able to entertain visitors—"

"It was Caroline," the dowager countess replied, as if he had not spoken. "Fretting me to pieces with her 'Now, Mama, should you eat that?' and 'Now, Mama, you know the doctor said that isn't good for you.' Couldn't abide it another moment. So I packed up and came to see you. For there's one thing about you, Giles, you don't fret me. Don't bore me, either, like John there—" her finger jabbed at the harassed Mr. Manfield "—or throw me into high fidgets like Cassandra. If ever a child was well named, it's my Cassandra! Between her and Caroline—well! I must say, Giles, you are the best of the lot. Could be it's because I don't see you that often. But whatever the reason, I like you, boy. Always have. There it is. No understanding it.''

His grandmother's speech did not appear to gratify the earl unduly, perhaps because he too was acquainted with his Aunts Caroline and Cassandra, and did not find an admission that his grandmother considered him better company than either of her daughters any huge compliment. But it did a great deal to restore Miss Tolliver's tranquility, appealing as it did to her ever-ready sense of humor and making her like the outspoken little lady before they were ever introduced.

That might have been remedied had not Lord Marletonthorpe picked that moment to approach the dowager countess to make his bow and to inquire if she was enjoying her stay in the country.

The old lady, who, as she was want to put it, did not suffer fools gladly, frowned haughtily at the unfortunate Chuffy and replied, "Enjoying, you idiot? I just got he—''

"Back.'' her last word was interrupted as Giles finished for her. "You just got back, Grandmother. And we hope you and John and Nurse''—for that good woman had some moments ago climbed down from the coach and was staring at him as if he were five again, and had just gotten into the cherry tarts—"had a good drive.''

"Nurse?'' Chuffy questioned, striving to understand the situation. A light struck. "Feeling a bit under the weather are you, Countess?''

"Never—'' The old lady began, frowning at him again. But before she could voice the word *better*, the earl interrupted her again.

"Never one to complain, is Grandmother,'' he said. "We sent her off this morning with John and Nurse because we thought fresh air might avert the migraine she felt coming on. Did it, my dear?''

"Migraine?'' his grandmother echoed, glaring up at him. "What on earth are you talking about, Giles? You know I never get the—''

By this time she had read the warning in his eyes, and broke off abruptly. "Oh yes. The migraine. As a matter of fact, I feel it coming on again, right now.''

"I feel one coming on, too,'' Miss Tolliver said in hollow

tones as the door of the second carriage opened and her
brother painfully descended, groaning as his heavily wrapped
foot came in contact with the ground. He stood for a
moment, leaning heavily on his cane and glaring balefully at
them all. Then he started forward.

"You, too, ma'am?" Chuffy inquired with real concern.
"Dear me! Never knew the migraine to be catching."

"Oh, yes," Miss Tolliver said, the sight of her brother
spurring her to desperate measures. "Quite catching. In
fact, sir, if I were you, I would make haste to leave here
because you never know when you, too, might feel a
headache coming on."

Chuffy tried to demur, saying he was never ill—unless
you counted that inflammation of the lungs he had last
Christmas.

Miss Tolliver assured him that the migraine almost always
attacked persons who had suffered an inflammation of the
lungs last Christmas.

"Really?" He looked to the earl for confirmation and that
gentleman nodded as, with Miss Tolliver, he started moving
his friend back toward the horse on which he had arrived.

"Margaret!" Sir Charles shouted, furious to see his sister
moving away from him.

"Oh dear!" The words were involuntary and the earl,
watching her deeply flushed face, motioned to John to
accompany Lord Marletonthorpe to his horse as Giles, with
a most interested Grandmother and Nurse looking on, turned
with Miss Tolliver to meet her brother.

"Margaret Marie!" Sir Charles thundered just as the
confused Chuffy climbed onto his horse. "What is the
meaning of this?"

"Noisy fellow," Chuffy observed to John. "Wonder what
it is he wants to know the meaning of?"

"Wouldn't know," the harassed John said, raising a hand
as if to wave good-bye to his friend. The friendly Chuffy
was waving back as John's raised hand came down—
accidentally, Chuffy thought, but hard—on the rump of Lord
Marletonthorpe's horse, and Chuffy galloped from the innyard.
So overwhelmed was he by all he had heard and seen that it
didn't occur to him until he reached home and Harry asked

that he realized he still didn't know what the earl was doing at the small out-of-the-way inn, attended by so many members of his family. Chuffy shook his head thoughtfully and hoped Giles wasn't growing too eccentric in his middle years.

By the time Chuffy Marletonthorpe exited the innyard, Sir Charles had made his painful way up to his sister, pausing only when he stood mere inches from her, waving his cane for emphasis as he repeated his question.

"What is it, Margaret Marie? What have you done?" he demanded.

Miss Tolliver, acutely aware of their interested audience, and of the display her brother tended to make of himself when in a temper, tried to forestall a public washing of family linen by suggesting that they go into the inn and talk about it, but her suggestion was ignored. His mind too fully occupied even to hear her words, Sir Charles continued.

"My coachman," Sir Charles said, stabbing his cane toward that individual, who stood several paces back but definitely within earshot, "returns to my home, rousing me from my sickbed—my sickbed, Margaret Marie—with some faradiddle about kidnappers and a holdup on the Great North Road."

"It was a mistake—" Miss Tolliver tried. Her brother was having none of it, and charged ahead with his accusations.

"*Then*," Sir Charles said, frowning greatly, "*then* he tells me that when, in the line of duty, he wounded one of the ruffians and had his sights on another, you told him to put up—to put *up*, Margaret Marie—so that not only did you keep him from doing his duty, and ridding the world of one more highwayman, you also ordered him to bring you and the villains to this inn. And when he tried to represent to you the impropriety of your actions—when he told you exactly what I would have told you in the same circumstances—you sent him about his business."

"Your coachman," Miss Tolliver said, frowning angrily at that individual, who took a thoughtful step backward, "is a fool—"

Still Sir Charles was not listening, and he plunged on. "I

am *shocked*, Margaret Marie! *Shocked* and *sickened* that a member of my family—a gently nurtured female, given every advantage from the moment of birth—could behave in this manner, as if she were a common . . . a common—''

Words failed him, and he stood glaring at his sister, his eyes fairly bulging from his head, the muscles of his jaw working as his chin jutted forward.

''—and so are you,'' the gently nurtured female completed his thought. Mortified that he had played out his scene in front of such an audience, she turned without a word and walked away.

''Margaret!'' he roared, taking a hasty step forward. He was stopped by a heavy hand on his shoulder, and looked up to see the earl, his face devoid of expression, staring down at him. ''Unhand me, sir!'' he bellowed.

The earl did not. Instead he bowed slightly, his eyes never leaving Sir Charles's face. There was something in them that made Sir Charles shift slightly and tug at his neckcloth.

''How do you do?'' Giles said. ''I am the Earl of Manseford. This is my brother,'' he said, indicating John, whose face showed that he would rather be anywhere but in that innyard at that moment, ''and this is my Grandmother, the dowager countess.''

Sir Charles, feeling as if control of the situation was slipping from his hands, but not understanding how, nodded begrudgingly to John and made a stiff bow to the countess. She favored him with a very slight nod, and her eyes, remarkably like her grandson's despite the difference in color, returned to Giles's face.

''Pleased to make your acquaintance,'' Sir Charles mumbled, because it seemed to be expected of him. Once again he tried to twist out of the earl's grasp. Giles's hand only tightened.

''I hope so,'' the earl said. ''I hope so, indeed. Because we are all about to become related, Mr. Tolliver. Your sister and I are betrothed.''

Chapter

12

"What?" The word came from several mouths, and several pairs of eyes grew wide at the earl's announcement.

"Betrothed?" Again the word was said by several voices, but after that questions pelted the earl with such speed, mixing and mingling with each other to such a degree, that he could not distinguish one from the other. He raised a hand for silence, and when that did not work, he barked the word *"Quiet!"* with such force that even his grandmother, the most redoubtable of dames, was startled enough to stop speaking.

"That's better!" the earl said, frowning at them all. "Now then. One question at a time, if you please."

"How?" The question was a chorus again, and there was a slight lessening of the earl's frown as he surveyed their faces and considered the ridiculousness of it all. For some curious reason he felt he was onstage, playing the lead in a period farce. For a moment he almost smiled, then his brows snapped together.

What, he asked himself severely, was there to smile about in this situation? True, the people before him had all the appearances of a gaggle of startled geese, and that struck him as funny. But the reason for their consternation was also a matter of deuced inconvenience to him, and that, he had to admit, was anything but laughable. Accustomed to running events, the earl was not pleased to find events running him, and he was brusque as he turned toward the bristling Sir Charles. .

"Your sister," Giles told him, "probably saved one of my brothers' lives yesterday when she prevented him from bleeding to death and brought him here so that a doctor might attend him."

"*What*?" his grandmother interrupted, horrified.

"Gillian," Giles said briefly, and the old lady sighed.

"Gillian," she repeated, as if that was enough of an explanation.

"She kept another of my brothers from being shot by your overanxious servant there." The coachman eased back a step, his eyes on the ground, but the earl's attention was diverted from him as the dowager countess stared at her second eldest grandson.

"Surely not you, John?" she questioned. His vigorous denial and explanation that it was Peter made her sigh again. "I thought not John," she said sadly. "Not that kind of spirit. Poor Peter!"

"And she sat through the night nursing them," Giles continued, ignoring his grandmother's interruption and John's manner of ill-usage at her comments, "even though they were not her charge and many people in our set certainly would have driven on and left them to their fate. It was the act of a kind and generous lady."

"Yes, well..." Sir Charles shrugged a shoulder angrily. "That's all very well, but what I say is that if Margaret would just think... It isn't like she had to leave my hearth and home at that strange hour..." His voice trailed off as the earl raised his quizzing glass and stared at him through it.

"Isn't it?" the earl inquired politely, and Charles, unsure of what had been said about his sister's abrupt departure before his arrival, decided to change tack.

"Yes, well... water under the bridge, I'm sure," he blustered. "But what is this about your being engaged to my sister? To my knowledge you never met her before today!"

"Last night," the earl answered briefly.

Sir Charles's color rose alarmingly. "Last night? And what happened here last night?"

The earl merely looked at him again.

"I met your sister for the first time last night," Giles said. "Not today."

"Well—but—" Sir Charles stuttered. He was interrupted by Nurse, who had a romantic soul.

"Love at first sight!" that worthy trilled. It occurred to Giles that he had never heard her trill before, but that thought was superseded by her next extraordinary action as she so far forgot herself as to throw her arms around him and give him a crushing hug, exclaiming as she did, "Ah now, your lordship, it's always the quiet ones you have to watch for. 'Still waters run deep,' I always say."

She stepped back, beaming, only to be interrupted by an imperious "Hogwash!" All eyes turned toward the dowager countess.

"Hogwash," she repeated, waving one hand toward Nurse and adjuring her to stop her foolish drivel and be off to the injured boys while she—the Countess—got to the bottom of the situation. Seeing Nurse poker up, Giles quickly seconded the notion and sent her off with John, whose last words as he stepped into the inn were, "But Giles, you said you'd loan her a carriage. Decent thing to do. Thought so at the time. A *carriage*, Giles—not *marriage*!"

The bewildered note in his voice was such that Giles almost laughed. That feeling vanished swiftly as he turned to the two figures still waiting for him.

"Now, sir—" Sir Charles began, but the countess overbore him.

"Now, sir," she interrupted, fixing Sir Charles with a minatory eye, "we are going to get to the bottom of this—that is, *I* am going to get to the bottom of this, for you don't strike me as a man who could get to the bottom of a stair without directions—but we are going to do so inside, out of the dirt and away from the gawking eyes of the masses."

Since the only "masses" present were the earl's coachman and groom and Sir Charles's coachman, all of them extremely interested bystanders but hardly enough to qualify as a crowd, the countess could have been accused of exaggeration. Neither of the gentlemen was unwise enough to level the accusation, however, and in silence they followed her straight little figure into the inn. There they were welcomed by Mrs. Murphy with the intelligence that if they wanted to use the small parlor they were welcome, and if the gentlemen liked, her husband could bring them a pint of his best ale, but for the lady she was that distressed, there was naught in the house for a lady to drink but tea.

"Tea!" The countess shuddered delicately, interrupting the jumbled speech. "I left home to avoid forever maudling my insides with tea! I," she pronounced, staring straight at her grandson, "shall drink ale. If you will be so kind."

Her most winning smile was fixed on Mrs. Murphy, who dropped an open-mouthed curtsey along with her "Well, I never," and hurried off to tell her mate about the strange ways of the quality.

"Now," the countess commanded after they had entered the low-ceilinged parlor with its white walls and brass candlesticks above the mantlepiece, and she and Sir Charles had disposed themselves, in varying degrees of comfort, on the two straight-backed chairs found there, "you may begin."

But Giles, who had walked to the single window in the room and now stood staring out it, unaware of the innyard bustle unfolding before his eyes, showed no disposition to do so. After several moments his grandmother prompted with, "You were about to tell us how you became engaged."

"Was I?" he asked with a slight smile as he half-turned toward them. "I rather thought Nurse explained all that."

"Giles," his grandmother said impatiently, "I am an old woman. I have lived a long time and seen a great many things. There may be such a thing as 'love as first sight' —although I doubt it myself; always seems to me like it's the province of silly cawkers—but if you have experienced it in the last twenty-four hours, I would be much surprised."

"Still waters run deep," he murmured, teasing her. Majestically she ignored him.

"And if the lady in question has experienced it in relation to you, I would immediately relinquish to Cassandra *my* grandmama's diamond tiara which she has wanted since she was three, and which I fully intend to be buried with, just to show her.''

"Such a loving mother," the earl commented, but his grandmother would not be diverted.

"Are you going to stand there and tell us the lady is in love with you?" she demanded. "Because I was watching her face in the innyard, and it seemed to me that she would more cheerfully strangle than marry you."

Ruefully he shook his head. "I fear, Grandmama, that you are right. Miss Tolliver was not best pleased by my announcement of our upcoming marriage."

"Then why—" the old lady began, puzzlement wrinkling her brow.

"Because we must."

"*What?*" Sir Charles fairly roared the word as he rose from his chair, surging forward onto his bad foot and wincing at the pain. "You blackguard! You scoundrel! Taking advantage of my poor sister—although how you could do so is beyond me, because I've never been able to beat her even at cards—"

"Oh, take a damper, Tolliver," the earl advised, disgusted at the evident meaning Sir Charles put on his words. "Nothing improper passed between your sister and me in our time here. In fact, few words have passed between your sister and me in our time here. But this morning when Chuffy Marletonthorpe walked through the inn door and found her in my arms—"

"*What?*" Both his grandmother and Sir Charles were staring at him, and the earl shook his head.

He told them with some asperity that he wished they would do both Miss Tolliver and himself the honor of believing in their integrity and their ability to conduct themselves credibly in all circumstances. Neither seemed particularly chastened, and it was with a great deal of stiffness that he explained that he and Miss Tolliver had collided in the hall, and he had put out his arms to keep her from falling just as Chuffy Marletonthorpe walked through the door.

"Well, silly cawker that he is, he assumed just what you

two were assuming," the earl concluded, "and I had no choice but to inform him of our imminent engagement."

"Then you did it to protect the lady's reputation," his grandmother said thoughtfully, and he nodded. She fixed him with a keen eye. "But the lady wasn't grateful?"

"No." The earl shook his head, and his eyes darkened as he considered Miss Tolliver's indignation. "Far from it. She even tried to tell Chuffy it was a mistake—"

"But you didn't let her?" Again the countess's eyes and voice were sharp, and he shook his head in irritation.

"I couldn't," he said. Then he thought a moment. "Could I?"

About to speak, the countess was interrupted by Sir Charles, who had had time to assimilate all that had been said to him, and to consider its implications. This time Mr. Tolliver rose from his chair with real enthusiasm, almost forgetting his gout as he limped forward. "No," he assured the earl as he grasped Giles's hand and pumped it heartily, "you couldn't. Very gentlemanly thing to do. Most decent of you. Going to marry my sister. Make her a countess. I never thought she'd be a wife, much less a countess, for a more headstrong, sharp-tongued—"

It occurred to Sir Charles that these remarks were hardly felicitous, and he changed the topic as he lowered his voice and said confidentially to the earl, "I've heard of you, you know—good stock, good estates, lots of ready—and what I say is, it's a good thing you're taking a wife. I would imagine you'll make a healthy settlement, too . . ."

His words trailed delicately off as he turned a hopeful face toward the earl, who bowed with an irony even Sir Charles could not miss. Mr. Tolliver colored slightly.

"Well, I've got to look out for my sister," he said defensively.

The earl agreed and said he would be quite happy to make a handsome settlement—if Miss Tolliver should find herself able to accept his suit. The thought that she would not so upset Sir Charles that he said he would go to her immediately, and stomped out of the parlor and groaned his way up the stairs to the room the harassed landlord, coming down the passageway with three pints of his best ale, told him Miss Tolliver occupied. A short time later Sir Charles was seen exiting the room in a great hurry, two large pillows and a vehement description of his character following his departure.

The countess, who had seen his movement through the open parlor door, raised her half-full mug of ale to her grandson. "To your affianced wife," she said, her eyes twinkling.

"To my affianced wife," Giles responded, drank deeply, and then put down the mug before he, too, started up the stairs.

Chapter
13

The earl's gentle knock upon Miss Tolliver's door was met with a sharp, "I warn you, Charles, if you come in here again I shall heave the mattress at you! And anything else I can find!"

"Well, my dear," the earl said, slowly opening the door, "I beg you will not further dismantle the bed, for it is I, and not your brother, and while I do not wish to have things . . . er . . . 'heaved' at me, I am most assuredly coming in."

Miss Tolliver was wiping angry tears from her eyes and turned away at his entrance to make one more vigorous swipe at her cheeks before facing him. "I should tell you, my lord, that I am in a dangerous mood," she said, chin up and hands clenching and unclenching at her sides.

"I shall heed your warning," he promised, noting her flushed cheeks, made redder by her recent cry. "And since I fear that my brothers and I are to blame for it, I think it behooves me to do what I can to rectify the situation. Don't you agree?"

Miss Tolliver did not, and said so. She told him that as far as she was concerned, there was no 'situation.' She had done what she could to aid two boys who through their own folly and misplaced adoration of an older brother—a point she made darkly—had come to grief.

Now, she said, they were in good hands; the inn fairly overflowed with their family, and she was ready to be off to her own home, there to forget she had ever traveled the Great North Road—a mistake she would not make again.

The earl heard her out in silence, but when she would have shaken his hand with a stiff good-bye, he took the hand held out to him and drew her to a chair, asking her to be seated. Miss Tolliver told him she preferred to stand.

"My dear—" he began.

"I am not your dear!" She cried, nearly stamping her foot in vexation. "Why does everyone persist in thinking I *am*? First a woman in a bonnet—a massive woman in a massive bonnet, really—positively *envelopes* me in an embrace when I stopped in to check on your brother Peter—"

"Nurse—" he explained.

"—and then would not accept my explanation that it was all a mistake, calling me a sly puss and wishing me happy despite my best efforts to assure her that marriage and happiness were not closely matched in my mind."

"She has a romantic soul," the earl explained, ignoring her comments on the matrimonial state, and Miss Tolliver glared at him in vexation.

"And then my brother—my *brother*—" the loathing in her tone made the earl smile "—*barges* into my room and tells me I should thank my lucky stars for such a catch. And when I tell him I have not caught and certainly do not plan to keep you, he *harangues* me about my duty to my family—and God and king and country, I think; somewhere in there I quit listening—and assures me that if we are not married, I shall be disgraced in the eyes of the world forever and ever. As if I cared for the eyes of the world! As if society had not consigned me to the shelf these many years past! As if that wasn't where I wanted to be! When I think of the shifts I was put to to prevent the marquis from applying to my brother for my hand, while as for young Mr.—"

All at once she focused on her exceedingly interested audience, and Miss Tolliver stopped abruptly, her hands pressed to her hot cheeks before they moved to cover her mouth, her eyes wide with dismay.

"I do beg your pardon," she stammered, almost overcome by her own carelessness. "I had forgotten there was anyone else here."

"Not at all," the earl replied politely. Then a thought occurred to him. "Do you often rage to empty rooms?"

"Oh yes." Her eyes twinkled. "All the time. One gets into far less trouble that way."

"I see." The earl considered her for a moment, his head to one side. "Are you often in trouble, Miss Tolliver?"

Candidly she replied that it did not occur so much anymore, adding that when she was younger, she suffered from the most unladylike habit of speaking her mind; but as she grew older, she learned to be much more careful who she was speaking her mind to. "Why, some people hardly know I have a mind at all!" she finished.

She meant it as a joke, but his eyes were grave as he assured her that was certainly the other people's loss.

"No, no, no!" she scolded half-smilingly. "That is not what you are supposed to say! You are supposed to say, 'Well, madam, if that is the case I fear we will not suit,' or 'I will not have a termagent for my affianced wife,' and slip thankfully from the room."

"I am?"

"Yes." She shook her head in mock disgust. "Honestly! Sometimes I have to do *everything* myself."

"You certainly seem capable of doing everything," he remarked.

"Oh yes." Margaret agreed easily. "I am one of the most capable people you'll ever know. Everyone says so."

"They do?"

"Yes. I am known throughout my family for my great capability. It is, I believe, one of the things my relatives find most wearing about me. If only I would learn to—how do they put it?—*droop* a little. If I could only swoon at the sight of a spider, or if I were given to mild hysterics when the satin delivered for the chair covers isn't right. It would make me so much more appealing. Unfortunately, I have so little sensibility that the wrong satin only annoys me, and I do no more than send it back again. It is most distressing."

"It is?" The earl, with his male fear of any form of female hysterics, could not believe anyone could ever have said such things to her, but Miss Tolliver nodded gravely as she crossed to the bed and sank wearily onto it, her energy suddenly spent by that last explanation. With one hand she motioned him to the chair by the window, and he took it, watching her for several moments before asking curiously, "What would you rather be?"

"What?" The question startled her.

"What would you rather be, other than capable?"

"What an odd question!" she began. "No one has ever asked me before. But since you ask, I'd rather be—" She was twisting the strand of hair that had escaped its pins at the back of her neck, but she stopped herself abruptly and straightened, regarding him with some severity.

"I think, my lord," she told him, "that we would do better to discuss this ridiculous tangle we find ourselves in, instead of woolgathering after my silly thoughts and fancies."

"But I'm enjoying your thoughts and fancies," he protested. She frowned at him again.

"This must be the famous Earl of Manseford charm and address used to turn women to witless wax in your hands."

Now it was the earl's turn to frown. "You have been talking to my brother Gillian, I see," he said.

"Not at all, my lord," she denied, smiling sweetly at him. "Your reputation precedes you."

His frown grew. "I begin to think your brother was not mistaken about your sharp tongue, Miss Tolliver."

"No." She rose, one hand on the bedpost as she stood looking down at him. "He was not. Thank your lucky stars you discovered it before it was too late, my lord. Now I will bid you adieu."

It was an excellent exit line, she thought, but since it was her room, she had nowhere else to go, and the earl, who had earlier struck her as a quick-witted man, clearly did not take his cue. He rose, as she had intended, but he showed no inclination to leave. Instead, he stood looking down at her with such a thoughtful expression that she was moved to rail him on it, suggesting that he run before she changed her mind.

He considerably startled her by stating quite calmly that that was just what he wished her to do.

"It is?"

He smiled at her apparent confusion, and with the address for which he was renowned, reached for her unresisting hand and raised it to his lips before asking in the soft voice that was known to turn half of London's society matrons to jelly, "And what is it you wish, Miss Tolliver?"

With a great deal of resolution she removed her hand from his and, holding it behind her back in case he might decide to reach for it again, she swallowed and put her chin up firmly. There was something in that small determined act that touched him, and his practiced smile softened. It was a most dangerous smile, Miss Tolliver thought distractedly, and hurried into speech before she forgot what her good intentions told her she must say.

"I wish," she said, her anxious blue eyes meeting his enigmatic gray ones, "for you to tell Charles—and your grandmother, and your brothers, and your silly friend—that it is all a hum, and we are no more betrothed than we are Napoleon and Josephine."

"An interesting comparison," he said, raising an eyebrow in a way that made Miss Tolliver wish she could reclaim her last words—or hit him. "But I find I cannot grant your wish."

"What?"

"Come, come, Miss Tolliver," he said, stepping toward her. She stepped away, and he did not follow her again, contenting himself to watch her as he spoke.

"I'm afraid we must both make the best of a bad bargain," he continued, realizing as the lady flinched that it was an unfortunate choice of words. "That is—I mean—" He paused and looked down at her, and his face was kind. "It is through the actions of my family that you find yourself in this predicament, and I must offer you a way out of it. Not for the world would I have you ridiculed or shunned by society for your innocent—if ill-judged—behavior."

"Ill judged?" Miss Tolliver, who had felt a ridiculous urge to cry in the face of his apparent kindness, found those words all she needed to overcome her emotions and to fire up her temper again. "Ill judged?"

"Well," the earl said reasonably, "if you had been traveling with your maid—"

"Oh yes," she said, the palm of one hand striking her forehead as she considered his words. "How ill judged of me—how blatantly wrong—to give a woman who has served me faithfully for fifteen years a few days off to visit her ailing mother! What a fool I am! I see it now! You are right, my lord—quite right. Not for the world must you take such a foolish, foolish wife! Please—flee immediately!"

"Miss Tolliver." This time he did step forward, and placed his hands on her shoulders. Margaret, who could see no way to rid herself of them without a most unladylike struggle, did of necessity stand and listen.

"Miss Tolliver," he said again, one hand moving to raise her chin until she was looking into his face. "I am saying this badly. I apologize. But I believe it is important that both you and I realize that in the eyes of our world, your spending the night in this inn with me, unchaperoned—"

"But the boys—Mrs. Murphy—" she started.

"In the eyes of the world, you were unchaperoned," he repeated, cutting her short, "which makes it imperative that I offer you the protection of my name, and that you accept. Really, Miss Tolliver, to save your reputation, and mine, we *must* be engaged."

"But—" Margaret stared at him helplessly, aware that the one thing she hated more than the feeling that *she* was being pushed into this was the conviction that *he* was being pushed into it, too. Then a thought occurred to her.

"For how long?" she asked him.

He stared at her. "What?"

"For how long must we be engaged?"

"Well . . ." His hands dropped from her shoulders, and his eyes grew cold as he seemed to consider. More calculating women than she had spent years trying to trap him into marriage, and this abrupt change from not wanting to be betrothed to wondering how soon they could marry made him suspicious of a plot—and the most devilishly fiendish plot he had yet seen, for how she had managed to inveigle Gillian and Peter in it he did not know.

Miss Tolliver was aware of his change of mood, and her

chin came up again as he said, his voice devoid of expression, "I suppose that, with special license, the engagement need not be long . . ."

"No, no, no!" This time Margaret did stamp her foot in vexation, and her next words proved his suspicions unworthy. "*Will* you get marriage off your mind? Much as I dislike admitting it, I do understand your concern for your reputation."

About to note that it was her reputation that also concerned him, the earl watched her take a hasty step around the room, and changed his mind.

"Before I was thinking only of my reputation," Miss Tolliver said. "It was most unfair of me. I see that now. But when you said we must be engaged, it occurred to me that that does not mean we must marry! We can pretend to be engaged now, and later, when the—er—unusual situation surrounding our engagement has been forgotten, we can simply declare that we do not suit and that the engagement is at an end. My lord, it is the most wonderful idea!"

The earl, who did not want to think what his friends would have to say now, when they heard he was to be leg-shackled at last, or later, when the word was spread that his betrothed had cried off, regarded the eager face before him consideringly. There was something about a lady who did not want to marry him that piqued him almost as much as did those who had for years sought to share his name and fortune.

"Are you saying," he asked, watching her closely, "that if it is only for a time, you will agree to this engagement?"

"Yes." Miss Tolliver gathered up her resolution and spoke firmly. "Yes, I will."

The earl bowed. "Miss Tolliver, you do me a great honor."

"Stuff!" Miss Tolliver replied.

Chapter
14

When the earl descended the stairs a short time later, he was met by an anxious Sir Charles, who looked him over carefully before inquiring what Margaret had heaved at him.

"Nothing," the earl said tranquilly, and passed into the parlor where his grandmother awaited him. Sir Charles hobbled along behind.

"Well?" the old lady questioned, glaring at him over her second pint of ale.

"I'm sure you shouldn't be drinking that," he answered, looking down at her. "I haven't a doubt Aunt Caroline would tell me so. And that I should remove it from your presence this instance."

"Stuff!" his grandmother replied, taking another sip. The earl, who had heard the expression recently, smiled and picked up his own mug.

"If you must drink, then, let us drink to my betrothal," he said, raising the pint and partaking deeply. The dowager countess choked and spit ale.

"*What*?" she cried.

"*What*?" Sir Charles echoed.

"You mean she'll have you?" the countess asked.

"You mean she'll have you?" a dumbfounded Sir Charles repeated.

The earl smiled and bowed, telling them with great irony that the obvious high regard in which they held him did him

111

honor, and that he would endeavor to live up to their apparent expectations.

His grandmother ignored him. "Thought the gal had more sense than that," she grumbled into her ale, and took another sip to refresh herself.

Sir Charles was regarding her in horror. "You thought Margaret had more sense? My dear madam, she has no sense at all! Never did!" Then he surged toward Giles to shake his hand warmly and, ignorant that it was his last remark and its various implications that had placed the smile on the earl's face, congratulated Giles, Margaret, and himself roundly, and called for the landlord and a bottle of his best champagne to celebrate properly.

Before Mr. Murphy could respond, a quiet voice from the doorway cut into Sir Charles's sounds of jubilation.

"It is hardly a matter for champagne, Charles," Miss Tolliver said, eyeing her brother from the doorway. "Our engagement is only for a time—for propriety's sake. Didn't his lordship tell you that?"

The happy glow faded from Sir Charles's face and his head swiveled around toward the earl. "No," he said, "he didn't."

"No." This time the echo was the earl's grandmother. "He didn't." She took another gulp of her ale and held the mug out toward Miss Tolliver. "Knew you had too much sense to hook up with my grandson, my dear. Could tell it just by looking at you. My congratulations."

Miss Tolliver curtseyed, a small smile playing across her lips as she caught his lordship's eye. He bowed again. When she rose she regarded her brother with a critical eye and asked, "Yes, Charles? Is there something you want to say?"

Since his jaw had been working for several moments as one hand played with his cravat, tugging on it as if it chafed him unbearably, her observation was just. And true. Sir Charles had a great deal to say. He started with "What do you mean, it is just for a time?" and ended, seated with his head in his hands, saying "I wash my hands of you Margaret Marie. This time, truly, I do."

"Promises," she said softly, moving to pat his shoulder. "Always promises."

The dowager countess choked on her ale again, and Sir Charles raised his head to glare at both ladies impartially. The earl decided it was time he took control of the situation.

"Now, now, Sir Charles," he said, moving forward from his place by the window and stopping to perch on the room's only table, one leg swinging freely as he looked down at the suffering face before him. "I believe we have devised an excellent scheme. You and your sister—and any other relatives you should wish to have join us—shall retire with us to Willowdale shortly for an extended visit. That should set the tattlemongers' tongues to rest. Then, if at some later date, your sister and I decide we do not suit—"

"*When* we decide we do not suit," Miss Tolliver interrupted firmly.

The earl bowed in her direction and continued, "—you will depart, with no scandal attached to your sister's name."

"Or to yours." Miss Tolliver was watching him closely.

"Or to mine," he agreed, smiling again at Sir Charles. "In the meantime you will, I hope, have enjoyed a happy visit at what is, although I am sure I shouldn't say it, commonly considered one of the prettiest country homes in the district."

"Come, Charles." Miss Tolliver patted his shoulder again. "Half a loaf is better than none, surely? Accept his lordship's invitation and be thankful."

"I would rather see you married," Sir Charles grumbled.

This time the pat on his shoulder became a sharp squeeze. "*Half* a loaf, Charles," Miss Tolliver said. "And if you do not care for it, you may wash your hands of me, as you've promised, and return to London. In fact, your carriage awaits."

Her brother twisted his head to stare up at her. "You never have had any wit, Margaret Marie. Whistling a fortune down the wind—"

"Charles!" she said warningly.

"—and all for some damned scruple—and it's all very well to talk about not forcing a man into marriage, but here's his lordship offering, and some women would jump at the chance, but not you, oh, no—''

"Charles!" The warning was stronger as Miss Tolliver perceived the arrested look in his lordship's eyes, and the significant glance his grandmother directed toward him. This time Sir Charles subsided.

"Oh, very well." His feeling of ill-usage was strong. "But here's the earl, a perfectly good man, I'm sure, and what's more to the point, rich as Croesus, and what must you do—"

"Charles!" Two red spots stood out on Miss Tolliver's cheeks, and one fist was clenched as if to hit him.

"Oh, very well," he repeated, eyeing the fist with some misgiving. "I'm mum."

"Never!" she answered bitterly.

He looked at her, then at the others in the room. "But what did I *say*?" he asked plaintively.

"Nothing untoward," the earl assured him, watching Miss Tolliver. The countess, watching them all, drained her ale and said nothing until the silence in the room had lengthened far past what she considered seemly. Then she put her mug down with a snap, and with a brisk "Well, what's to do now?" stood up and glanced, bright-eyed, from her grandson to his betrothed. Miss Tolliver seemed momentarily at a loss, so the countess directed her attention toward Giles. He did not disappoint her.

"I think," he said with the decision that characterized him, "that it would be best if you and John return to Willowdale today, accompanied by Miss Tolliver and her brother."

"What?" Miss Tolliver demurred. "But sir, your brothers! You certainly are not the one to take care of them—"

The earl was not used to being argued with, and it showed. "Nurse and I shall stay here with the invalids, Miss Tolliver," he said with a frown. "There is no need for you to trouble yourself further on our behalf."

"Well!" Miss Tolliver's chin came up and her eyes snapped. "Don't you think that's rather autocratic, my lord, to be deciding who will go and who will stay, with nary a thought for the wishes or the suggestions of others?"

The dowager countess grinned at the surprised look on her grandson's face; it was, she decided, high time he got used to having his decisions questioned.

"Autocratic?" the earl said in amazement. "My dear Miss Toll—"

"I am not your dear anything! I have told you that before. And there is no need to patronize me, my lord. Just because I do not have a lower voice or grow a beard does not mean that I do not have a brain."

"Margaret!" Sir Charles gasped, watching his hopes of a still-happy outcome to this unlooked-for opportunity vanish before his eyes as his sister and the earl stared daggers at each other.

"Quite right!" The countess interrupted in satisfaction and reached for her grandson's ale mug that he had set down on the table near her. Finding it not yet empty, she drank heartily, ignoring both the earl's and Sir Charles's frowns.

"Not right at all." Sir Charles hurried into speech, trying unsuccessfully to catch his sister's eye as he grinned placatingly at the earl. "You'll have to excuse her; shock of it all, you know—"

"Oh, do be quiet, Charles!" Miss Tolliver interrupted.

"Yes," the countess seconded her, frowning at him. "Quiet."

The earl looked down at his grandmother and stepped forward to remove the ale from her grasp. The countess glared at *him*, too.

"I believe," he said to Margaret, the words coming between slightly clamped lips, "that if you will allow me to continue, I can convince you of the propriety of my plan." She gave a most unladylike snort, but refrained from speaking. The earl's jaw tightened further.

"There obviously is not enough room in this inn for all of us to stay," he said. "Four bedchambers, two of which are already filled with invalids, cannot accommodate my grandmother, you, your brother, and myself, to say nothing of Nurse, the maid grandmama would be lost without, and our valets, Miss Tolliver."

She bit her lip at his logic, and his jaw muscles relaxed slightly as he saw a rueful look come into her eyes. *Ah ha!*

he thought, and continued aloud. "When the invalids are well enough to travel—hopefully in a day or two—we shall all join you at Willowdale."

"But—" Miss Tolliver was not ready to give up. "It doesn't seem right, my lord. You are no hand in the sickroom, and I would be so happy to stay—"

"But then, Miss Tolliver, there would still be the question of your chaperone, wouldn't there?" he inquired silkily.

She glared at him. "With your nurse present—"

"But I could not for the world ask Nurse to add to her duties that of chaperoning you, Miss Tolliver. Really. I wish you would have a care for others in this whole situation—"

About to fire up, Margaret realized in time that he was roasting her, and subsided, contenting herself with a fulminating glance which, to her disgust, only seemed to increase his enjoyment of the situation.

"Quite right," he murmured, bowing to her before he continued. "In the meantime, Miss Tolliver, you can contact any of your relatives that you wish to have join you at Willowdale."

The offer had been made before, but it registered in Sir Charles's mind for the first time, and he started uneasily. "No, no," he said, shifting in his chair and looking from the earl to his sister and back again. "No need for that. Can't have the relatives descending on you. Wouldn't be polite." The earl said he did not mind, and Sir Charles lowered his voice confidentially. "Thing is, rather odd sort, the relatives."

The dowager countess choked, and Miss Tolliver sighed heavily.

"Yes, Charles," she told her brother. "He knows about my odd relatives."

"Oh?" Missing her meaning, Sir Charles was surprised. "You've met our Aunt Henrietta, then?"

The earl said he had not had the pleasure, and Charles regarded him with anxious eyes, shaking his head from side to side in a manner that reminded his sister of a large and not quite bright dog. "No pleasure, I assure you. Wouldn't want Aunt Henrietta at Willowdale. Wouldn't do at all. Would it, Margaret?"

It was a mistake, asking his sister, and he knew it immediately.

"Yes," Miss Tolliver replied, her chin up and her eyes sparkling. "If I am to be there, Aunt Henrietta must certainly come."

"But—" Charles protested.

"And Lazarus. You must fetch them immediately, Charles."

"Lazarus?" the earl inquired politely. Sir Charles stamped his cane angrily on the floor.

"Stap me, Margaret Marie, if that isn't beyond all bounds, and you know it. Can't bring Lazarus into another man's home; wouldn't have him in mine."

"He must be some fellow, this Lazarus," the countess ventured, enjoying herself immensely. "Is he your aunt's son?"

"No." Miss Tolliver answered promptly. "Her rooster."

"Her—" The countess shook her head and gazed accusingly at the second ale mug. "I'm sorry, my dear—it's an old woman's hearing. I would have sworn you said this Lazarus fellow is your aunt's rooster!"

"Yes." Miss Tolliver was smiling, her head held high. Her eyes met the earl's and there was a definite challenge there. If she did not expect him to meet it, she was disappointed.

"Dear me," the earl said, "and how does one entertain a—er—rooster?"

The earl's expectation that he, his two youngest brothers and old Nurse would arrive back at their ancestral home in "a day or two" was optimistic; Peter's recovery was slower than all might wish, and when it rained for five days straight, the doctor could not recommend that he make the twenty-mile drive in his condition. It was over a week before the sun came out, Peter perked up to the doctor's liking, and the earl and his entourage arrived back at Willowdale. It was a week during which there had been many moments when he wished he had accepted Miss Tolliver's offer to stay with his brothers, and that he had beat a hasty if undignified retreat. The earl felt he had borne much, and was ruefully aware that he was not given to appreciate time spent in the sickroom, or catering to the whims of convalescing patients. But if he had borne much, it became clear after several moments home that Miss Tolliver had borne more. Much more.

When his affianced wife and the rest of his household turned out to welcome home the invalids, they were joined by his Aunts Caroline and Cassandra, and the Honorable Harry Marletonthorpe, who, John said in a loud aside, had arrived that morning on the pretext of a visit on his way back to London, and who had—again, John's voice was quite loud as he said it—inexplicably stayed.

The elegant Harry, wearing a grin almost as bright as the enormous stickpin in his cravat, approached the two eldest brothers as they stood by the coach watching the careful unloading of their younger brothers.

Despite Gillian's vociferous objections that he was much better and intended to go to the drawing room and not his bedroom, thank you, and Peter's assurances that he had suffered no chill on the trip and was indeed feeling quite chipper, both were being shepherded by Nurse and Willowdale's attentive housekeeper up the stairs and indoors. At the same time, Aunts Caroline and Cassandra hovered ineffectually about them, Caroline offering tea while Cassandra drooped and told them stories of boys in much better health than they who had died of mysterious complications for not taking care of themselves. Giles had no doubt that each of the invalids would be tucked up in his bed with a hot brick at his feet in five minutes, and grinned at the thought. The grin faded as Harry approached, Miss Tolliver on his arm.

"Well, well, Giles, you've been having quite a time of it, I hear," Harry said, looking from him to Miss Tolliver and back again.

"Yes, we have had, Harry," Giles answered, removing his fiancée's hand from the other man's arm and considerably surprising her with a swift kiss on the cheek. "How are you, my dear? Keeping well, I trust."

Miss Tolliver, under Mr. Marletonthorpe's watchful eye, could only swallow her ire and answer, eyes on the ground, "Quite well, thank you."

"I am glad." The earl patted her hand and looked down his long nose at his uninvited visitor. "Was there something special we could do for you, Harry, or is this a purely social visit?"

John, who had never liked Harry Marletonthorpe when they were boys and young Harry would not share his famous kite, and who despised in him now his tendency toward dandyism, answered for him.

"Oh, he came for a reason," John said sarcastically. "He came to see if what Chuffy told him was true. Wanted a look at Miss Tolliver, if you ask me."

"But I didn't ask you, did I, John?" the earl asked pleasantly. John snapped his lips together, and Harry smiled uneasily.

"Well, I suppose in a way John is right—I did want to meet the future countess. Meant to ride over to the inn after Chuffy came home with that ridiculous tale, but then I heard the woman—I mean, Miss Tolliver here, was already gone. With your grandmother, too, they said. Most extraordinary. Of course, I found it hard to believe—" He stopped that sentence and bowed toward Miss Tolliver, who nodded slightly.

"You must excuse me, Miss Tolliver," he said. "I let my thoughts run away with me." Despite her best efforts, the lady appeared uncomfortable, and Harry smiled. He knew himself right in thinking something was untoward. With another bow toward the earl he said, "She is a gracious lady, Giles. You are to be congratulated."

"I am." The earl's voice was calm.

"I suppose you'll be puffing it off in all the papers soon," Harry said, his tone casual, his eyes sharp.

"A notice has already been sent to the *Gazette*," the earl replied.

"It has?" Harry, hearing the words come out of his mouth, realized they had been uttered by Miss Tolliver, as well, and his eyes narrowed.

"Yes, my dear," the earl patted her hand again. "Soon we will be receiving the felicitations of all our friends."

"We will?" Miss Tolliver's eyes were wide and her voice hollow.

"Well." Harry laughed. It was a forced sound, and Miss Tolliver wondered for the tenth time since his arrival what there was between him and the earl. "I guess I won't be ahead of the news when I reach London, then."

"No, Harry." The earl's smile had an edge to it. "You won't be making news at my expense—or that of my fiancée or family."

"Ha!" John couldn't contain himself, and his smugness made Mr. Marletonthorpe's face flush. But his words were pleasant as he bade them all good-bye, saying if he wished to arrive in London before midnight, he must be on his way. He charged them with get-well messages for the invalids, which John said later would more likely make them ill than well, and bowed himself away toward the light traveling coach that sat on the other side of the drive in front of the house. The three watched him go in silence, but once he was safely on his way, Miss Tolliver spoke.

"Well!" she said, turning toward the earl. "What was that all about?"

His eyes were on the traveling coach, and for a moment he did not speak.

"Harry Marletonthorpe is a—" John started roundly, but his brother interrupted him.

"It was nothing, Miss Tolliver," the earl said. "Nothing at all."

Chapter
15

The earl's suggestion that they go into the house was met by a wrinkled nose on Miss Tolliver's part, and a step back on John's, and Giles watched as a look of mutual sympathy passed between them. He was surprised to find that in the week he'd been away from Willowdale an easy understanding had sprung up between his normally formal brother and his betrothed, and, for a moment, he was uneasy about it. The latter feeling he dismissed as unworthy, and inquired if there was something wrong—some matter he should know about before entering the great hall.

"Oh, no . . ." Miss Tolliver began politely, but John was not as kind.

"You've seen what's wrong, Giles," John told his brother frankly. "Aunt Caroline and Aunt Cassandra are here."

"Oh." Giles digested the information. It was not a happy thought. Then another struck him. "Why?"

"They're worried about your grandmother . . ." Miss Tolliver began.

"That's what they *say*," John interrupted her. "I think they're just here to see what brought Grandmama to Willowdale, not realizing that it was not being able to bear with them that sent her off to us. And then, of course, when they got here, they decided it must be Miss Tolliver, because Grandmama didn't think it wise to tell them the whole story, their being such gossipy old things—"

"John," Miss Tolliver protested, half-laughing and half-

serious as she removed her hand from the earl's arm to place
it on Mr. Manfield's shoulder. "That is no way to talk about
your relatives."

"Perhaps," the earl interrupted, reclaiming her hand to
lay it on his arm again, "but quite true."

"Yes." John defended himself, "and you're a good one
to talk when I think of some of the stories you've told this
week about your nearest and dearest—"

"Oh." Miss Tolliver blushed. "How unhandsome of
you!"

"What?" John was thrown out of stride by her words,
and, wondering what he had done to offend, looked toward
her anxiously. The earl promptly intervened.

"Yes, John," Giles chided. "A gentleman never contra-
dicts a lady. *Particularly* when he is right."

Miss Tolliver raised her candid gaze to his face and eyes
him consideringly. "Yes," she decided, "I can see why
your brothers consider that quite your most disagreeable
trait."

Now both John and Giles were startled, John uttering a
sheepish protest as Giles said "*What*?" in a tone that would
have made Gillian and Peter gulp. Miss Tolliver remained
unmoved.

"That habit you have of always understanding *exactly*
what is happening. *Particularly* when one would most wish
you did not."

The earl's eyes glinted. "It will do you well to remember
it, my dear," he said, ignoring her protest that she was *not*
'his dear' and had told him so before. Blandly he requested
his brother to continue.

John did, and the tale he told made his brother grimace in
sympathy. The aunts, as John lumped them, had descended
on them one day after John, the dowager countess, Sir
Charles, and Miss Tolliver arrived at Willowdale. Not being
privy to the real truth behind the earl's and Miss Tolliver's
engagement, they had jumped without difficulty to the same
conclusion reached by Nurse—that it was love at first sight.

"Although your Aunt Caroline will have it that you spied
me many years ago in London, but I vanished before you
could learn my name, and you have been searching for me

ever since," Miss Tolliver said thoughtfully, slanting a sidelong glance toward his lordship.

Giles was clearly surprised. *"What?"*

"It is most romantic," Miss Tolliver informed him, her lips pursed exactly as he had seen his aunt's time out of mind.

"What a ninnyhammer!" the earl exploded.

Miss Tolliver patted his arm kindly. "She never called you that," she told him sweetly. "We all thought it, of course, but no one said—"

"He means Aunt Caroline, Margaret—Aunt Caroline is the ninnyhammer!" John interrupted, anxious to set her straight.

"Ooooh!" Miss Tolliver's eyes opened wide as she digested John's information. "So silly of me—" She was brimming with laughter as John continued his explanation, and the earl, watching her, was amazed at how hard he had to work to keep his mind on his brother's words.

"Anyway," John continued glumly, "they have been here ever since, trying our patience to the utmost. Grandmama locks herself in her bedroom most afternoons just to avoid them—says she is going to take a nap, but *we* know she smuggles in one of those high-flying romances and a bottle of the best sherry. That has left most of the entertaining upon Miss Tolliver's shoulders, really, and I must say, Giles, she has been a real trooper about it."

"The capable Miss Tolliver," the earl murmured, looking down at her.

Yes, she told him, she had been most capable. Yet she didn't want him to think it had been all duty—far from it. She had, she assured him, enjoyed the most informative week! Before coming to Willowdale and meeting his Aunt Caroline, she had never known how many things tea can cure until said aunt arrived to suggest it for everything. Nor did she know how many innocent circumstances and happenings a person can die from, ranging from choking on a toast crumb to sticking oneself with a brooch dipped in poison and dying the most affecting death, until his Aunt Cassandra had acquainted her with the facts. It had, she repeated, been most informative.

"Poor, capable Miss Tolliver," the earl murmured again, favoring her with a smile that made her pulse jump oddly. To squelch it, she smiled right back at him.

"Do not lavish all your sympathy on me, my lord," she said at her sweetest, "for you might require some of it later for yourself. My brother Charles returns tomorrow. With Aunt Henrietta."

Surveying his assembled guests the next evening as they sat at the large mahogany dinner table acquired some years earlier by the fourth earl, Giles could barely suppress a chuckle. Miss Tolliver's Aunt Henrietta was all his betrothed had suggested, and more. At present she was busy out-Cassandraing his Aunt Cassandra—coughing twice for each time Cassandra uttered a small *achoo*. She seemed entirely unconscious of it, too—something Aunt Cassandra most definitely was not. It was a situation that had Miss Tolliver and his grandmama nearly in whoops, and that was causing his brothers John and Gillian a great deal of amusement as well. The earl knew himself incapable of dampening the spirits of the ladies, but he was quite willing to frown his brothers down. And he planned to do so before Gillian's high spirits at once again being allowed from his sickroom took him beyond the line of what even the most self-concerned individuals—such as the aunts—could ignore.

For that reason he drew his brother's attention from the ladies in question to the footman at Gillian's side as he recommended his brother help himself to the viands offered there.

"Yes, Gillian," Miss Tolliver seconded at once. "Do help yourself to the chick—chick—chicken!" Her eyes met the dowager countess's at the worst possible moment, and both ladies dissolved into laughter behind their napkins.

Not so Aunt Henrietta, whose head snapped to attention and whose eyes grew wide with horror at sight of the large fowl resting comfortably amid piles of chestnut stuffing on the footman's platter.

"*Chicken*!" the old lady said, shuddering. She pointed a finger at the hapless Gillian who had just helped himself to a large wing, and with a cry of "You *heathen*!" swept from the room. Giles noted that she was not too upset to forget to take her plate with her.

Gillian sat with his mouth open, as did Giles's two aunts, while John, in the midst of swallowing, started to cough, and reached for his wine. The dowager countess, wiping her eyes and giggling as if she were in her teens again, looked across at Miss Tolliver

"Oh, my dear," the countess said, "I do *like* your aunt! So true to her convictions!" Then she was off in giggles again. Giles, watching the stunned faces of his Aunts Caroline and Cassandra, could only be thankful that Miss Tolliver's brother had chosen to take his supper in his room that night, to recover from the rigors and indignities of his day. The thought of those rigors and indignities made the earl smile again.

It had all started at teatime that afternoon—or rather, the earl thought reasonably, it had started earlier that day, but they were not then aware of it. What they were aware of was the arrival of a coach in the midst of tea, and putting down their cups, all went out to welcome the newest guests—despite the fact, as Cassandra told them, that it was drizzling outside, and they would all no doubt take a chill and inflammation of the lungs from it. She begged her mother not to put herself in such jeopardy, but the dowager countess only eyed her daughter in disgust and said she would not miss meeting Miss Tolliver's Aunt Henrietta for anything.

"Bound to be better than a circus, if half of what Margaret has been telling me is true," she said, surprising the earl with the familiarity upon which his sometimes starchy grandmama stood with his fiancée. It seemed, the earl thought rather wonderingly, that Miss Tolliver was on the best of terms with everyone in his household but himself. It was a circumstance he planned to rectify as soon as possible, and how to do that was on his mind as he followed his grandmother and his betrothed from the room. One quick glance out the front door toward the just-arrived carriage made him think the dowager countess would not be disappointed.

The first sight to greet their eyes was that of Sir Charles, propped up beside the coachman on the box, his afflicted foot out before him and a look of great martyrdom on his face.

"Charles!" Miss Tolliver cried in real consternation, hurrying down the steps despite the drizzle to stand looking anxiously up at her brother. "What on earth—My dear, *why* are you riding out in the rain instead of inside the carriage? Your poor foot . . ."

Sir Charles sat stiffly erect as he gazed down at her, his mouth tight as water dripped off his beaver and down his neck. "I do not ride with poultry, Margaret," he said.

"Oh, Charles!" Miss Tolliver shook her head, torn between vexation at his stuffiness, and real concern for his discomfort. "You silly thing! Do come down from there and let us help you into the house and up to a nice warm bed and a hot toddy. You'd like that, wouldn't you?"

Sir Charles knew he would like that very much. So much, in fact, that he was willing to overlook his sister's ill-considered "silly thing" epithet, and would have done so if at that moment his Aunt Henrietta hadn't stuck her head out of the coach to demand Margaret's assistance in descending from the carriage—despite, Charles noted bitterly, the fact that two perfectly able-bodied footmen stood ready to assist her, as well as the earl himself. Charles was further outraged to discovered that the reason his aunt required Miss Tolliver's assistance, and claimed her attention over his far more deeply felt need, was to hold "that confounded chicken," as he phrased it.

Miss Henrietta informed everyone in sight, in the tones of the slightly deaf, that Lazaurus was a high-strung aristocrat who could only be handled by someone he knew well or someone who understood the temperament and soul of a rooster—and that someone was Margaret. Smiling, Miss Tolliver took the bird, stroking his feathers with one hand as she cradled him to her side with the other.

Miss Tolliver did suggest that it was most unkind of her aunt to make Sir Charles ride on the box in the rain, with his bad foot, but her aunt only looked at her and said in the most reasonable tones imaginable, "But my dear, Charles makes Lazaurus nervous. We can't have that!"

Once she descended, in a wave of trailing shawls and tangled fringe, her gray crimped curls covered by a black mantilla because, as she would later tell them, she could not abide hats, Aunt Henrietta took the bird back again. Then she suggested that they all go into the house because, as she confided to one of the footmen who so far forgot himself as to look astonished, "travel *always* makes Lazaurus bilious." She considered for a moment before jerking her head backward toward the coachbox, and adding, "Just like Charles there." Her long-suffering nephew sighed heavily.

Aunt Henrietta took several steps forward, then stopped suddenly, nearly tripping John, who followed behind her. She turned and her eyes sought her niece as she said, "Oh yes. Almost forgot. Come to meet your earl, Margaret. Charles says he has 20,000 pounds a year. I am sure I shall like him excessively."

She gazed about her in expectation while Sir Charles sat on the box as if turned to stone. Margaret cast him a reproachful look before stepping forward to make the introductions. She was relieved to find the earl appeared amused rather than irritated, and had opened her mouth to present her aunt to him when she realized that his amusement did not surprise her. There was something about him that was so—well, dependable, that way . . . Trying to figure out what it was, she became so lost in thought that, after a brief moment, the earl stepped forward and performed the introductions himself.

Aunt Henrietta gazed up at him placidly, paying particular attention to his face. "Oh yes," she declared, "you'll do nicely. Twenty thousand pounds! You may carry Lazaurus!" And so saying, she thrust the rooster into his hands and made her stately way up the steps, trailing shawls and hosts behind her.

"Oh my!" Miss Tolliver said, hurrying forward. "I am so very sorry! She has never allowed anyone but me to carry Lazaurus before—I never thought—" She reached for the bird, but the earl was before her.

"No, no, my dear," he said, handing the rooster off to an

unsuspecting John, and catching Miss Tolliver's hand to lead her after her vanishing aunt. "Do not be concerned. John will take care of the bird. Won't you, John? And you'll see to Miss Tolliver's brother, too, won't you?"

They had reached the top step when John's indignant "Here! I say—*ouch!*" stopped them, and both the earl and Miss Tolliver looked back questioningly.

"This obnoxious fellow bit me!" John said, regarding Lazaurus in indignation.

"How terrible!" Miss Tolliver cried, preparing to descend the steps immediately. The earl held her hand to keep her from it even as he agreed with what she said.

"Yes, John," he told his brother gravely. "Terrible indeed. Roosters don't bite, my dear fellow. They peck. He did not bite—he pecked you. One must always try to be correct, John even in matters of little moment. You must remember that if you hope to make your way in politics, as you say you do." And with that, he smiled benevolently at brother and chicken, and drew an astonished Miss Tolliver into the house.

"You, sir, should be ashamed," she told him, trying to look severe as she gazed upward, biting her lip to hide her amusement at her last glimpse of John's shocked face.

"Do you think so?" he asked whimsically, brushing a raindrop from her forehead. "I rather thought it was something to crow about!"

Aware that the spot he had just touched felt warm, while all the rest of her face was cool from the outside damp air, Miss Tolliver strove for composure, telling him roundly that she could not be put off by rooster jokes, and making a case for returning to the steps to help John with his charges.

"No, no," the earl said, retaining her hand and leading her toward the morning room to which the other members of their party had already disappeared. "John must learn to deal with all kinds of circumstances, both fair and—er—fowl."

Despite herself, when they walked through the door, Miss Tolliver was laughing.

The remembrance of that laugh continued to make the earl smile as he sat now at his supper table, and his smile grew as he heard her laugh again. Glancing up from a joke she shared with the dowager countess, Miss Tolliver found him watching her, and smiled back unconsciously in that easy, unaffected way that the earl had seen her exercise with all members of his household but himself. Without thinking, he reached out and picked up his wineglass and raised it to her as if in a toast. Suddenly Miss Tolliver seemed to recall her surroundings as well as their relationship, and her smile disappeared as she consciously directed her attention away from him.

With a frown and a slight snap of his wrist, the earl set his glass down again, and picked up his fork, spearing a piece of the chicken on his plate with it, and transferring that chicken to his mouth. Somehow, it was not what he had hoped for, and he thought it a tough and most unpleasant bird.

Chapter
16

After the arrival of Aunt Henrietta and the return of Sir Charles to Willowdale, life settled into its own routine at the manor. People seemed to get up earlier, the earl noted—no doubt due to the exertions of Aunt Henrietta's Lazaurus, who slept in her room and who stood each morning on the sill of her window, greeting the first rays of light with such cries of delight as must awaken anyone sleeping in or near the wing where the old lady and rooster presided. It was not a circumstance that won the bird friends, of course; in fact, the earl was sure that only Miss Tolliver's timely suggestion that they all practice a little trick she herself had learned several years earlier, of tucking cotton into their ears and pulling pillows over their heads at Laz's first crow, that kept the bird from being found one day with his neck mysteriously wrung—a service Miss Tolliver told him she had seriously considered, and would have done, if it wouldn't have so upset her aunt, who loved the rooster dearly.

That, the earl observed, was very true; although Miss Tolliver had, by means unknown to him, convinced her aunt that the earl's dining room was no place for a brown rooster, Lazaurus could be encountered everywhere else in Aunt Henrietta's company. He accompanied her on walks; when they went out driving, a red-crowned head was always seen poking from the back of the landaulet, keeping an eye on the world and sundry; when Aunt Henrietta sat knitting one of her interminable projects in the evening, Lazaurus was comfortably perched in her bag amid the large skeins of wool.

The arrival of Aunt Henrietta and Lazaurus did mean, the earl found regretfully, the departure of all kinds of fowl from his dinner table—a departure that brought him a rather tearful interview with his cook, who told him that he had always understood that m'lord liked his way with a green goose and quails in sauce, and if that were not so, he was sure he would be happy to take himself elsewhere, where his skills were more appreciated.

Because the earl had gone to considerable time and expense to lure his chef from that worthy's former employer, and because he did not want to lose him, he was rather at a loss as to what to do until the redoubtable Miss Tolliver, who had been present for the interview by the mere chance that she wandered into the library from the left just as the chef sought him out from the right, came to the rescue.

With one of her friendliest smiles she explained that the departure of all fowl from the earl's table was a temporary—and to be devoutly hoped not too extended—change in the Willowdale menus. She suggested that the chef look upon it as no more than his host giving up a favorite dish for Lent.

"It is not Lent, mademoiselle," the chef told her severely, his Gallic eyebrows raised alarmingly as he held one wooden spoon like a sword at attention before him, "and m'lord, he is not Catholic."

"No," the lady replied pleasantly, "it is not Lent, and his lordship is not Catholic. But it never hurts to experience the habits and hardships of others, to give one a better understanding of self, don't you agree?"

The chef, whose English was never good, and who lost it almost completely when he was excited, did *not* agree—in fact, he did not understand—but by means unknown to him he found himself nodding yes and being ushered from the room by the smiling lady whose gentle touch on his sleeve as he passed through the door she held for him, and whose polite "thank you for being so understanding" made him nod again. As she closed the door behind the chef, the earl eyed Miss Tolliver warmly.

"That was very well done," he said.

"I have had a great deal of experience with difficult people," she replied, but so absently that he knew her mind was not on the disappearing chef. He was proven right a moment later when she came toward his desk, her distress evident in her large blue eyes. She stopped before him—in the same spot where Gillian had stood when he started this whole ridiculous venture, his lordship realized suddenly, and smiled. Miss Tolliver returned his smile automatically, before becoming most serious again.

"My lord," shes aid, "this cannot go on."

The earl, who had risen at her entrance, invited her to take a chair, an invitation she declined as of no moment. The earl disagreed.

"You may find it of no moment, my dear," he told her, in a fair imitation of his Aunt Cassandra at her most irksome, "but I am fatigued nigh to death, and since civility decrees that I must remain standing until you are seated, I beg of you, take a chair."

A reluctant smile touched Miss Tolliver's lips as she sank into the chair nearest to her and the earl, with a great show of relief, sank back into his. "Fatigued nigh to death, my lord?" she asked, with a quirk of an eyebrow.

"Such scenes as the one just endured with my cook always overcome me," he said gravely, his shoulders down as if he were indeed spent.

Miss Tolliver laughed. "As if you couldn't—and wouldn't—handle any number of crises without a flicker of an eye, my lord! I have been watching you. I know! Doing it up too brown—" She caught herself up on the slang and blushed guiltily, but his lordship, who was pleased to hear she had been watching him, appeared not to notice.

"No, no," he assured her with the utmost earnestness. "You misunderstand! My nerves—of the most delicate! My feelings—the tenderest flowers—"

Miss Tolliver laughed again but refused to be drawn into this discussion, which he had hoped would lead her from the conversation she had begun before his interruption.

"You are in a funning mood, my lord," she told him, "but I will not be drawn off what I have come to say to you, and which I started before your flight into fancy. And that is—"

"Do you know, my dear, you bring out my 'flight into fancy,' as you so aptly put it, more than anyone I have ever known?" his lordship interrupted musingly, picking up a letter opener that lay on his desk and using his right hand to tap it gently against his left.

The lady eyed him with some severity. "This is no time for such talk," she told him. "I am sure it is all very well for your flirts and your fine lady friends—"

"I do wish I knew who has given you this unfair opinion of me," his lordship complained, his brow furrowing as if he were hurt. "It is not as if I have women waiting in the hall, you know—"

It was at that point that they were interrupted by a knock. When the earl called "Enter" the butler walked in to announce, stone-faced, that there was a lady—er, woman—waiting in the hall for his lordship, a woman who said she would not leave without seeing him. Miss Tolliver bit her lip to prevent her laughing at the outraged astonishment on the earl's face. The butler, trying to protect himself as best he could from what he knew was sure to be a thundering scold, if not outright dismissal, excused himself by explaining that it was the newest footman who let the woman in, him not being fully trained and thinking that if she was with Mr. Harry Marletonthorpe, who had been here so recently—which, his lordship would remember, he was—it must be all right. Although, the butler added with strong feeling, anyone with a particle of sense could see that she wasn't quite the thing...

The earl's brow, which had been black before, darkened. "You're telling me," he said, "that there is a strange woman in my hall in company with Harry Marletonthorpe? And you did not show them into the morning room? Or the back parlor?"

The butler, who knew the woman was not as much a stranger to the earl as the earl might like, was torn between trying to explain why he had left the company in the hall, and not wishing to say a word before the exceedingly interested—and, he had decided since her first day at

Willowdale—exceedingly nice, Miss Tolliver. In the end he
compromised with a wooden "I did not think it best, my
lord."

"Might I ask why?" His lordship said the words softly,
between his teeth, and the butler quailed inwardly. Usually
an easygoing master, the butler knew that, like his father
before him, the sixth earl could be dangerous when angered.

"Oh, for heaven's sake!" Miss Tolliver interrupted, taking pity on the butler and winning his lifelong gratitude.
"Obviously there is something the poor man doesn't want to
say in front of me, and you are putting him in an impossible
position! Let us go see what this is all about, at once!"

She rose as if to put her plan into action, but it was not
necessary; another moment, and the noise coming from the
hall would have drawn them there immediately. Even through
the closed library doors the occupants of that room had no
trouble recognizing John's voice, raised in acute astonishment.

"What in heaven—" that worthy started as he entered the
hall from the back, coming in after a most satisfactory day
of shooting. His eyes fairly bulged at the sight of the
grinning Harry Marletonthorpe and the statuesque woman
by his side. Gillian, who accompanied his brother, recognized Harry, whom he too had never liked, but not the
woman, and gazed at John in puzzlement. "It's the actress,
you idiot!" John hissed at his younger brother just as the
library door opened and Miss Tolliver entered the scene
ahead of the earl.

"Oh, no!" John said, his face horrified at the sight of
Margaret. "I beg of you, Miss Tolliver, you must return to
the library immediately! Bit of a misunderstanding here. Go
on back inside and read a book. That's the dandy!"

John had hold of her arm now, and would have literally
thrust her back into the room had not the voluptuous
redhead standing beside Harry caught sight of the earl,
immediately behind his betrothed, and with a most unladylike
shriek of "Giles-y!" hurled herself toward the astonished
earl, brushing the smaller Miss Tolliver out of her way and
into John's arm as she flew past. The woman's arms en-
circled the earl's neck, clinging there despite his best efforts
to remove them, and her tears poured down his waistcoat.

"Don't!" she cried noisily. "Don't, I beg of you! I cannot let you! Oh, oh, oh!"

Miss Tolliver, who had by this time been set on her feet by John, met the earl's desperate eyes above the improbably colored red hair.

"Dear me." Miss Tolliver's voice was cool. "This must be—Vanessa."

It was Vanessa in all her glory, from the purple bonnet with magenta feathers that adorned her improbable curls, to the low-cut sapphire gown that clung to her curves and did much more to reveal than to conceal her many charms. She was a big woman, and tall, and Miss Tolliver thought dispassionately that she would probably run to fat in her later years. Her later years were not now, however, and Margaret, extremely just, could understand what it was that had drawn the earl—and any other number of men—to her.

"Yes," the actress said, raising her head from the earl's chest to dab tragically at her eyes. "It is I. Vanessa."

"Well, by George, Giles," Gillian, who had been studying her intently ever since John's disclosure, suddenly entered the conversation. "If this is who we were looking for, I'm certainly glad we didn't find—oof!"

His sentence ended abruptly with a swift kick to the shins from John, who, when he had Gillian's reproachful attention, nodded warningly toward Harry, whose ears had pricked up at Gillian's innocent remark. Coloring, Gillian subsided into the background. It was just as well, for in a moment a sharp "What is the meaning of this?" drew all eyes to the landing where the dowager countess stood surrounded by her daughters and Miss Tolliver's Aunt Henrietta, armed with her rooster.

To complete the scene Peter wandered down the stairs with the rector, drawn to the hall by the noise, just as Sir Charles, leaning heavily on his cane, appeared at the top of the stairway irritably demanding to be told what all the noise was about. He stopped abruptly at the sight of the woman still clinging to the earl, despite Giles's continued efforts to be rid of her, and the name "Vanessa!" exploded from his lips.

The actress turned her head at the sound of her name, and gave him a friendly wave and a "Hi, Charles-y!"—an action that loosened her grip enough to at last allow the earl to set her firmly away from him.

"Charles!" Miss Tolliver said, astonished, and her brother, who stood for a moment as if he were stuffed, bethought himself of his bedchamber and with a muttered "won't detain you" took himself off to it as fast as his sore foot would carry him.

"Well, I never . . ." Miss Tolliver said thoughtfully. A twinkle appeared in her eye as the earl murmured, "But your brother obviously did."

The twinkle disappeared at once, however, when her glance returned to the earl and the actress, who was doing her best to get her arms around Giles's neck again, and who, failing that, had caught him about the waist and was holding tight, begging him to tell her it wasn't so.

Miss Tolliver was about to recommend that he tell her, and find out later what it was that wasn't so, just to get her to let go, when the dowager countess again entered the fray.

"Unhand my grandson, you hussy!" she cried, hurrying down the stairs and leaving the aunts goggling on the landing. "It's a fine thing when a man isn't even safe from your kind in his own home!"

Peter, whose eyes were wide at the sight of his brother in the arms of a heavily painted woman, and who had missed hearing her name, was heard to ask the vicar, "What kind is that?"

That worthy man, so at home in the world that should be and so out of place in the world that was, bethought himself of a prayer left unsaid at home, uttered something inarticulate, and told his pupil he would see him tomorrow. Then he rushed down the stairs, snatched up his hat from the stand by the door, and with a "so nice to see you all—sorry I can't stay—would be pleased to meet your company—"got himself outside where he stood for several moments as if dumbstruck.

Finally, with a shocked "Well! I never!", he pulled a handkerchief from his pocket and mopped his brow. Starting off home, he was so overcome that he was halfway there before he realized he had ridden his trusty old cob to Willowdale that morning, and had to go back for it.

The earl, who never in his worst nightmares had imagined himself in such a scene, wished heartily that he could follow him, but did not. Instead, he stood his ground and watched as his grandmother literally tore Vanessa's arms from around him, and thrust herself between Vanessa and the earl, to the delight of Harry Marletonthorpe, who laughed.

The countess turned her baleful glare toward him. "This is all your doing, isn't it, Harry?"

He raised one hand as if to ward off the accusation, smiling in delight. "No, no," he disclaimed. "I am only here as cavalier to the fair Vanessa who, reading of Giles's engagement, was so overcome . . ."

His voice trailed off delicately, and the actress took up her part in the story. "Yes," she said, raising soulful eyes toward the earl in a way that, strangely, made Miss Tolliver itch to slap her (a reaction Margaret did not question too closely), "when Harry told me—" Marletonthorpe cleared his throat and, realizing she had missed her lines, the actress quickly changed to "—that is, when I read of your engagement, Giles, I had to come see you, for I know it can be nothing more than the desperate act of a man on the rebound, and I cannot let you do that. Had I known how much you were hurt when we parted—"

Watching critically, it occurred to Miss Tolliver that the earl had at last found his cue, for his mouth tightened and he looked down his nose at the woman in distaste, so obviously disgusted that her words petered out, and Vanessa at last stood in silence, her eyes tear-drenched—and attractively so, Miss Tolliver noted, wondering why some women could do that while she and others like her always ended up with a red nose when they cried—her lips pleading and her hands raised in prayerful supplication.

"Grandmama," the earl started, "Miss Tolliver—" His eyes were beseeching as they sought Margaret's. "Really—"

He got no further for Miss Tolliver took up her part in the scene, applauding gently as everyone stared at her in surprise.

"Really," she said, walking up to Vanessa and extending her hand, "you are very good!" She turned toward the earl and said accusingly that he had not told her how talented the actress was.

"What?" The word echoed from the earl's, Vanessa's, and Harry Marletonthorpe's mouths, and she turned toward Harry approvingly, too.

"And you, sir!" she said, sweeping toward him and holding out her hand which he automatically received and bowed over. "It was quite clever of you to cook up this little scheme, to bring Miss—" she turned and looked consideringly at the actress before turning back again and continuing smoothly "—Vanessa here to embarass Giles. But it won't work, you know. He told me all about it a long time ago."

"He did?" Vanessa was staring uneasily up at his lordship, and Miss Tolliver returned to her side, taking her elbow solicitously.

"But of course, my dear," Miss Tolliver said, "and we have had many a good laugh—"

"Laugh?" Vanessa, unaware that she was being moved slowly but inexorably toward the door, looked back toward Giles in indignation. *"Laugh?"*

"Oh, no, my dear, not at you," Miss Tolliver soothed, "but at the very idea that someone might think my knowing about your former—er, alliance—would give me a disgust of the earl, or that someone might think that now-dead alliance could be rekindled—"

By this time they had reached the place where Harry Marletonthorpe stood, a smile still on his lips but a hard look growing in his eyes. Vanessa glared at him.

"'Ere now," she said, dropping some of her carefully cultivated accent in her anger, "I told you he said we was through when he left me, but you said—"

"Oh, be quiet, you idiot!" Harry growled, "can't you see she's guessing?" But that was enough for Miss Tolliver, who smiled up at him.

"Guessing, Mr. Marletonthorpe?" she questioned. "Well, perhaps I am. But if I were a guessing person, I would also guess that this might be a good time for you and Miss—Vanessa—to leave."

A slight backward motion of her head indicated the

purposeful advancement of the earl, John, and Gillian, and Harry's lips thinned as he watched them.

"All right," he said. "Fine. My compliments to you, Miss Tolliver. If truth be told, I didn't expect to find you still here, but you are, and this hand is yours." He took her fingers and bowed over them with an easy grace, then raised his eyes to hers, and then to the earl's. "But you win only this hand. All gamblers know that the game isn't over until the last card is played."

And so saying he bowed himself out of the door, stopping with exaggerated courtesy for Vanessa to precede him. He ignored the actress's "And what was that all about?" as he waited for his coachman to bring the coach forward, and was equally impervious to her lament that this whole day had cost her a night's wage at the theater, and a very pretty supper afterward, she had no doubt. "And for what?" Her voice rose on the last word as she was helped into the carriage, and it was apparent that she was fast working herself into a rare temper. A repeat of the question floated back to them as the coach drove away.

"The capable Miss Tolliver." The earl smiled warmly as he approached Margaret and laid a hand on her shoulder. "Thank you. That was very well done. I am in your debt."

With a "Don't touch me!" the lady twisted away and glared up at him. "How dare you? You say you're in my debt when I want you out of my life! I came to you today to tell you that we must put an end to this 'engagement,' and instead I end up more deeply embroiled in your scheme than ever! I did very well before you came into my life, my lord, and I shall do very well when you go out of it again. Which cannot happen too soon!"

"Miss Tolliver—" He held out his hand to her and she pushed it crossly away.

"And in the meantime," she said, "I do not believe I shall ever speak to you again."

Then the capable Miss Tolliver considerably astonished her assembled audience by issuing one angry sob before turning and rushing away.

Chapter
17

The earl's first inclination was to follow her, but as he took the steps two at a time and reached the wide doorway, his grandmother stopped him.

"No, no, no!" she told him, clicking her teeth in vexation. "Let her go. First she'll have a good cry, and then I'll talk to her."

"But Grandmama," the earl protested, "she is distressed—"

"Well, of course she is distressed, you ninny!" the countess responded fiercely. "Who wouldn't be distressed after such a scene? I'm quite distressed myself, let me tell you. A fine thing when I am forced to encounter one of my grandson's inamoratas in the hall of his family home! I don't know what the world is coming to, Giles, truly I don't!"

It was useless for the earl to point out to her that the previous scene had not been of his making; his grandmother told him severely that if he intended to consort with "that type of person," such happenings were inevitable. His response that he was no longer consorting with "that type of person" and that he never planned to again brought a sharp "And let that be a lesson to you!" as his grandmother stomped into the house, shepherding the aunts, who had crept out onto the doorjamb, their eyes big with wonder, before her.

"I swear," the old lady said irritably, "I can almost feel my palpitations coming on! To think that you, Giles, should be the cause of the death of your dear old grandmama—"

Since she seemed to be enjoying herself immensely, the

earl was not unduly concerned, but her daughters took her words to heart. Anxiously clasping one of her hands, Cassandra recited chapter and verse of who knew how many cases where the circumstances had been just the same, and someone *had* dropped over dead, while Caroline fussed on her mother's other side and declared that what they all needed was a nice spot of tea.

Henrietta merely frowned at the earl, and told him that he could *not* carry her rooster. That, he decided, was the unkindest cut of all, and with a black brow that made both his butler and several footmen steer clear, took himself off to the library to sooth his feelings with a bottle of his best port. His grandmother, watching him go, smiled consideringly.

Miss Tolliver had had her good cry and was in the midst of packing her valise when the first gentle knock fell on her door.

"Go away!" she cried, expecting the person in the hall to be the earl or her brother.

"Now, now, my dear," a soft voice said as the dowager countess's face appeared around the door. "Is that any way to talk to an old lady?"

"Oh." Margaret stopped, holding a skirt in midair at the sight of her guest, and half-smiled. "Oh, it is you, madam. Of course *you* may come in. I thought it must be my brother, or Gi—your grandson."

"Oh, well then," the countess agreed, nonchalantly ignoring Miss Tolliver's almost use of her grandson's given name and moving into the room to seat herself on Miss Tolliver's bed to watch the packing with interest. "You would be quite right to send them away. Men are such ninnies, my dear. I don't know how we abide them."

"Ha!" Miss Tolliver gave a most unladylike snort signifying her agreement. "You're quite right, dear Countess. And I, for one, have no intention of abiding them further!"

"Ah!" The countess nodded intelligently. "That would be the reason for the packing!"

"Yes!" Miss Tolliver gave up her efforts to correctly fold

the skirt and stuffed it instead into the only space left in the bag. "*I* am going *home!*"

"Quite right," the countess approved. "In fact, I am thinking of going home myself. I have never been so disgusted with Giles in all my life." She lowered her voice as if sharing a great secret. "It grieves me to tell you this, my dear, but he is really the best of my family."

"You have my condolences," Miss Tolliver answered, setting the valise on the floor and picking up another to place on the bed.

"Yes," the countess said. "It is a most sobering thought." She watched Miss Tolliver throw open the large cupboard behind her and reach into it for the dresses newly acquired in London. Out came the salmon walking dress and the blue velvet riding suit, the morning dresses and the evening gowns trimmed in lace, chosen with such care by their owner and now treated so ruthlessly as she strove to deposit them in her bag. "Oh, my dear, have a care!" The countess was moved to protest at the treatment of one particularly fine blue silk gown that matched its owner's eyes to perfection. "You'll wrinkle that past bearing! Here, let me help!"

She reached for the gown and smoothed the silk tenderly as Miss Tolliver tossed the other dresses onto the bed and stared helplessly at them.

"It's no use," Margaret said. "I'll have to have my trunks sent on later."

"Quite right," the countess agreed. "A much better plan! After all, when one is running away, it is such a bother to have to pack first."

"What?" Margaret let the dress she had just picked up fall again as she stared at the old lady.

"I was merely saying, my dear, that it is such a bother to pack—"

"No," Margaret said. "The part before that."

"Before that—?" The countess seemed doubtful, and Margaret supplied the words for her.

"You said I was running away," Margaret said.

"Oh, that! Yes, of course!" She looked at Miss Tolliver inquiringly. "Well?"

"I'm not running away!" Miss Tolliver exclaimed.

"No?" The countess's face was doubtful. "I must have misunderstood! I thought you said you were going—"

"I am going!" Miss Tolliver told her. "But I am not running away!"

The countess shook her head slowly, one hand absently twisting the lace spread that covered Miss Tolliver's bed. "Let me understand this," she begged. "You are leaving because of what just happened here, but you are not running away!"

"Well, yes—" Miss Tolliver said. "I mean—no. I mean—" She put one hand to her head and took several hurried steps around the room. "I don't know what I mean!" she cried, falling into a chair near the countess and pulling distractedly at the doilies that covered its arms. "I feel as if I have no hand in ordering events—as if they are ordering me—".

"Well," the countess comforted, "you certainly ordered events this afternoon! And they say this Vanessa person is an actress! My dear, you were superb!"

"But I didn't wish to be superb!" Miss Tolliver told her, harassed. "I went out of this room this afternoon with the firm intention of telling his lordship that we must put an end to this pretend engagement before it becomes even harder to do so—" It was as if she suddenly realized how those words sounded, for her color heightened, and it clearly required resolution to pretend they had never been said as she continued. "Now I've come back into this room less than an hour later more firmly embroiled than ever! Well, I won't have it, I tell you! I won't!"

The countess told her she understood. Without hesitation she joined Miss Tolliver in every aspersion she cared to cast on the male sex in general and the sixth Earl of Manseford in particular, even going so far as to say that she quite understood why Miss Tolliver would like to hold him and his family up to the ridicule they so abundantly deserved . . . although she rather thought it would be hard on Peter . . . and on herself, of course, for she was an old woman.

Miss Tolliver eyed her consideringly. "Ridicule?" she repeated.

The countess nodded mournfully, and said that when the

story got out—as Harry would no doubt see that it did when
he realized his plan had chased the earl's intended away—
Giles wouldn't be able to hold his head up, "for you must
know, my dear, that he is a proud man, and would find it
hard to bear the whispers and innuendos that an actress
appeared at his home and gave his betrothed such a disgust
of him that she left immediately. And then, of course, there
is John—"

"John?" Miss Tolliver questioned, surprised.

Sadly the countess responded that just a whiff of scandal
could ruin the most promising political career.

"But it is not John who is scandalous!"

The countess shook her head despairingly. "It doesn't
matter," she sighed. "It is scandal by association in our
world, and Giles is John's brother. And if we think it will be
hard on John—oh, my, just think of Gillian!"

"Gillian?" Miss Tolliver's head was reeling, and she
wished that she had never heard of the Manfield men. The
countess continued.

"Oh, my dear, yes. I know Gillian could never bear to
hear any slings cast upon his brother, so you can imagine
the fights . . . perhaps duels . . ." The old lady sighed again.
"I should not tell you this, but he is not a very good shot,
our Gillian."

"Oh." Miss Tolliver sank down further into her chair. "I
did not think—I certainly would not wish—perhaps I could
stay . . ."

The countess was smiling to herself when Miss Tolliver
took her aback by looking up and shaking her head with
resolution. "No, dear madam, I cannot. This farce must be
ended—"

Willingly perjuring herself, the countess agreed that it
must, but added, "Could you not wait just a little longer,
my dear? Until we are sure Harry has relaxed his vigilance—"

Miss Tolliver regarded her with doubt and curiosity.
"What is there between Harry Marletonthorpe and his
lordship?" she asked. "I knew the first day I met Mr.
Marletonthorpe that there was something, but all the boys
are remarkably closemouthed about it, and when I asked the
earl—"

"He said it was nothing at all," the countess supplied, accurately gauging Miss Tolliver's darkling look.

"Yes."

"His grandfather was just as exasperating," the countess complained. "And nothing I ever said could move him from that code of honor . . . Well, I suppose I didn't really want anything to move him because I was in love with an honorable man. . . ." She sighed heavily, and her eyes took on a faraway look. "How I miss him! What a dear, proud man he was! Giles is a great deal like him, although Giles was thrust into his responsibilities at such an early age that he never had the opportunity to develop the playfulness my Robert had . . ."

She was silent several moments and then, noticing Miss Tolliver's look of quick sympathy, gave herself a shake and said briskly, "Well, what a silly old woman I am, going on like that when you asked me about Harry Marletonthorpe!"

"Not silly—" Miss Tolliver assured her, but the countess interrupted with a firm "Very silly" before starting her tale.

She told Miss Tolliver that she had heard the story from Chuffy Marletonthorpe because that poor soul felt so bad about the entire situation that he had poured the information into her ears upon their first meeting after it happened.

"It?" Miss Tolliver questioned.

The countess nodded. "It seems that one night there was a card party at Giles's house in town—a few of his intimates, and Harry, because he was visiting Chuffy at the time—not because he was a friend of Giles. Actually, Harry is more John's age, but they never have been friends, either. I don't think Harry has many friends, really . . . but there— I'm off the story already!"

It seemed, the countess continued, that Harry was dipping pretty deep the night of Giles's card party. There was nothing new in that—Harry often did. It also seemed, she told Miss Tolliver, that the younger Marletonthorpe hadn't a feather to fly with—a circumstance that also was not new. What was new was that he was apparently more desperate than usual, for he tried cheating at cards.

"*What?*" Miss Tolliver exclaimed.

"Yes." The countess nodded. "Tried cheating Giles's friends. And wasn't very good at it, either, because Giles saw him. Out of consideration to Chuffy, Giles merely told Charleton about it and requested that he remove his brother from Giles's house immediately. Chuffy did, of couse—he was so embarrassed, and I understand Charleton and Harry had quite a turn up over it—in fact, Chuffy told me later that they didn't speak for months, until Harry's more pressing debts made approaching his brother for relief far more important than his pride. So the brothers have reconciled— uneasily, perhaps, but they do speak—but Harry has hated Giles ever since and would love to do him mischief if possible."

"But he should be grateful Giles didn't expose him in front of all the guests!" Miss Tolliver objected.

"Yes." The countess smiled inwardly at Miss Tolliver's unconscious use of the earl's name. "But I've often noted that the people who should be most grateful for a kindness are those who dislike the person who was kind to them. It is a sorry case, but true."

"I see," Miss Tolliver said absently as she stood and returned to the clothes cupboard.

"Does that mean you'll stay?" the countess asked hopefully, straightening from her drooping position on the bed.

"Yes—"

"Oh, good!"

"But only for a little while!" Miss Tolliver said. "Only until enough time has passed to make it clear to Mr. Marletonthorpe and all other interested parties that our decision that we will not suit is based on mutual agreement and *not* on the presence of an actress named Vanessa!"

"Quite right!" the countess approved, hopping down from the bed and moving toward the door, where she paused a moment and peered at Miss Tolliver. "My dear," she said, "forgive an old woman her terrible curiosity, but would marriage with my grandson really be so dreadful?"

The question surprised Miss Tolliver, and for several moments the countess thought she would not reply. Then Margaret raised her head and smiled at her. "Why, no,"

Miss Tolliver said in a brittle tone that hung in the air as if the slightest jar would crack it. "I'm sure marriage with your grandson would make any number of women happy. Any number at all—if it were not a marriage forced by circumstance, but rather a marriage of love."

Chapter
18

The dowager countess shut the door quietly behind her before allowing the laughter that had been threatening to overcome her to escape, floating softly on the air as she moved down the hallway, one hand on the old oaken bannister. She looked thoughtfully over the railing to see his lordship's footmen in close and speculative gossip, one eyeing the library door while the other looked upward toward Miss Tolliver's room. When that second servant saw his lordship's grandmother, he blushed and signaled to his friend, and the two melted away, leaving the countess smiling at the place they had been.

Ah, the servants are aware of it too, she thought, staring down, *and that is a very good sign, for the servants almost always know what is happening long before the people they serve do.* "Oh, I haven't had this much fun for an age!" she said aloud to the family armor of the first earl, which stood as silent sentry at the top of the stairs. "Now to see that silly grandson of mine!" And so saying, she hurried down the stairs and toward the library. There, after one sharp knock, she entered to see Giles seated gloomily by the fire, a bottle of his best brandy by his side, and a snifter in his hand.

"Well?" His one word was sharp as he rose at his grandmother's entrance, and she smiled benignly at him.

"Yes," she answered gently, "I am well. And you?"

The response took the earl by surprise, and he stared at

her for a moment before, recalled to his manners, he asked her to take a chair by the fire. The countess did so at her leisure, pleased to see the impatience in his manner as he awaited her pleasure, flinging himself into his chair and downing his brandy before setting the glass down with a snap.

"Did you talk to her?" his lordship demanded, leaning forward. His grandmother beamed at him again.

"Why yes," she said, "I believe I will have a sip of your brandy. Since you ask."

His lordship almost ground his teeth as he reached for the decanter and a clean glass. After pouring a splash of the amber liquid into it, he handed it to the countess who shook her head reproachfully at him.

"Really, Giles," she chided, "as your grandfather used to say, a gentleman should never be stingy with the price of his boots or the dispensing of his brandy."

The earl's brow almost lightened as he reached for the decanter again and added a generous amount to his grandmother's glass. This time she accepted it with becoming thanks, and sipped the liquor slowly, her eyes watching him over the snifter's rim. She seemed in no hurry to begin their conversation, and so the earl, after several moments, said, "Yes, Grandmama, you're quite right—there is a chill in the air today, and no, I don't think the country can continue to let Prinny set this ruinous course; although I quite agree with you that it is not wise to say so outside these walls; and yes, I have heard the latest crim. con. story, and agree it is quite scandalous, so—now that we have covered all the social niceties, perhaps we can get to the heart of this conversation. And that is—did you speak with Miss Tolliver? What did she say? What was she doing?"

The countess, upon whom her grandson's best brandy was having a mellowing effect, nodded. "Yes," she said. "I did speak with dear Margaret. She said a great deal. And she was packing."

"*What?*" His grandmother's last sentence ended all amusement the earl had heretofore felt at her tactics. He sprang from his chair and with a "She must not!" had half-covered the distance to the door when his grandmother stopped him.

"My dear Giles," she complained, "how is it I used to think you the most restful of my relatives? Really, dear boy—I cannot have this. Come back and sit down. I said Miss Tolliver *was* packing. She is doing so no longer."

"What?" The word, not as sharp as his first explosion moments earlier, was still strong enough to make his grandmother frown at him as he stood, looking back at her over one well-tailored shoulder, his eyes narrowed and his jaw tightened.

"Oh, do stop glaring at me and come and sit down!" his grandmother said irritably, placing her glass on the small table beside her. "If an old woman can't even enjoy a glass of brandy in peace, without being badgered to fix all and tell all—well!" Giles had not moved, and the countess straightened, regarding him with the same regal gaze she had used when he was a boy of twelve who had broken a shoulder after taking out his grandfather's high-spirited hunter. To her delight it still worked, for after one more impatient step toward the door the earl stopped, looked back at her again, and, muttering, returned to his chair across from her.

"Now," his grandmother said, favoring him with her most severe frown, "do strive for a little of the sense God gave you, Giles! I don't know how any grandson of mine could be such a—but there!" She reached forward and patted his knee. "I suppose some allowances must be made for a man in love!"

"*What?*" It was that same sharp tone again, and the dowager stared at the earl's frowning face in blandest surprise.

"I beg your pardon?"

The earl straightened, jerking on his cravat in a manner that well illustrated that this man of fashion was seriously upset. "Really, Grandmama! A man in love! You mistake my—that is—I mean—"

His grandmother did not help him, merely opening her eyes wider as he glared at her.

"It is merely," he said at last, his back as stiff as hers had been moments before, "that I do not wish Miss Tolliver to be unhappy—or inconvenienced—or worried. It is also that

I do not want her to so happily refuse what any number of other women would be so delighted to—''

The way his grandmother was smiling at him—almost as if she were laughing—made him stop that thought and hurry on.

"While I will agree that she is a pleasant woman," he continued, frowning at the countess, "—the pleasantest of my acquaintance, actually; and that it has been agreeable to have her here—more agreeable than I would have imagined, really; and that she has that trick of knowing just what is funny, and of making little arrangements with the cook, and the housekeeper, and of keeping Gillian in line and Peter and John happy . . ."

He seemed lost in that sentence as his gaze shifted from his grandmother to the fire, and he continued almost to himself. "But on the other hand, she is impertinent and strong-willed and sharp-tongued, and she isn't above giving me a piece of her mind on almost any subject! And it isn't that she's a beauty—far from it!"

"I like her eyes," his grandmother interposed.

The earl nodded abstractly, his gaze still fixed on the fire. "She has fine eyes," he agreed. "So kind, and laughing. And she has one of those smiles that makes a person feel important. I've seen her talking with Peter, and the servants, and my aunts—just the way she smiles at them makes them feel better. You can tell."

"She has a good mind," his grandmother offered.

"Almost too good!" his lordship agreed with feeling, looking back at the countess. "In fact, only yesterday she was saying—" There was something about the way his grandmother was smiling at him that made Giles stop, and his jaw dropped in amazement as if for the first time he, too, heard his words.

"Good grief, madam, you're right! I *am* in love with her! Of all the preposterous—foolish—Oh, Grandmama! *What* am I going to *do*?"

The dowager countess told him. She told him—among other things—that his handling of the situation so far had convinced his betrothed that he had offered for her only out of chivalry, and that that lady, having her own chivalrous ideas, was determined not to hold him to an agreement she felt he had been driven into and did not want.

His lordship's protest that he had been driven into it—at first—was met with a vehement "Hogwash!" and the severe request that he pay attention and not talk like a ninny. After that Giles subsided meekly, listening as his grandmother said she had done what she could for him, detailing several aspects of her conversation with Margaret and continuing uninterrupted until she announced that she had persuaded Miss Tolliver to stay a while longer to protect the earl from embarrassment and scandal.

The countess was rather pleased with her stratagems and success at that point, but the earl did not take her last disclosure in good part; in fact, he was moved to protest quite strongly that he did not want either the lady's pity *or* her charity. The very thought was repugnant to him, but his grandmother brought him up short by asking if he would rather Miss Tolliver departed that day, never to be seen again?

Of course he would not, he told her; it was just that—just that—

"Just that you've got the Manfield pride." His grandmother nodded. "I know. Pride is a fine thing, in moderation, but it can't share a joke or hold your hand, so you'd better decide if you'd rather have all of the former or some of the latter, because—"

Seeing all the signs that the countess was ready to launch into one of her famous pungent lectures, the earl agreed hastily that he could do with a little less pride, and his grandmother continued. She gave him several pieces of good advice on the wooing and winning of a spirited lady—not, she added crossly, that she expected him to take them, for even men of usual good sense acted like such idiots when it came to love—but declined to venture an opinion when the earl, an anxious crease across his forehead, asked if she thought Miss Tolliver might care for him—a little—or might learn to?

"I wouldn't know," the countess said mendaciously, keeping to herself the brittle tone and the overly bright eyes that had punctuated the end of her interview with Margaret, and comforting herself with the thought that it did not hurt a gentleman as used to being in control as Giles was to be a bit unsure now and then. "I think she could do better myself, but there! You never know when an otherwise sensible woman will be smitten in the most foolish ways!"

The earl smiled at her. "Thank you, Grandmama! Your opinion is always elevating for me!" And so saying he rose and kissed her cheek before reaching for the brandy decanter and adding to her diminished glass. "You will excuse me," he said with a bow. "I believe I have a great deal of work to do!"

His grandmother nodded tranquilly and reached for her glass, smiling into it as she heard the soft closing of the library door behind him. She sat for several moments, watching the fire dance up the chimney, then raised her glass in quiet salute to the picture of her son that hung above the mantle. "You've got a good son there, Richard," she said. "I know how important that is. I was lucky. I had a good son, too."

The painting above the mantel smiled back at her as she issued a relaxed sigh then touched her lips to the snifter, and drank.

Chapter
19

The earl, hunting in earnest now, found his quarry remarkably elusive in the next few days, and his frustration had peaked when he came upon Miss Tolliver by accident one afternoon in the Willowdale gardens. She was dressed with the elegant simplicity that had become familiar to him. She wore a high poke bonnet that framed her face, its light blue ribbons matching the flounce on her high-waisted gown and setting off to advantage the soft blue of her eyes. She also wore a light silk shawl against the day's breeze, and was untangling its fringe from an inquisitive rose bush whose branches brushed the bench upon which she sat.

"My dear, let me help you with that!" the earl said, hurrying forward.

"There is no need—" Miss Tolliver began, but he did not listen, and in a moment had the fringe free. Looking up with thanks, Margaret found him smiling down at her in such a way that she quite forgot for a moment what she was going to say, and had to give herself a severe inward shake before the words returned to her.

"My dear, you look charming," the earl said in a warm voice. "May I join you?"

Miss Tolliver had the time neither to issue an invitation nor to decline his request, for Giles seated himself on the bench beside her, picking up the fan that had lain there and opening it to view the scene painted upon it.

"Very pretty," he approved.

154

"Yes," Miss Tolliver agreed. "But not half so beautiful as your gardens, my lord. I wish we had but half these blossoms at my home in Yorkshire!"

The earl regarded her curiously, asking if she liked to garden, and when she acknowledged that it was a favorite pastime, he told her that the gardens were largely the work of his mother, who had enjoyed gardening, too.

"It was she who drew up the plans for the grounds," he said. "I can remember how my father used to tease her about them—saying she cared more for her flowers than she cared for her family, and that her desire to import this or that exotic bloom would be the ruin of him. But after she died, he was often to be found here. He said the gardens were a continuation of her beauty, and he felt closer to her here than anywhere else. I think sometimes—"

He stopped suddenly, and Miss Tolliver put an unconscious hand out to cover one of his own. "You think, my lord?" she asked softly.

He looked down at her hand and then up into her face before shaking his head. "I do not wish to bore you."

"I am not bored," she answered in that quiet voice that made him want to stroke the hand that covered his, but he refrained. "Tell me what you think."

"I think," he said at last, looking out at the well-kept shrubs and flowerbeds, "that it is the best part of herself she could leave us, this growing, flowering place she created with love."

Miss Tolliver agreed that it was a fine gift, but added that his mother had left them all something else. At his questioning look she smiled. "She left you each other. And there is a lot of love apparent there, too."

This time he could not help himself—his second hand covered hers, and hastily Miss Tolliver withdrew, her color high as she directed his attention down one of the garden paths. "Oh, look," she cried. "Lazaurus is taking Aunt Henrietta for a walk!"

Obediently his eyes followed her pointing finger. "Don't you mean your aunt is taking her rooster for a walk?" he asked, smiling, but she shook her head, and in a moment, he saw that what she said was true. The rooster strutted ahead of the absentminded Henrietta, its head cocking from side to side as it kept a watchful eye out for bugs unwise enough to be in the garden at the moment. Laz also kept an eye on Henrietta, and whenever she stopped to admire a particularly lovely bloom or to gaze at the sky or the small pond that the earl's mother had made part of her garden, he went hopping back to her, scolding in such a way that she invariably started forward again with a "Yes, yes, Laz, I'm coming!"

They proceeded in this manner until they reached the earl and Miss Tolliver, and Aunt Henrietta stopped for a moment to pat her niece's cheek and to gaze consideringly at the earl, who had risen at her approach. "Twenty thousand pounds!" she breathed, looking nearsightedly up into his face. "My, my!" Then, to the rooster clucking at her feet, she said, "Yes, Laz, yes!" and drifted past.

The earl, left smiling behind her, remarked to the air that he was glad Miss Tolliver's family found him so agreeable.

"Oh, yes," Miss Tolliver agreed, her eyes alight. "My aunt and brother both find you—enchanting!"

"Both find my twenty-thousand pounds enchanting, you mean," he corrected her.

She assured him that, to her brother, he and his twenty-thousand pounds were one and the same.

"And to your aunt?" he was smiling back at her in that odd way that made Miss Tolliver feel the air growing closer about her.

"Well, the twenty-thousand pounds is a powerful inducement, of course," she said, "but there is also the fact that Lazaurus likes you. That goes a long way with Aunt Henrietta."

"Lazaurus—likes me?" the earl repeated. His popularity had never rested with a rooster before.

"Oh, yes," Miss Tolliver assured him, her lips prim, her eyes still alight. "You sit quite well with Lazaurus. He never pecks at you, as he does at Charles, nor does he fly in your face, as he did the day poor Gillian was napping on the morning room sofa."

"He flew in Gillian's face—?" the earl, who had not heard this story, questioned. Miss Tolliver nodded.

"Lazaurus," she informed him in a perfect imitation of

her aunt's tone when an indignant Gillian applied to that lady to constrain her wild bird, "does not approve of sloth. An early riser himself, he cannot condone people whiling away the day's most productive hours in slumber. A bit of a high stickler, is Lazarus."

The earl laughed. "I am sure Gillian was moved."

"Well," Miss Tolliver confessed, "I think he was nearly moved to wring poor Laz's neck. And if it had not been for his inherent good manners—and your brother John's timely intervention—he would surely have done so. But now he has learned to leave no door ajar when he enters or leaves a room, and if he only remembers to also close all windows, I have great hopes that we won't have a repeat of that unfortunate scene."

The earl, saying that he would certainly remember such precautions if he, himself, ever felt an attack of sleepiness— or sloth—coming on, added that Lazarus might be the best guardian he could find to keep Gillian at his studies. Miss Tolliver smiled, and they sat for several moments in silence, the lady surveying the gardens before them, and his lordship surveying the lady.

"It really is too bad," he said suddenly, and Miss Tolliver turned to him in surprise.

"Too bad, my lord?" she repeated.

He nodded, and his expression grew mournful as she watched him. "Yes. Too bad."

"But—" Quickly she reviewed their conversation, seeking the sadness in it. "Are you thinking of your mother—"

"No." His lordship shook his head. "I am thinking not of my family, but of yours."

"Mine?" Miss Tolliver was startled, and then she stiffened. "If it is about Lazarus, my lord, I am sorry, but I warned you before Aunt Henrietta ever came—"

His lordship said it was not the rooster.

"Oh." Miss Tolliver thought again, and sighed. "Well," she said, "then it must be Charles, and I am sorry for that, too, but he is what he is, and—"

Solemnly the earl told her that his thoughts did not lie with her brother.

"Oh." Miss Tolliver cocked her head to the left, considering, while one hand absently played with the fringe of her shawl. "Well, then . . . I do not understand. What is it, my lord, that is too bad?"

"You." He watched in enjoyment as her eyes widened, and she sat back a little on the bench, regarding him. Instantly the alert rosebush tangled in her shawl again, and his lordship reached over to free it. Miss Tolliver continued to regard him.

"Me?" she said at last, and the earl nodded.

"You, Miss Tolliver."

"But Giles—" the lady started, then stopped, blushing. "I mean, my lord—"

"No, no, no," he complained. "You were quite right the first time. My name is Giles, and there is nothing wrong with your using it. You say it quite charmingly, you know. I would like to hear you say it again."

Miss Tolliver shook her head, watching her hands clasp and unclasp in her lap. "We are not on terms—" she began primly.

"My dear Maggie, we are engaged!"

"Not really—and you shouldn't be calling me Maggie!"

"Margaret, then," he said placatingly.

"No. You shouldn't call me Margaret, either!"

"But it is your name!"

"But you are not at liberty to use it!"

"Make me at liberty," he coaxed, but Miss Tolliver shook her head.

"It would not be right."

"But my dear!" He appeared astounded. "I have 20,000 pounds. A year!"

Her lips quirked slightly, but she refused to succumb.

"And a fine home. Several of them, in fact!"

"I do not care for such—"

"I am considered a fine dancer and a fair conversationalist; I can hold my own at whist and piquet—"

Miss Tolliver eyed him consideringly. "You play piquet?"

Now it was his turn to nod. "Well. And besides—Lazaurus likes me!"

He said it as if it were the clincher, and in spite of herself, Miss Tolliver smiled.

"There," he said. "That's better. Now all you have to do is say 'Giles' to make me quite happy again."

Severely Miss Tolliver told him that she could not be accountable for his happiness, reminding him that he had been about to tell her what it was that was 'too bad' about her before they dwindled into this silly conversation.

"But my dear," he protested, "this is just it. It is too bad that my 20,000 pounds a year and my way with poultry make me acceptable to every member of your family but the one whose opinion I value most!"

Miss Tolliver was heard to murmur that it was not that he was unacceptable to her, it was just that—just that—

"Just that?" his lordship pressed, leaning forward to capture one of her hands as it moved restlessly in her lap.

Miss Tolliver watched her small white hand disappear into his two large brown ones, and gulped.

"Giles, really—" she began weakly, trying to pull her hand away.

He smiled. "Yes, really, Margaret," he agreed, leaning forward just as an irate squawking was heard from the western edge of the gardens, followed immediately by an indignant demand that someone get that infernal bird away from him before he made fricassee out of it.

"Oh, dear!" Miss Tolliver rose quickly and picked up her skirts to hurry toward the sound. "Gillian!"

The earl, following more slowly behind her, repeated the name with disgust. "Gillian! Of course. Where there's trouble—always Gillian!"

Chapter
20

In this instance, however, Miss Tolliver and the earl wronged Gillian, for when they rounded the last hedge in expectation of seeing the earl's second youngest brother, they found instead an angry John, his color heightened, as with the judicious waving of his hat and riding crop he kept the ruffled Lazaurus at bay, while Aunt Henrietta stood severely by, shouting at him not to harm her rooster.

He was shouting back that he wasn't going to have the rooster hurting him, either, when he caught sight of Miss Tolliver and his eldest brother and, considerably aware of the ridiculous picture he must present, clamped his lips together and restored his hat to his head, whereupon Lazarus, seeing his advantage, rushed in, wings flapping, to do a scuff and scratch dance on John's highly polished riding boots.

"Oh, dear!" Miss Tolliver said, hurrying forward to rescue the astounded gentleman, who stared with bulging eyes at the results of the assault on his new boots. "Lazarus, it is too bad of you!" she said, shooing the rooster back to her aunt, who stood glaring at John.

"Sloth!" the old lady said succinctly, picking up her bird and tucking it under her arm, where it sat sounding off angrily at those around it. "Lazarus never can abide sloth!" And so saying she turned on her heel and, ignoring the open-mouthed John and his now amused brother, stalked

160

off, clucking softly to her rooster and promising him a nice bowl of corn to soothe his nerves.

"To sooth *his* nerves?" John repeated after her, watching them go with a disapproving eye. "Well, of all the—"

He became aware of his brother's laughter and turned to glare at him with the same disapproval. "Oh, yes, it's all very well for you to laugh, Giles. The crazy bird likes you! But look at these boots! My valet will never get the scratches off, and I shudder to think what he is going to say, for very particular about my boots is old Timms, and—"

"As well he should be," Miss Tolliver seconded him warmly, interrupting the earl's response that his brother ought to be able to deal with his valet—hopefully better than with a rooster! Miss Tolliver's eyes were reproachful as they turned toward the earl, before busying herself again with removing the random feather from Mr. Manfield's coat and cravat. "Boots are very important, I'm sure."

"Well, yes—that is—" It again occurred to John that he was cutting a ridiculous figure, and he stopped his sentence to brush his riding crop against his breeches. "Thing is, that bird is a menace! Attacks an innocent man—"

The earl, prepared to enjoy himself, interrupted to ask what his brother had done to earn the rooster's ire. John said it was no such thing; he had returned perhaps a half hour earlier from a visit to one of the estate's tenants and, it being such a beautiful day, had stretched out on the grass, his back to a tree, there to contemplate the world. And if he had happened to doze off for a few moments—well, surely there was no harm in that . . .

"Sloth," the earl pronounced, echoing Aunt Henrietta's word. "Sloth, sloth, sloth."

John's chin came up, and he regarded his elder brother with disfavor. "No such thing," he said, and stalked off toward the house, an errant feather floating on the air behind him as he went.

"Oh dear!" Miss Tolliver's eyes were rueful as she watched him go.

The earl grinned, and said, "Quite!"

* * *

Miss Tolliver had, through quiet means, acquired the habit of spending part of each afternoon with the earl's youngest brother, Peter. Although he was certainly better, the fourth of the fifth earl's sons still had the remnants of a cough, and those remnants were enough to make the family doctor charge him most forcefully not to overdo. It was a difficult task for someone Peter's age, a boy who possessed a powerful intellect and a not so powerful body, and who would much rather have been able to be out and about, but he bore with it cheerfully, even striving—difficult as it was—to heed the doctor's advice and leave his books several hours a day to rest his eyes.

Toward that goal he was aided by Miss Tolliver, who took it upon herself to join him in the library for a game of chess or a discussion of various art exhibits she had seen, or books they both had read. Sometimes, when the others were out, they made use of the billiards room, Miss Tolliver explaining guiltily that although it was probably not quite the thing, she had always wished to learn the game, and would be ever so grateful if he taught it to her. Peter, anxious to please his new friend, was glad to comply, not realizing that what he did as a favor for Miss Tolliver was a relaxing exercise for himself.

Occasionally, too, they met in the music room, where Miss Tolliver played the piano and Peter joined her in duets of some of the old country tunes for which they found music tucked up in one of the room's bookcases. A casual question to Giles brought the information that the music had belonged to their mother, and that increased Peter's enjoyment of it.

He was awaiting Margaret in the music room several days after John's encounter with the time-vigilant Laz, and was idly strumming the keys of the piano when Miss Tolliver rushed through the door, her color high and her eyes sparkling.

"Your brother—" she began when she saw him, "is the most high-handed, disagreeable, overbearing—oh!" She put her hands to her cheeks and took a quick turn around the room. "It does not bear thinking of!"

Peter, who had several brothers, regarded her, consideringly. "Have you been quarreling with Giles again?" he asked.

Miss Tolliver nodded. "And quarrelsome! That is a good word, Peter! He is one of the most quarrelsome men I know—"

Peter, who had always thought the earl quite calm, interrupted to ask what they had been quarreling about. Miss Tolliver ground her teeth.

"All I did," she told him, one hand running distractedly through her hair while the other hand tapped a rapid tattoo on a convenient table, "was tell him that I thought we needed to develop a timetable for ending our engagement, and he said—he said—"

"Aren't you happy here?" Peter asked, his tone of voice as anxious as the expression in his eyes.

"That's exactly what he said!" Miss Tolliver exclaimed, staring at the boy in surprise. "As if being happy had anything to do with it!"

"Doesn't it?" Peter asked, again in that anxious tone that made Miss Tolliver cease her mutterings and come forward to place a hand on his shoulder.

"Being happy is very important, Peter," she told him gently, one hand pushing the hair back off his brow, "but it is not everything. Not always."

"Oh." He considered for a moment, then asked in a small voice, "but do you really have to go away?"

"Yes," she said with resolution. "I do."

"Why?"

"Peter." She joined him on the piano bench, one arm around his shoulder. "You know it is all a hum, this engagement between your brother and me. You know we're not really to be married—"

"But why not?" Peter cried. "Don't you *wish* to marry Giles? Because he is really a very good sort, and perhaps if you knew him better—"

Miss Tolliver's throat constricted as she told him it was not a matter of wishes; it was simply the knowledge that circumstances had dictated their engagement, but they did not—could not—dictate their marriage.

"But Giles wouldn't have told everyone you were engaged if he didn't think it was the right thing to do!'' Peter objected.

Miss Tolliver was heard to say that his lordship's motives had been most pure, but . . .

"Then you have to marry someone!" Peter told her.

She assured him—with every sign of loathing—that she did not, but he persisted.

"It is all our fault—Gillian's and mine. I do wish you would consent to be Giles's wife, and stay here at Willowdale with us."

Miss Tolliver thanked him for his kindness, but said quite firmly that nothing could prevail upon her to marry his brother.

"Are you sure?"

She met Peter's anxious look with a resolute one of her own. "Quite."

The boy took a deep breath. "Then," he said, the words coming in a rush, "would you like to marry me?"

Miss Tolliver sat back suddenly on the piano bench, her arm dropping from around Peter's shoulders onto the keys behind them, which made a loud and a not tuneful *kerplunk* as she regarded him in amazement.

"My dear!" she exclaimed.

"I would try to be a good husband," he assured her. "Truly I would. And then you wouldn't have to go away—"

Miss Tolliver reached for his hand, and pressed it warmly. "Peter," she asked, "how old are you?"

He looked away, then back. "Thirteen," he said. "Two months hence. Does it matter?"

Miss Tolliver sighed. "Quite a bit," she told him. "I am twenty-eight. Fifteen years older."

"Oh." He bit his lip, and it was apparent he was considering deeply. Then he looked at her, and his eyes were hopeful. "I shall grow older, you know. In seven years, I shall be twenty!"

"Yes," she agreed, her graveness matching his own as she willed herself not to laugh. "But in seven years, I shall be older, too. When you are twenty, Peter, I shall be thirty-five!"

It was plain that that thought had not heretofore occurred to him, and his lips parted slightly. "That old!"

"That old, Peter," she agreed.

He rallied like a gentleman, declaring stoutly that he did not care. She smiled, but although she was deeply touched, she added that she could not accept his kind offer.

"But you have to marry one of us," Peter objected, "and you won't have Giles, who is quite old, too, so age shouldn't matter there, and you won't have me, and I don't think Gillian would make a good husband for you—"

Gravely Miss Tolliver agreed that Gillian would not.

Peter looked at her doubtfully. "Would you like me to speak to John?"

Her mind occupied by the feeling that she was getting deeper and deeper into a web of the Manfield men's weaving, she had been half-listening. Peter's last words, however, made her straighten with a loud *"What?"*

"I asked if you would like me to speak with John," he said, "because I would—except that—well . . . well I think John would marry you, out of duty, if we made him see it, but somehow . . . I don't think . . . You wouldn't wish to be married out of duty, would you?"

"No." Miss Tolliver squeezed his hand, and her voice was firm. "No, my dear, I would not."

Chapter
21

In Miss Tolliver's mind the discussion was ended, but in Peter's mind it went on. He felt responsible for the situation in which the lady now found herself—after all, he knew, if it hadn't been for his and Gillian's kidnap attempt and subsequent bungling, Miss Tolliver would be at her home in Yorkshire now, and she and the inhabitants of Willowdale would never have met. That thought left him feeling curiously bereft, and he did not dwell on it. Instead, after much private thought in which he could not hit upon a solution as to how best to help her out of her predicament, he took the matter up with his brother Gillian. Thus it was that, two days later, on one of the early morning rides that Miss Tolliver and Gillian had fallen into the habit of taking, Miss Tolliver received her second proposal from a Manfield male.

They had paused together at the top of one of the small rolling hills that characterized the earl's estate, and Miss Tolliver was quoting Shakespeare:

> *"Full many a glorious morning have I seen*
> *Flatter the mountain-tops with sovereign eye,*
> *Kissing with golden face the meadows green,*
> *Gilding pale streams with heavenly alchemy..."*

At least, she said it was Shakespeare, and Gillian, not one to judge, and lending only half an ear to the lyrics he did not appreciate nor fully understand, surprised both the lady and himself by suddenly blurting, "Will you marry me?"

Miss Tolliver's quote ended abruptly as she turned a startled face to his bright red one.

"I beg your pardon?" she asked, thinking she had not heard right.

"I said," Gillian repeated manfully, trying not to feel as if his life were passing before his eyes, "will you marry me?"

Later he could not say what reaction he anticipated, but hers was not the one. Miss Tolliver began to laugh.

"Here—I say—" Gillian stared at her in surprise and not a little chagrin, and the lady did her best to stifle her giggles.

"Oh, Gillian—" she started. "I am sorry—but if you could see your face! My dear boy, you look as if you'd rather have a tooth drawn—have all your teeth drawn—than asked me, and yet—"

"No, no!" Gillian assured her, abashed. "Not at all. Would be most happy to marry you. Really. That is—"

His voice trailed off at the infelicity of the thought, and helpfully Miss Tolliver took it up for him.

"That is, if you wished to be married," she said gently.

Head down, he nodded. "I knew I wouldn't do it right," he said, voice and face glum. "Told Peter so. Told him no matter how many times I rehearsed it, I was bound to make a mull . . ."

"Ah." Miss Tolliver nodded too. "Peter. I might have known."

Gillian looked at her worriedly. "Mustn't blame Peter, you know. He's right. It's our fault you're in this predicament. And if you don't wish to marry Giles . . . Well! Stands to reason you should marry one of us. Peter is too young. You told him he was too young. But me—well!"

Unwilling to spoil his self-image as a man-about-town, Miss Tolliver pointed out that he, too, was underage, and that it was not to be supposed that his guardian would consent to his marriage before he attained his majority. Gillian stared at her in surprise.

"Hadn't thought of that," he admitted. Miss Tolliver said she thought he had not.

"But still—" Gillian was torn between relief and his desire to acquit himself as a gentleman. "Would make a push . . . That is, if you wanted . . ."

The words trailed off, his face so hopeful that Miss Tolliver had trouble containing herself once again. She told him, voice grave, that she was convinced they would not suit. Relieved, Gillian confided that he had told Peter the same thing, but he would have done his best if she'd had her heart set on marrying him. The reassurance that Miss Tolliver's heart was in no way damaged by their being unbetrothed seemed to clear away the last of his doubts, and happily he suggested that they ride on. Miss Tolliver agreed it was the best thing they could do.

Peter was as near to angry as he ever got with Gillian when that young man reported back on the lack of success of his mission, even going so far as to call his brother a gudgeon in a tone that put Gillian remarkably in mind of John. Gillian demanded to be told just what Peter thought he could have done, since the lady obviously did not wish to marry him. Peter's explanation that no lady of any spirit or self-respect would want to marry a man who so obviously did not want to marry her struck Gillian forcibly, for he had not thought of it before.

"Oh," he said, the good fortune he had felt at his narrow escape from matrimony easing away as the knowledge that he had not behaved as he ought slipped in. "I never thought—"

Severely Peter told him that one of his chief problems was that he never thought. Privately Gillian agreed it might be true, but he was not going to admit such a thing to his younger brother. Instead he asked what could be done, and Peter frowned deeply before answering. Miss Tolliver had told him she did not wish it, but still . . .

"I think," he said finally, "that we should apply to John."

The interview with John came in the library, and it did not, in his brothers' minds, at least, go well. For one thing, they interrupted him in the midst of some weighty correspondence that he was loathe to leave, and when they did at last persuade him to leave it to discuss their problem with them, he was so shocked at what they had done that Peter could not help agreeing with Gillian that they would have been better off to keep their own counsel, and not to seek his. John told them severely that it was wrong of one brother to propose to a woman betrothed to another brother; in fact, he said, his eyebrows beetling together in a good imitation of their grandfather, who was always awe-inspiring when angry, he thought even two such numbskulls as they would know that—

"Yes, well," Gillian interrupted, trying to save them from a lecture, "It doesn't matter, does it? Because she wouldn't have either of us, and now it's up to you."

Caught like that, in the middle of pontificating, it took John some time to assimilate Gillian's meaning. When he did, his brows rose and his face purpled alarmingly, while his jaw worked several moments before he could stutter out the words to ask, in effect, if his brothers had lost their minds.

"Not that you have one to lose, Gillian," he ended, glaring at his brother, "but I thought Peter had better sense . . ."

His gaze turned toward their youngest brother and Peter, with a sigh, said he thought it best that he tell John all about it. He started with the kidnapping—which, John said, his face austere, they should all try to forget about as soon as possible—and hit upon the engagement entered into by the earl to save Miss Tolliver from scandal. John told them that was the earl's business, and no one else's.

"But it isn't!" Peter cried. "It's Miss Tolliver's business, too, and she doesn't wish to marry Giles. She told me so. And I asked Grandmama one day if it would be such a terrible thing if Miss Tolliver and Giles didn't get married, and she—she was on her way to her bedchamber at the time, with a bottle of sherry—said it would be a very terrible thing indeed. Then I asked Aunt Caroline what would happen to a lady who spent a night at an inn with a gentleman, unchaperoned, and she blessed herself and said whatever was I thinking of to ask such a thing, but that such a lady would be ostracized—''

His voice trailed off as his brothers regarded him with amazement.

"You asked Aunt Caroline *that*?" Gillian said, his voice tinged with awe.

Peter said that he had, and Gillian clapped him on the back. "Peter, my boy, you're a braver man than I am, and that's a fact! It's a wonder she didn't faint dead away at the very thought! Lord, I'd have given a coachwheel to see her face!''

John reminded him that he was talking about his aunt and should keep a civil tongue in his head, but Peter grinned and whispered that she had been quite pink at the thought. Then it was John's turn to frown at Peter, too, and both of the younger brothers thought it best to hold their tongues while John, his fingers tapping rhythmically on his chair arm, sat pondering the conversation.

It was difficult for him to believe that Miss Tolliver did not wish to marry their brother Giles. She had spoken of a pretend engagement, but as her time at Willowdale lengthened, he had pushed the thought to the back of his mind, thinking that she and the earl had realized they would indeed suit and had come to an understanding between them. It was very probable, he told himself, that Peter had misunderstood, but if he had not . . . Well . . .

Like his brothers, John had come by insensible degrees to find Miss Tolliver a part of their world. Usually ill at ease with the ladies of his acquaintance, there was something about her that made it almost effortless for him to talk. She was an attentive listener, and she was informed on so many of the topics that turned other females of his acquaintance glassy-eyed at the mere mention. She played chess, too——in fact, they had gotten into the habit of playing almost nightly. He had mentioned once that Giles might not like his brother taking up so much of Miss Tolliver's time in the evening, but she had smiled and said it could be of no moment to the earl, and so . . .

In the wake of Peter's and Gillian's disclosure, those words took on new meaning, and John sighed heavily. He was so used to thinking that *everyone* wanted to marry his brother, that he could not believe there was a lady who did not. But perhaps . . .

Gillian's clearing his throat for the third time made John conscious of his brothers, who had stood forgotten before him for several minutes. He frowned heavily at them and said that although he did not credit their story, he would take it upon himself to ascertain the lady's leanings, and if she indeed did not wish to marry Giles—something he was in no way certain of—why then, he would see . . .

Peter and Gillian, realizing it was the best they could do, nodded and slipped quietly from the room, leaving John to his thoughts and his reading. It could not be said that in the rest of the afternoon he accomplished much of the latter.

It had occurred to Miss Tolliver at supper that something was heavy on John's mind. The earl was aware of it too, she knew, for she had seen him direct several sharp glances toward his brother who sat unmindful of the comedy between the aunts, Caroline so determined and so loud in her protests that tea would and could cure any and all of the many ills Cassandra was suffering, that Cassandra was at last moved to snap, "For goodness' sake, Caroline, I do not *wish* to be cured!"

As soon as the words were out of her mouth, Cassandra knew what she had done. As her sister stared at her in astonishment and her mother cackled in glee, Cassandra, her face red and, for once, her posture not drooping, rose and offered a polite "excuse me" to the assembled company— of which, she noted, only the earl and Miss Tolliver, and John seemed to have retained their composure, while the others sat laughing or at least grinning at her faux pas. Indignant, she stalked to the door, only pausing there long enough to inform the group that she would be leaving on the morrow. She was further incensed by her mother's frank assertion that it was about time.

The earl told her politely that they would all be sorry to see her go—earning him an appalled glance from his grandmother—and offered the use of his coach to convey her to whatever destination she chose. She thanked him with

dignity, saying she rather thought she would visit Cousin
Elizabeth for a time. That drew a "poor Elizabeth" from
her unrepentant mother, and with her shoulders back and her
head high, Cassandra left the room. If she shut the door
behind her with unnecessary violence, no one seemed to
notice.

"Really, Grandmama—" the earl started, shaking his
head at the dowager countess, but she, paying him no mind,
turned to the puzzled Caroline and remarked pleasantly that
she understood Cousin Elizabeth was becoming quite an
aficionado of tea in her old age; some people even said that
her storeroom rivaled that of Mr. Petersham's.

"In fact," she said mendaciously, watching her daughter's eyes light up, "I don't know how I came not to
mention it to you before, Caroline. I was thinking just the
other day that Cousin Elizabeth could surely benefit from
your opinions and knowledge. Don't you agree?"

Caroline left off trying to understand what had provoked
her sister to anger—surely, she assured herself, it was not
something she, Caroline, had said—and gazed at her mother
in wonder.

"Why, really, Mama," she said in a soft complaining
voice, "I do think you could have told me about it sooner."

The countess, meeting the eyes of no one else at the table,
agreed that she could have, and lamented the loss of
memory that comes with old age.

Caroline sighed. "Well, yes, I quite understand—you
didn't mean to. But mama, if you had told me earlier, it
could be I off to visit Cousin Elizabeth, and not Cassandra!
It really is too bad of you!"

For the thousandth time the dowager countess wondered
what she had done to deserve her daughters, and as she
raised her eyes to heaven, she caught sight of the earl's
face, and knew he was reading her thoughts exactly. She
frowned at him for his impertinence, and with great patience
suggested that perhaps Caroline could *join* Cassandra in the
earl's coach the next morning. If she really wanted to . . .

That the idea had not occurred to her was apparent in the
way Caroline brightened. She said it was a splendid notion,

and only hesitated to leave her mother alone when she might need her.

Nobly the countess promised to bear up, and when Caroline still showed signs of protesting, she pointed out that Miss Tolliver and the earl could be depended upon to see to her needs if any should arise. Miss Tolliver, knowing what was asked for in the look the countess directed toward her, agreed, and Caroline was able to relinquish that worry. In a moment the second of the earl's aunts was on her feet, saying that she must go at once to tell Cassandra, for they would have such a good time, and must make their plans as to where they would stop on the road for tea. She heard the George served a good cup...

With an abstract "excuse me," Caroline left the room. The earl gazed at his grandmother sternly.

"Really, Grandmama!" he said. "*Does* Cousin Elizabeth have a tea collection?"

The countess's voice was tranquil as she said she did not know. But, she added, she was sure that if she did not have one now, she certainly would in the near future.

The earl shook his head. "Do you think it kind to let my aunts descend on her in this way?"

The dowager sat for several moments, sipping her wine. "The last time I saw Elizabeth," she said at last to the room at large, "she wore a puce gown. I detest puce. *And*," she continued, as her grandson was about to argue, "she told me I was looking quite old. Aged, even." She sipped her wine again and said no more. But everyone in the room— with the exception of Charles, who was too busy eating, and John, who had heard none of the evening's conversation— understood perfectly. Henrietta even offered to lend the countess her rooster.

Chapter 22

When the countess rose from the table and Miss Tolliver and Aunt Henrietta rose with her to withdraw, Miss Tolliver stopped for a moment beside John's chair to ask him if he wished to play chess that evening. Her question was low, and the earl could not hear it, but there was something about the anxious way she looked at his brother that troubled him, and he raised his voice to ask if she would care to join him for a game of piquet that evening.

Sir Charles, whose thoughts had gone from the earl's excellent dinner to the earl's excellent port, which the butler was now placing on the table, started at that, and eyed the earl with misgivings.

"Better not," he said, his face earnest. "Doesn't do to play piquet with Margaret. *I* should know."

The earl smiled at him, but raised the question again. "Miss Tolliver?"

Margaret, who had bent to hear Johns' answer that he would join her in the library directly, returned an abstract "perhaps later" to the earl and, ignorant of his frown, walked out of the room with a smiling "thank you" for the footman who held the door for her. The earl, wondering why everyone in his household was capable of winning the lady's smiles but himself, picked up the port and poured it. Liberally.

He poured another round several minutes later when his brother John excused himself to join Miss Tolliver in the library, so far forgetting himself and considerably surprising his brother Gillian when he filled Gillian's glass yet again. Not given to deep cogitation, Gillian did not long wonder why; he just thanked his lucky stars and drank deeply.

Miss Tolliver had the chessboard ready when John walked into the library, and had the gentleman for whom she waited been in a less serious mood, he might have better appreciated the charming picture before him.

The lady had set the chessboard in front of the fireplace, and the flames therein crackled and snapped cheerfully, their blues, oranges, and yellows ably aided by several candelabras as together they cast a cozy glow over the area. Two large leather wing chairs were drawn up to the small mahogany table on which the chessboard sat, and in one of them a smiling Miss Tolliver awaited him. He took his place in the other chair without comment and stared at the board, while Miss Tolliver watched him. It was clear his abstraction had not lifted; if anything, it had deepened. He appeared nervous; in fact, her quiet "Would you like to begin?" made him start, and after a fleeting look up, which made him gulp and look hastily down again, he did not meet her eyes as the game progressed.

Usually the most deliberate of chess players, tonight John moved his pieces very much at random, and when at last Miss Tolliver deliberately put her king in danger, only to have him miss the correct move for one in favor of an insignificant pawn, she reached out her hand to cover his as it rested on the chess piece, and said, "My dear John, whatever is the matter? Can I help?"

He looked first at her hand and then into her concerned face before sitting back as if her touch burned him. Both bewildered and alarmed, Miss Tolliver watched as he tugged hastily at his cravat and rose to pour himself a glass of the brandy that sat on the library table before one of the room's large windows. He drained the glass quickly, and poured out another before turning to face her. He seemed about to speak, changed his mind, and downed the second glass. Miss Tolliver watched in amazement.

"My dear sir!" she said. "Surely whatever is distressing

you cannot be so bad that we cannot make it better if we put our heads together—''

She was interrupted by a strangled sound from John's throat, and words that sounded suspiciously like "That's it!''

"I beg your pardon?''

John picked up the decanter, changed his mind, and put it down again before returning to stand by his chair before the fire, twirling the empty glass in his hand, setting it on the mantlepiece and then picking it up again. "Thing is—I mean—want to talk to you—''

"And I want to talk to you!'' Miss Tolliver assured him, rising to lay a hand on his arm. He gazed at her hand, and swallowed deeply. Hastily he took a step back, then moved to the other side of the chair, keeping it between them as if for protection.

"Miss Tolliver!'' he said. Words failed him.

"Yes?'' the lady questioned.

"Miss Tolliver!'' His jaw worked several times. "Thing is . . .'' His eyes turned wistfully to the brandy again, and a thought occurred to him. "May I offer you a drink?''

She brushed the offer aside with the information that she never drank brandy, and politely he said that he could have some sherry—or ratafia, if she wished—brought in. Miss Tolliver assured him she was not thirsty.

"Oh. Well.'' There was a small table behind him, and John set the glass he held on it. "I seem to be making quite a mull . . .'' Miss Tolliver, who wished to help him but had no idea what he was talking about, stood listening, her head to one side. She really was a good listener, he thought . . . Drawing a deep breath, he plunged in.

"Miss Tolliver,'' he said. "Do you wish to marry my brother? My brother Giles, that is,'' he added conscientiously, remembering too late that she had already been proposed to by his two youngest brothers.

"My dear sir!'' Surprised, she stepped back a moment. "What on earth has that to do with what is troubling you?''

It had a great deal to do, she learned shortly, for when, upon his repeating the question and her answering firmly that she was convinced she and the earl would not suit, he took another of his deep breaths, picked up the glass behind him and put it to his lips, removing it without ever being aware that it was empty, and he had had nothing to drink, and said in strangled tones, but with a perfect bow, "Then, madam, would you do me the honor of becoming *my* wife?"

"Becoming—your—" Miss Tolliver repeated the words slowly, tottering backward with each until she found herself in front of her chair, and sank into it gratefully. She gazed up at his flushed and anxious face, and passed a hand over her own in bewilderment. "But, John—"

Humbly he told her that he knew he would not be the best of husbands; that he realized he had a manner that was by many considered too stiff and formal; that he was aware he was not an exciting man, or one given to flattering speeches and conversant with all the little niceties so dear to the feminine heart.

But, he told her with real sincerity, he held her in high regard, and he would do his best to make her happy.

"Oh, John!" Miss Tolliver said the words softly, reaching out to take his hand between both of hers. "You do me a great honor. But truly. You do not wish to be married, either. And truth be told, you know we would not suit."

He sighed heavily. "But you must marry one of us. And if you don't wish to marry Giles, and you won't marry Peter or Gillian or me—"

"Ahhhh." Understanding came. "It is so dear of all of you to ask, but I do not wish to be married. In a short time I shall go away, and you can all be comfortable again—"

"But we don't wish to be comfortable without you!" John said. "In fact—"

He was interrupted as the door to the library opened and the earl walked in, frowning at the sight of Miss Tolliver clasping his brother's hand between her own. Miss Tolliver, following his glance, hastily dropped her hands to her lap, unaware that her high color had led the earl to his own inaccurate conclusions.

"I believe you said we might have our game of piquet later, Miss Tolliver," he said, bowing in her direction while he watched his brother's face. John, his color also high,

turned away and picked up the glass behind him before
moving to the brandy to pour himself another splash.

"We are not finished—" Miss Tolliver began, but the
earl, walking forward, moved one piece to put her king in
check.

"Now I believe you are." His tone was pleasant, but
there was something in it that made both the lady and John
look at him sharply, and John took a step forward.

"Perhaps Miss Tolliver does not care to play—" he
began, and the earl turned to stare at him in a way that made
the lady rise hastily and say that yes, she thought it would
be nice . . . The earl bowed again and presented his arm and
she, after a moment's hesitation, put her hand on it and
walked with him from the room.

Miss Tolliver had thought they would join the others in
the drawing room, but that was not the case. Instead, the
earl ushered her to the back salon—known in his family as
the green room because it was hung with spring green
draperies, and the chairs upholstered to match—and after he
had seen her seated, and shut the door firmly behind them,
took up a post with his back to that room's mantlepiece, and
his arms folded before him.

"Now, Miss Tolliver," he said, "perhaps you would be
good enough to tell me why you were holding my brother's
hand."

"Oh, really!" Miss Tolliver had endured a trying time,
and his question was not helping it. "That is between your
brother and me—"

"Ah." The word was quiet, but it interrupted the lady
abruptly. "How foolish of me! Of course it was! As your
betrothed, I could have no reason to wonder why you were
holding another man's hands—"

"Oh, for goodness' sake!" Miss Tolliver rose and took a
hasty step away, turning to face him. "This has gone far
enough! In fact, this has gone much too far! Here you are
talking about our betrothal as if it is real, and there are you
brothers, proposing—"

"Proposing?" The earl straightened suddenly. "John—
proposed—to you?"

"Well, yes—"

"Of all the—" The earl took several purposeful steps toward the door. "We shall see about *that*!"

Miss Tolliver stared at him in amazement before crying out that if he planned to have words with one brother, he must have them with all three, because all three had proposed to her recently, and she was most tired of it.

"*What?*" Now it was the earl's turn to look amazed. Slowly he turned and walked back toward her.

"Miss Tolliver," he said. "Perhaps you had best tell me what this is all about."

In as few words as possible, she did. She told him that his brothers—with the best motives possible, and realizing that she was resolute in her promise not to hold the earl to their false engagement—had all proposed to marry her, "so that I won't be ruined in the sight of the world. It is most honorable of them. But I, too, have my honor, and I would no more force a man into marriage with me than—"

The earl was looking at her with a strange glint in his eye, and Miss Tolliver broke off to return his gaze inquiringly.

"Is that all—" he started. "Well, of all the—" With one quick movement he stepped forward and grasped her hand, raising it to his lips as he gazed down into her stunned face. "Margaret," he said, "will you marry me?"

Miss Tolliver, retrieving her hand to put it to her head, uttered a small sound of fury and, with a rustle of skirts and one short stop to glare in astonishment and say "Oh!" to him again, left the room.

Chapter
23

The earl stood stock-still for several moments, cursing himself for his heavy-handedness before, with a short, under-his-breath oath, he bounded after the lady. He did not think himself more than five seconds behind her, but as he rushed from the salon into the great hall, it was to collide with Sir Charles who was standing at the stairway watching his sister disappear up it with a melancholy sigh. At the sight of the earl's face, Miss Tolliver's brother sighed again.

"Told you you shouldn't play piquet with my sister," he said, and limped off toward the library in search of the earl's brandy.

"We didn't—" the earl snapped, but Sir Charles was no longer listening. That was not true of the earl's family, however. The doors to the drawing room stood open, and Giles turned to find his brothers' and his grandmother's very interested eyes upon him. Frowning, he advanced upon them.

"I would like a word with you—" he began, glaring at his brothers, but his word was brought up short at the sight of Aunt Henrietta, ensconced in a chair by the fire, doing her best to retrieve a bit of yarn from Lazaurus's interested beak. She seemed to feel Giles's eyes upon her at length, for she looked up and, finding all heads turned her way, smiled distractedly.

"He thinks it's a worm," she said, indicating the yarn and the belligerent rooster. "Poor boy. Perhaps he's hungry."

The earl agreed that that must be the case, and suggested that the lady go immediately to feed him. Corn would be nice, he said.

Aunt Henrietta agreed, but hesitantly. "Perhaps. But it won't do if he is hungry for worms."

"I beg your pardon?" The earl was looking down at her, his brow knit, and she kindly explained it to him. "Lazaurus is very picky. If he's hungry for worms, corn won't do. I know just how it is—no matter how many vegetables I eat, they'll never substitute if what I really want is a sweet."

The dowager countess, appearing much struck, vowed it was true. She noted that all the tea Caroline had poured for her had never been one whit as satisfying as a bottle of her husband's best claret. She beamed at her grandson as he turned to frown at her.

"Don't encourage her," Giles hissed, but the countess did. She recalled times out of mind when she had wanted one thing but substituted another, only to find that it would not do. Aunt Henrietta nodded agreeably and the earl, much frustrated, paced the room. His suggestion that they might at least *see* if Lazaurus would accept corn was pooh-poohed by everyone, his brothers, not eager to face his wrath, joining their grandmother in her objections. At last he hit upon the very thing and, calling his butler into the room, left that worthy bereft of words when told he was to take a lantern, Aunt Henrietta, and the rooster and search the garden for worms.

"For—worms, my lord?" the butler repeated, sure he could not have heard right. When assured that he had, his entreaty was almost tearful. "For *worms*, my lord?"

The earl's ruthless repetition of the words left him wondering if it was time he sought employment elsewhere, but the earl's suggestion that if he was busy, he might have one of the underfootmen do it did much to restore his peace of mind, and with a bow of great dignity he said that it would be done, merely waiting for Aunt Henrietta and Laz to precede him out of the room before, with lofty pomp, he shut the doors behind him.

"Now," the earl, who had escorted Henrietta to the door

said silkily as he turned to face the other occupants of the room. "*Now*, my dear family . . ."

His brothers, who had stood for some moments enjoying the scene before them, became suddenly busy. John bethought himself of some correspondence that required his immediate attention. Peter yawned and said he rather thought it was time for bed. And Gillian, usually the most casual of scholars, recalled a book that required his immediate attention in the library. All would have made good their escape but for the fact that their eldest brother stood in front of the door, and showed no disposition to move. On the contrary, he invited them—in a tone that brooked no argument—to take a seat because, he said, he wanted to talk to them. "*All* of you," he stressed, as his grandmother rose to leave. As she raised her eyebrows at him, he amended the statement to "If you would be so good, Grandmama."

Graciously the dowager countess said that she would.

"Now then." The earl advanced into the room, eyeing his brothers sternly. "I have had the most interesting conversation with Miss Tolliver."

The countess objected that Miss Tolliver could not have found it interesting, based on the way she had stormed from the salon and up the stairs. The earl ignored her.

"And I am given to understand," the earl continued, raising his quizzing glass and polishing it carefully on his sleeve before gazing at his brothers through it, reducing them to squirming silence as he did so, "that my brothers— *each* of my brothers—" and here he inspected each of them in turn, "has proposed to the lady."

"Really?" The announcement, which had John, Gillian and Peter shifting uneasily in their chairs, intrigued the countess, who sat up straight and clapped her hands together. "By all that's famous! What fun!"

"Fun?" The earl repeated the word, his tone making it clear he did not agree with her. The countess ignored him.

"You, too, John?" she questioned. "And Peter?"

Neither of her named grandsons seemed to find her incredulity flattering, nor did they appreciate her wistful "I wish I could have seen it!"

The earl told her crushingly that he had had the misfor

tune to observe the end of John's proposal, and the sight of Miss Tolliver holding his brother's hand had not filled him with any great pleasure.

"Why, John!" The countess was approving. "You sly dog! Perhaps there's hope for you yet!"

John cleared his throat and said it was no such thing; Miss Tolliver had been comforting him, that was all—

The earl's brow darkened and he said with some asperity that he hoped his brother would not require such comforting again. Nor did he appreciate the way they—*all* of them, he said, favoring his grandmother with a black look, too—had interfered in his life. He started to tell them that he did not want to find them meddling in his affairs any longer when his grandmother, who made it a policy never to let anyone younger than she was talk to her in such a way (and, as she liked to tell her friends, there were few people older than she anymore to scold her), straightened and, with a declared "The best defense is a good offense," launched an attack.

In a few well-chosen and extremely pungent words, she gave her eldest grandson to understand that he was *not* capable of handling his affairs; that they would be more than happy to refrain from "meddling," as he so rudely put it, and go on about their lives, if only he *would* get his affairs in order; and that if it *hadn't* been for their help—well, she said reflectively, gazing at her other three grandsons, for *her* help—Miss Tolliver would have left Willowdale several weeks earlier.

The earl had to admit that was true, but pointed out that if his brothers did not take up so much of Miss Tolliver's time—with Gillian capturing her morning rides, and Peter for afternoon talks, and John for interminable evenings of chess—he, Giles, might have more of an opportunity to fix his interest with her. His brothers stared at him in amazement.

"To *what*?" they echoed.

"To fix my interest," the earl returned. "It hasn't been easy; I can barely find a moment—"

"Then you *want* to marry Miss Tolliver?" Peter asked, eyeing his brother in surprise.

"Of course I want to marry Miss Tolliver!" the earl said

impatiently. "I'm a Manfield of Willowdale, aren't I? From what she tells me, we *all* want to marry Miss Tolliver!"

"But she doesn't know you do!" Gillian objected. The earl stared at him.

"She—what?"

"She doesn't know you want to marry her."

"Well, of all the—" The earl ran his hand distractedly through his hair as he glared at his brothers. "Doing it a bit too brown. I proposed to her, didn't I?"

"No," the countess said, unexpectedly entering the fray. "You didn't."

All eyes turned toward her in surprise. "You announced to Chuffy Marletonthorpe that you and Margaret were betrothed. In so doing, you announced it to her. You announced it to her brother. You announced it to us. But you never—as far as I can tell—*asked* her."

"So she thinks," John said, "that Giles—" he was eyeing his grandmother, but transferred his gaze to his older brother—"that you—are only marrying her out of chivalry."

"And she," the countess continued, snatching the conversation back again, "having impeccable manners, is determined to prevent you from a course that she feels has been thrust upon you. If only you had *asked* her—"

"I did," the earl replied grimly, surprising them all. "I figured out what you're saying this evening, and asked her moments ago. With disastrous results."

His brothers seemed to take his announcement seriously, but the dowager countess eyed him with disgust. "Honestly, Giles!" she said, "you put me all out of patience with you. Asked her this evening, did you? After no doubt yelling at her about finding her in the library holding John's hands—"

The earl's dark flush proved her words true, and his brothers glared at him. "You—yelled—at Miss Tolliver?" Peter said, springing up. "Shame on you!"

Never before had Peter spoken so to his eldest and most adored brother, and the earl stepped back, surprised.

"Yes, shame on you!" John seconded. "For if you could really have thought that I would try to steal a march on you with the woman you loved . . . Not that you ever let us know before that you loved her, and I'm sure we all believed, as

Miss Tolliver does, that you were continuing the engagement out of duty—"

"*I* didn't think so," Gillian said, surprising them all with his sudden entrance into the conversation. "Well, it stands to reason. She offered to cry off any number of times; Giles wouldn't have it." He noticed he momentarily had robbed John of speech, and nodded, satisfied. "I'm a lot smarter than you think I am—*Johnny*."

John was heard to say that if Gillian had any brain at all it would make him a lot smarter than John thought he was, and ended by asking why, if Gillian was so sure Giles cared for Miss Tolliver, he, too, had offered for her.

Gillian had an answer for that, too. "Thought she didn't want to marry Giles. Thought she ought to marry someone. Thought it might as well be me. After all, the whole kidnap confusion was a little bit my fault—"

"A little bit?" The words came from four mouths, and Gillian hunched a shoulder and subsided, muttering that all right, all right, he was the one responsible . . .

John seemed inclined to drive his responsibility home but the dowager countess interrupted him to say it was all water under the bridge, and they'd be wise now to turn their attention to what was the next best thing to do.

She had everyone's attention but the earl's; he was on his way to the door, saying over his shoulder that he intended to make a push that very night—

"And to lose," his grandmother called after him. "Really, Giles! *Do* try for a little sense! No doubt Margaret is upstairs right now packing—" The earl had turned at her first words, but at the last, started forward again—"and all she'll need to send her into the night will be you, pleading and storming at her, both at the same time, and swearing that you love her when all you've given her is reason to believe you're acting from honor. Do you think she's going to change her mind because you tell her differently?"

"But—" The earl was listening, and his grandmother's last sentence made him object. "But if she doesn't believe me when I tell her, what am I to do?"

"Show her!" the countess responded.

"But I can't do that if she leaves!"

"She won't leave."

"How can you be sure?"

The countess crossed her fingers behind her back. "I'll think of something."

Slowly the earl walked further into the room, his eyes narrowing as he scanned his grandmother's face.

"You will?"

She crossed her fingers again. "I always do."

With that the earl had to be content and, ignoring the sound of light rain on the windows, he and his brothers gathered close around the dowager countess who, with a wave of her hand, as if she were a magic sorceress, lowered her voice and said, "I have a plan."

Chapter
24

The countess lay awake most of the night, trying to hit upon a plan to keep Miss Tolliver from leaving the next day, and when she fell asleep in the early hours, nothing had yet occurred to her. She went down to breakfast that morning with a heavy heart, only to be met with the intelligence that Miss Tolliver's plans had indeed changed, and she and her family would be staying a while longer. Unable to take credit for this abrupt about-face, she asked her grandsons what had transpired, and was told that they all owed a debt of gratitude to Lazaurus, who was, at least indirectly, the cause of the Tollivers' postponement of departure.

"To the rooster?" the countess asked, pausing in mid-bite, a bit of egg hanging precariously from her fork as she frowned at the faces before her. "Don't try to gammon me, my boys! I'm too old for it! Now tell me truthfully—what happened?"

The earl told her—truthfully—that they really did have Lazaurus to thank. It seemed that Miss Tolliver had informed her brother of their imminent departure last night and, immune to both his threats and cajolings, had told him to pack or they would leave without him. But when she had visited her aunt's bedchamber, Henrietta had not been there and, Miss Tolliver thinking that the older lady was still below stairs, had determined on second thought to allow her aunt a good night's sleep before telling her that they were leaving.

To that end she had visited her aunt's room this morning, only to find that lady still in bed, a handkerchief to her nose and her voice husky as she informed her niece, with a great deal of dignity and a loud "achoo!" that Lazaurus had a cold.

One quick glance toward the supposedly ailing bird convinced Miss Tolliver that it was not he who was ill, and she hurried forward to place her hand on her aunt's forehead, and to exclaim with some concern that it was hot. Her aunt agreed, saying Lazaurus, too, had a temperature. Plus, she announced, he was achey and feeling chilled.

Miss Tolliver asked how that ever could have happened, and was told that it must have occurred last night when they were on their worm hunt.

In the process of tucking the blankets up around her aunt's shoulders, Miss Tolliver fell back a step to gaze at her in surprise.

"Worm hunt?" she echoed.

In a voice that was rapidly dwindling to a thread, Aunt Henrietta told her how Lazaurus, the underfootman, and she had spent much of the night in the garden, gathering worms until Lazaurus positively refused to eat another of the tender morsels the footman so—or at least, Aunt Henrietta said—willingly fetched for him.

"But my dear!" Miss Tolliver said, patting her aunt's hand sympathetically. "It rained last night!"

With great dignity her aunt told her that made for a productive worm hunt. "Worms come out when it rains, you know."

Miss Tolliver shook her head in amazement. "How did you ever—" she started.

Aunt Henrietta explained that Lazaurus had been hungry for worms—he had made that known by refusing to give up her yarn, and the earl—"truly a gentleman, he understands a rooster's needs so nicely"—had recommended that they go in search of worms immediately.

"The earl!" Miss Tolliver said wrathfully. "I shall have something to say to him!"

Aunt Henrietta said she had something to say to him, too, she wanted to thank him . . . But it would have to be later, after she had napped . . . And with that and another "achoo!" she snuggled under her bed covers and left her angry niece to go in search of the earl.

"And the long and the short of it is, the doctor has come and pronounced Aunt Henrietta suffering a severe cold, and said that she must stay in bed at least a week. Which means the Tollivers will be with us until she is better."

"Wonderful!" his grandmother approved, delighted. "Nothing could be better!"

"Well." The earl swirled the coffee in his cup and watched it consideringly as he replied. "Perhaps they could be a little better. Miss Tolliver says that although my actions have forced her to stay in my home, there is no way I can force her to speak to me."

His grandmother waved her hand and said that was nothing.

Even though her resolution was firm, Miss Tolliver found she could not long refrain from speaking with the earl. When she softly entered her aunt's bedchamber that afternoon, it was to find the invalid propped up on her pillows, her eyes upon a bouquet of flowers thoughtfully presented by the earl, one hand stroking Lazaurus and the other holding her handkerchief in ever-readiness.

"So kind (achoo!) of you (achoo!)" Henrietta was whispering to the earl, who bent politely forward to hear her. "Oh, look, (achoo!) Margaret," she said when she spied her niece, who would have slipped out again if her aunt were not so quick, "the earl has brought me these lovely (achoo!) flowers. And even"—she stroked her rooster fondly—"a worm for Laz."

"A worm?" Miss Tolliver, not wishing to carry her feud with the earl on in front of her aunt, cocked an eyebrow at the earl, who had the grace to appear contrite even as he rose to place a chair for her. "I thought Laz had had his fill of worms last night."

"Oh, no," Aunt Henrietta assured her gravely. "He was feeling decidedly peckish." Busy stroking the rooster, she did not see the grin that passed involuntarily between the earl and Miss Tolliver at her choice of words. Catching

herself, Miss Tolliver sobered immediately, but she knew
her moment to be lost, and replied quite civilly when his
lordship asked if she had gotten out to enjoy the day.

No, she told him, she had not. She had been busy
unpack—er—with other things. Aunt Henrietta looked at her
in concern and told the earl that Margaret was wont to
exercise every day, whether riding or walking. "The sun-
shine is good for her," Aunt Henrietta said seriously,
unaware that a person who spent the night in the rain
looking for worms was hardly an authority on good health.
"You must get out, Margaret! Really (achoo!) you must."

Her niece promised that she would do so, and the earl,
seeking an advantage, suggested that she might like to go
driving with him. "I know you like to ride, Miss Tolliver,"
he told her, "and I would be delighted if I might take you
driving. Perhaps, if you like, I could even teach you to
handle the ribbons."

Miss Tolliver had reached forward to soothe her aunt's
covers, but her hand stilled suddenly and she shot him a
sideways look before repeating, in an odd voice, "Teach
me, my lord?"

"Why, yes," the earl said, misunderstanding her tone. "I
would be happy to. There is nothing to be afraid of, I
promise you."

Miss Tolliver straightened and batted—yes, positively
batted—her eyes at him while replying in a too-bright voice,
"Why, how kind of you! But perhaps you are one of those
gentlemen who does not like his horses driven by a lady."

The earl *was* one of those gentlemen, in general, but, he
assured her gallantly, in this case his horses would be
honored. And, he added, speaking his thoughts aloud, there
would be no danger of his animals coming to grief while he
was in the carriage.

"But—" Aunt Henrietta whispered. Miss Tolliver patted
her hand.

"Yes, yes, Aunt," she said. "It is time you got some
rest. We are going."

She rose, and the earl, perforce, rose with her, following
her to the door as she asked him in a properly hesitant voice
if they might go driving that very afternoon. Happily the

earl agreed, and Miss Tolliver told him she would be with him as soon as she changed her dress. Thus it was that when she met her brother in the hall a half hour later and he asked where she was going, she told him with breathless pleasure that the earl was going to teach her to drive, and passed on to where that gentleman stood awaiting her at the door.

Charles, who found the earl's cellars and the earl's servants infinitely superior to his own, and who had no objections to the earl paying his living expenses indefinitely, was glad to hear she and the earl were going out together, and said absently that that was nice before limping on. He had taken several steps before the full meaning of her words sank in, and then he turned to stare after her departing figure in surprise.

"Margaret Marie!" he called, but the just-closed door prevented her answering him. Aloud he asked the hallway how that could be, when in Yorkshire his sister was known as a notable whip.

Once in the curricle the earl, who knew how many women were nervous around horses, determined to do nothing to frighten or startle Miss Tolliver. With that intention in mind he drove at such a sedate pace that the groom, hanging on behind, wondered what had come over his master, even venturing at one point to ask if his lordship was feeling quite the thing. Upon being assured that the earl was fine—never better—Hobson gave himself up to a deep and thoughtful scrutiny of the countryside, never letting on that the scenery that interested him the most was the earl's and the lady's heads. He listened in stony silence as the earl explained the art of driving a team in detail, and in astonishment as the lady—who had visited the stables one day when he was present and who had asked extremely knowledgeable questions about the earl's horses, calling his team of grays and the chestnuts "proper high bred 'uns"—asked a number of naive questions, exclaiming over the earl's prowess and grasping his arm, as if in fright, when he let the team break into a gallop. At once the earl brought them to a fast walk again.

When they had driven some miles, the earl very kindly

asked Miss Tolliver if she would like to try her hand at the
ribbons and, after a display of maidenly fear and confusion,
and a great many reassurances on his part that there was
nothing to it, and that he was right there to help her if need
be—along with the information that he felt they had gone
far enough for the freshness to wear off the team—Miss
Tolliver was convinced to take the reins. She then sat up
straight, touched the leader with her whip and caught the
thong in a manner reminiscent of the best of the Four Horse
Club, and drove the horses well up to their bits for several
minutes before slowing them to a walk again. With a sweet
smile at the thunderstruck earl and his grinning groom, she
handed the reins back to Giles saying, "I do believe you are
right, my lord. There is nothing to it."

The earl took the reigns automatically but dropped his
hands, allowing the team to break into a canter. Miss
Tolliver told him kindly to mind his horses.

He did, but continued to stare at her for some minutes—a
stare that was met by her wide-eyed look of inquiry.

"You knew how to drive all along!" he said at last.

"Why, your lordship," she replied, in that sweet-shy
voice that he realized now should have warned him of her
hoax. "How can you think so? You must know I was able to
do so only because I had such a good teacher."

The earl agreed that was so, asking who the teacher had
been.

"Why, your lordship—" she began again, but he told her
he could no longer be taken in. With a cheerful grin she
shook her head and said nothing.

"Was it your brother?" he asked at last.

That *did* bring a response from her as, with a scornful
"Charles? Charles couldn't drive a wheelbarrow through a
gate with any dependence!" she said that it had been her
father who taught her.

"He must have been a notable whip," the earl said, and
she agreed warmly that he was, whereupon they rode in
silence until their return to Willowdale, the earl only speaking as he helped her down from the curricle. Then, his
hands on her waist, he detained her a moment to say, with
the whimsical smile that always seemed to interrupt her

breathing, "You know, my dear, I said it once before, and I think it more true now than ever."

Miss Tolliver cocked her head expectantly, then gulped as he raised her gloved hand to his lips and kissed it gently, smiling into her eyes. "My brothers really did kidnap an actress."

Chapter
25

The week of her aunt's illness passed quickly for Margaret. In fact, it passed into a second week and then a third. There was a change in the tenor of her days—a change born in upon her gradually as she realized that all of the earl's family was working together to see that she and the earl spent time with each other.

The first time it happened, when she and Peter were participating in one of their illicit games in the billiards parlor, she thought it must be an accident. So intent was she on her shot that she did not hear the earl's entrance, and when Giles's arms slipped around her and his voice, warm in her ear, said, "No, no, my dear. You must hold the cue like this," and he illustrated his point with his hands over hers, she had been aware only of that odd breathlessness again, and her joy at hitting the ball under his tutelage.

When he joined her and Gillian on their morning rides, she had at first found nothing amiss; even when Gillian had, after several days, begged off with talk of attending to his studies, she had refused to think too deeply about what was happening. Truth be told, the earl was a much better companion than Gillian, whose neck-or-nothing riding style left little time for enjoying the beauty of the day.

The earl, however, was never averse to pausing for a view of some particularly fine horizon, or to stopping when she spied some fragile wildflower heretofore unseen. In fact, the gentleman considerably surprised her when he was able to identify almost all of the specimens she found so intriguing and, when her surprise became apparent in her face, to murmur almost apologetically, "I am sorry to disappoint you, my dear, but I am not really such a frivolous fellow as you think me. Botany happens to be a particular interest of mine."

Of course Miss Tolliver then must cry out at his belief that she considered him frivolous; her opinion was far from it. Actually, she found him quite—quite—

"Quite?" he pressed, watching her face closely as she strove to find the right word. It did not come, for with a firm grip on heart and tongue she finished the sentence with a laugh and the words "abominable, for teasing me like this."

"Abominable" was not the word the earl wished to hear, and with it he could not be content.

But the big change—the one that finally made Miss Tolliver face up to what was occurring, came in the evenings when John forsook his love of chess in favor of a game of whist with the earl, Miss Tolliver, and his grandmother, even going so far as to partner his grandmama at the table, nobly bearing up under her constant—and pungent—criticisms of his ability to play. And if that were not enough, there were even nights when the countess, the most inveterate of whist players, vowed that she was "not in the mood, and would just sit by the fire with a nice little cup of tea" while Miss Tolliver and the earl played piquet.

It wasn't that Miss Tolliver minded; she enjoyed her games at piquet with the earl more than she cared to admit even to herself, for in him she found a skilled and worthy opponent who neither asked for mercy—as her brother Charles so often did in so many irritatingly indirect ways—or gave it, as many men made a show of doing whenever they were playing with a lady. She and the earl, both normally cool-headed and determined to be in control, were quite evenly matched, and the excitement of the luck of the cards, and trying to outguess what her opponent would hold, increased her enjoyment of the evenings.

But as she sat one night before her mirror combing her hair, feeling its long, heavy fullness caress her neck and back, she stopped abruptly and, pointing the comb at her image, said severely, "You're being seduced, Margaret Marie, and you must be careful." Her image looked gravely back at her, nodding, and she sighed. "The great problem, my dear, is that you like it. And you know it cannot go on."

Still resolute in her determination to leave Willowdale when her aunt grew well enough to travel, Miss Tolliver told herself that it could not hurt to enjoy the inhabitants of the hall (not especially the earl, she thought, although she knew it was not true) to the fullest while she was with them, just to provide kind memories to warm herself on the cold nights in Yorkshire. She did not question too deeply why those nights seemed colder than ever now...

And so Miss Tolliver at last gave herself up to the full enjoyment of all Willowdale had to offer. Knowing she was leaving, knowing there could never be anything between the earl and herself, knowing that he was just being kind, and appreciating his kindness, she allowed herself to talk and laugh and tease with him without constraint. And if, she told herself, that meant a pang or two (or four thousand or more) later, it was worth the enjoyment now.

The only uneasiness Miss Tolliver felt as one week lengthened into three was over her aunt's continued illness. Although the sneezes and red nose had long disappeared, as the doctor had promised they would, Aunt Henrietta remained firm in her assertions that Lazaurus and she still had a cold, were not feeling well, could not possibly travel all the way to Yorkshire, and, in fact, should not even be out of bed.

To that end she spent a great many days snuggled under the covers relishing both the blood-curdling books so thoughtfully provided by the countess and the unending supply of chocolates that were the gifts of the earl, and not sneezing until Margaret noticed she was doing better, whereupon her answer was always a loud "achoo!"

Lazaurus, too, seemed content to perch either upon the windowsill, in Aunt Henrietta's knitting bag, or on the turned wooden foot of the bed, and if his continued good temper was the result of a bewildered footman's constant forays into the garden in search of beetles and worms, Miss

Tolliver was not to know. And she did not know, right up until the day she walked into her aunt's bedroom to see if that lady had any needs before she, Miss Tolliver, joined the earl for a drive. In the act of pulling on her gloves, Margaret stopped stock-still at the sight of her aunt, waltzing about the room, while the approving Laz sat on the bedspread providing an odd little tune for a dance of his own.

"Aunt Henrietta!" Miss Tolliver said, her eyes wide. Her aunt turned inquiringly at the voice, and stopped suddenly.

"Margaret!" Face and voice revealed signs of guilt. "I thought you had gone!"

In the midst of explaining that she had just stopped by to check on her aunt before leaving, Miss Tolliver's words ended abruptly and her gaze grew accusing. "You're not sick!"

"Oh! Well!" Her aunt suddenly placed one hand to her forehead and another to her stomach as she tottered carefully back to the bed. "Why, of course I am. Very sick. Amazingly so." She lifted the covers and slipped under them.

"No, you're not!" Miss Tolliver said. "You were just dancing!"

"Dancing?" Aunt Henrietta opened her eyes wide. "My dear, did you think I was *dancing* just now? That wasn't it. Not at all."

"Oh?" Miss Tolliver's face was polite but skeptical, and she stood, one hand cradling the elbow of the arm that had a hand supporting her chin and the fingers tapping her cheek. "Then what were you doing?"

"Why, I was just—just—" Inspiration struck. "I was just demonstrating something for Laz!"

"Oh?" Miss Tolliver was politer still. "And what were you demonstrating, Aunt Henrietta?"

"What—was I—demonstrating?" The words were repeated falteringly, and the old lady gazed around the room for help. Several moments passed, in which her niece stood suggestively tapping her foot, but at last inspiration struck again.

"I was demonstrating," she said with great dignity and a hand extended to smooth the feathers of her favorite bird,

"what would happen to Lazaurus if he were to rise from
his bed before he is ready. He would be quite disoriented,
you know; going in circles, weaving this way and that.
What you thought was *waltzing*, Margaret, was really my
interpretation of a disoriented—"

"Deranged, perhaps," her niece suggested politely.

"—chicken!" Aunt Henrietta ignored the interruption
and stroked the rooster's feathers again. "And now, dear, I
think you had better go. For after all the excitement,
Lazaurus—perhaps even I—oh, let us say, we—are in dire
need of a nap."

"Aunt Henrietta—" Miss Tolliver began, but that good
lady showed all the signs of being asleep already, her head
turned and her eyes closed in a way that made it clear there
would be no further conversation now. With slow steps and
biting her lip, Miss Tolliver moved toward the door, there to
turn and, discovering her aunt watching with one eye open, to
pause and inquire in the most bemused tone possible, "Aunt
Henrietta, who was it that told you—that is, Lazaurus—that
you both are still sick?"

"Why, the doctor, of course!" her aunt replied, surprised. Then she thought a moment. "Or was it the dowager
countess?"

Miss Tolliver's "aha!" was almost as sharp as the sound
with which she shut the door to her aunt's room, and she
moved swiftly down the hall, a martial light in her eye. The
dowager countess indeed! That meant they all—every one of
them, from Peter to Gillian to John to Giles to the countess—
had been part of a conspiracy, enlisting her own family as
well. At least, she told herself fairly, they had enlisted Aunt
Henrietta. Sir Charles, happily ensconced amid the earl's
port and the earl's chef's way with a joint of beef, would
have needed no convincing. She should have seen it all
before, but she, she told herself severely, had been too busy
woolgathering, pretending nothing had changed when of
course it had...

Her eyes were stormy as she hurried down the stairs, and
her chin came up as the front door opened and Gillian
walked in, smiling at her pleasantly. His smile faded as he

looked closer at her face and, scenting danger, he told her that he was in a great hurry because he had a great deal of studying to do.

Miss Tolliver told him that his studying could wait, adding with biting sarcasm that since he, too, had thought so for months, he must not try to gammon her now that he was a reformed character. He strove in vain to tell her how that wounded him, in fact—

She cut him off with a curt "Where are your brothers?" and he goggled at her in surprise.

"I say, Miss Tolliver," he began, growing gradually aware—for he was never a quick study—that her behavior was most unusual. "Has something occurred to upset you?"

"Upset me?" Her lip curled, and she glared up at him in a way that made him feel she was much taller than she really was. "Oh, no Gillian, what could upset me? How could it upset me that there is a conspiracy, right under this roof—right under my nose!—and that I am the one being conspired against? How could it upset me that—" She grew aware that he was hedging off, and reached out to grasp his lapel, glaring up at him again.

"Where did you say your brothers are?" she demanded. Hastily he told her that John and Peter were in the library while Giles was awaiting her in the blue salon, along with their grandmother.

"Aha!" Miss Tolliver heard herself say the word again and told herself sternly to try for a loftier tone. She sounded, she thought, like a character in a bad farce; next she would be rubbing her hands together in anticipation. She looked down to see she was doing just that and quit abruptly, fixing Gillian with that frosty stare that had him tugging at his cravat as if it had grown much too tight.

"Fetch John and Peter and bring them to the blue salon," she commanded, and when he stood a moment longer goggling at her, she stamped her foot and shouted, "Immediately!" Gillian disappeared like a wild hare, and Miss Tolliver, her back as rigid as the proudest soldier's, proceeded to the blue salon.

Chapter
26

Next to the library, the blue salon was Miss Tolliver's favorite room in Willowdale. It was decorated in varying shades of blue, from the very pale shade of the room's large rug—a lightness Miss Tolliver was sure was the despair of his lordship's housekeeper but which she, as the person who did not have to clean it, could much admire—to the medium blue of the richly papered walls, to the cerulean shade of damask that covered the high-backed sofa and large wing chairs, and the deeper, almost midnight blue of the velvet curtains that draped the deep windows, shutting out both night and the grayest of days. A blue porcelain figurine sat on the mantlepiece, framing a gilded clock, and it was seldom that Miss Tolliver could enter the room without appreciating the beauty to be found there. This day, however, she did so without difficulty. Nor did she seem to notice the loud slamming of the door behind her, a sound that brought both the countess's and the earl's heads up in surprise, distracting them from the numerous cards they had moments before been discussing.

"Miss Tolliver!" the countess said, surprised. "By the sound of it, I was expecting Gillian—"

"Gillian," Miss Tolliver said through clenched teeth, "will be here shortly."

"Oh?" The countess was eyeing her with some misgivings. "He will?"

"He will." Miss Tolliver nodded in satisfaction. "So will John and Peter."

"I see." The countess was treading carefully. "How very—nice."

"Yes," Miss Tolliver agreed affably. "How nice. It will be a family gathering."

The earl, who had been watching her face since her entrance, but who had not yet spoken, rose now and walked toward her, reaching out to take her arm. "My dear," he said. "Whatever has occurred—"

"Don't 'my dear' me, my lord," she told him, wrenching her arm out of his grasp and taking a hurried step backward, out of his reach. "I am not your dear—"

"But you are," he told her.

"No!" She glared at him. "I am not! I am a pawn in your game and the object of your conspiracy—" She was striding about the room now, her face flushed and her skirts rustling as she smacked one hand into the other—"but I am *not* your dear!"

"Miss Tolliver—" The earl started hastily toward her, but his grandmother, thinking it best that she now take a hand before these two silly children out-misunderstood each other to the point of no retreat, entered the conversation to say, "My dear, you look magnificent, striding about like that, but please, do come sit down. Watching you is quite fatiguing."

Miss Tolliver halted in mid-stride to turn a startled face toward her. Words of ill-use warred with the one other thought crowding into her head. The other thought won. "I look—magnificent?" she repeated.

"You do," the countess assured her. "Doesn't she look magnificent, Giles?"

"She *is* magnificent," her grandson seconded her, with that peculiar smile that always made Miss Tolliver aware of how warm the rooms were.

"I—" Ruthlessly Miss Tolliver pushed the flattery behind her, and her frown descended again. "No, I am not," she said crossly. "And I wish you would not so confuse the issue!"

"But my dear," the countess said mildly, "we do not yet

know what the issue is! Come—" she patted the sofa seat beside her invitingly "—sit down and tell us all about it."

It was a reluctant Miss Tolliver who at last stepped forward, her eyes moving suspiciously from the earl to his grandmother. Both retained their innocent expressions as, with grave reservations, she took her place beside the countess. The earl, seeing her seated, pulled up a chair to her right and leaned forward. Then, with every sign of courteous bewilderment, they asked her to tell them what it was that had distressed her so.

"You know very well what has distressed me so, and these innocent airs are no—" Miss Tolliver began crossly, only to be interrupted as the door opened and three decidedly ill-at-ease gentlemen entered the room.

"You—" John cleared his throat "—wanted to see us— Miss Tolliver?"

"Oh, yes!" the lady said, rising to greet them. "I most certainly do!" As they showed no inclination to move away from the door, she begged them to be seated, and said, "Come in—do come in! Peter, you can take my place here by the countess. And Gillian—there's a chair for you, and one for John—"

She ignored all the gentlemen's claims to the right to give her their chairs, saying with great dignity that she preferred to stand for what she had to say. Gillian, Peter, and John exchanged glances, but the earl and his grandmother continued only to regard her with polite interest.

"It has come to my attention," Miss Tolliver told them, her eyes raking her audience in a way that made Peter and Gillian squirm and John clear his throat again, "that I have been the dupe in your conspiracy—"

"Conspiracy?" The dowager countess appeared much surprised. "Why, my dear—whatever conspiracy is that?"

"You know very well what conspiracy," Miss Tolliver returned. "All of you know. I just left my aunt waltzing in her bedroom—"

"Your aunt is—waltzing—" the countess started.

"—in her bedroom?" the earl finished for her.

Miss Tolliver frowned at them. "Yes, she is. And even if she told me some faradiddle about demonstrating for Lazaurus what happens when an ill chicken gets up before he is fully recovered—''

"She told you—" the countess's lips began to turn up in spite of herself, and Miss Tolliver was much incensed to see the earl's shoulders shake.

"Yes, well, it's all very well for you to laugh," she told him roundly, "but my aunt never used to lie to me, and—"

"But my dear!" he interrupted her, "a demonstration for an ill chicken!" This time he could not contain himself, and his laughter burst out; the countess followed suit.

"An ill chicken!" she said, wiping her eyes. "I do enjoy that woman!"

"Yes, well—" Miss Tolliver felt her own ever-lively sense of humor threatening to overcome her, and tried firmly to bring the situation back in hand. "That's all very well. But what I want to know is, *why*? Why have you constrained my aunt to act against me—"

Quickly the countess assured her there had been no constraint. "Your aunt likes it here, Margaret."

"Yes, but—" Try as she might, Miss Tolliver did not seem able to bring them to an understanding of the full depth of their perfidy. "That is all very well. But you all know it is only a matter of time until we leave, so why did you choose to postpone it this way—"

"Because we don't want you to go!" Peter said, rising suddenly to come forward to catch her hand and to gaze entreatingly up into her face. "We want you to stay with us. Always."

"Oh, Peter." She smiled, and put a gentle hand to his cheek. "My dear, you know I cannot."

"But why?" Peter cried. "Giles loves you! We all do."

A flush rose in Miss Tolliver's cheeks, and she turned her head away. "No, no," she said. "Gi—I mean, the earl—is acting only out of his code of honor—"

"No." Her startled eyes turned to the earl's as he too rose and came forward. "Gi—you mean, the earl—is not. Peter is right. Giles loves you."

Miss Tolliver cried that it could not be true, recalling to his mind the look of disgust that crossed his face that long-ago day when he first announced their engagement to

Chuffy Marletonthorpe. He possessed himself of both her hands and stood smiling warmly down at her.

"Did it occur to you, my dear, that my feelings might undergo a change since that time? That I might have moved from feeling obliged to marry you to feeling I cannot live without you?"

"No." Miss Tolliver's lips parted in amazement, and she seemed unable to move as she stood staring up at him. Clearly it had not.

"Lord, yes, Margaret," the countess seconded him from her interested post on the sofa. "He has been in love with you as long as you've been in love with him. Maybe longer."

"In—love—*with me*?" Miss Tolliver turned her dazed eyes toward the countess and then back toward the earl. With great resolution she pulled her hands from his and said that it could not be; it was just his chivalry, and his love of mastery, so that if one told him something could not be, he must say immediately that it could . . .

"Margaret!" The earl captured her hands again. "For a generally sensible woman, you say the most extraordinarily foolish things!"

"It's love," the countess interjected wisely, nodding at her other three grandsons. "Love walks in and reason goes out the window. It was the same with your grandfather and me."

Miss Tolliver, with the earl looking at her just so, was having great difficulty concentrating, but she turned her eyes to the countess again. "It—was?"

"Just like," the countess approved. "'In the end I had to marry him. Just to save him from himself. Couldn't let the whole world know what a gudgeon he was, you know. I liked his family. Had to protect their name."

"Ah." Miss Tolliver nodded wisely, and her eyes began to twinkle. "I see. I should marry his lordship for your sakes—"

"Yes!" chorused the countess and her three youngest grandsons, but they were overborn by a forceful "No!" from the earl. Miss Tolliver gazed at him inquiringly.

"You should marry his lordship," the earl said, each

word deliberate as he raised her hands to his lips and gracefully kissed each finger, "for his lordship's sake. And for your own."

"Gi—I mean your lordship—" A blushing Miss Tolliver was finding it difficult to speak. "You forget yourself—"

"Giles," he corrected her, kissing her fingers again and watching her face in enjoyment as she tried to pull her hands away. His hold remained firm.

"Your lordship—"

"Giles." He seemed to have a particular interest in the tip of her middle finger, rubbing his lips against it in a way that made the normally capable Miss Tolliver feel rather— well—incapable.

"Giles!" she said. "Really! There are other people in the room—"

"Yes," he agreed, smiling at her in approval and releasing her hands to turn to them. "I have noticed that. I cannot imagine why they are still here!"

"Oh!" The word came from four mouths as four very interested pairs of eyes met his lordship's and read the meaning there. "Yes! Of course!"

"Studying to do—" said Peter.

"Correspondence," said John.

"Got to see a man about a horse—" Gillian tried. The earl corrected him gently with one word. "Library."

"Library," agreed the crestfallen Gillian, and the brothers moved from the room.

"Grandmama?" the earl questioned politely as the dowager countess seemed disposed to remain on the sofa, smiling brightly at them.

"I have no place to go," she said, her tone tranquil as she smoothed the stiff black silk of her gown. "I have no correspondence, and no studying to do."

His lordship suggested that she could read a book—one of the lurid romances so dear to her heart. The old lady sighed and said she did not feel like reading. His lordship's eyes glinted.

"Did I tell you, Grandmama, that just this morning we laid in a new supply of sherry? I'm told it is the best we've had in years . . ."

"Oh?" The old lady looked up sharply, and rose. "Perhaps," she said, drifting across the room, "I will spend an hour or two reading . . ."

With a quick stride the earl moved to open the door for her. "I told you it would work out," she said, pausing to pat his cheek before she departed. "And in time for the ball, too . . ."

"Ball?" Miss Tolliver pricked her ears at the word. "What ball?"

"Oh." The countess turned dreamily to face her. "Didn't we tell you, dear? We're hosting a ball a fortnight hence to celebrate your engagement. Nothing large—perhaps 200 people. It will be a costume ball."

"Two hundred people—" Miss Tolliver began, aghast. "No, you *didn't* tell me—"

"A costume ball?" the earl interrupted. "We did not speak of a costume ball, Grandmama."

"Oh?" She turned vague eyes toward him. "Did we not, my love? How strange, for I distinctly remember writing it on the invitations . . ." She paused. "Your grandfather and I announced our engagement at just such a ball."

The earl was heard to say that he did not care for costume balls. His grandmother smiled, and patted his cheek again. "Dear Giles!" she said. "Neither did your grandfather!"

Then she drifted from the room, and the earl, with a philosophical shrug, turned to face Miss Tolliver.

"Well, sir?" she challenged, chin up.

He took a purposeful step forward. "Yes," he told her. "It is very well, Miss Tolliver!"

Chapter
27

It was some time before Miss Tolliver could bring the earl to a proper sense of duty, or to an understanding of his own duplicity, for he seemed much more interested in exploring the area between her right earlobe and the nape of her neck than in attending to her questions—an exploration that did not seem exerting to him, but which left her oddly breathless.

"Now, sir," she said for the fourteenth time, firmly removing his hands from her waist and turning resolutely to face him. "Do behave! I have asked you and asked you about the people who have been invited to this ball I know nothing about—"

"And—" she continued, resolutely pushing away his hands as he reached for her again, "I do not believe that I have yet received a formal offer of marriage." She bethought herself of John, Gillian, and Peter, and amended that to "from you." Then she remembered the scene in the green salon, and conscientiously changed her statement to "that I have accepted."

The earl grinned. "Miss Tolliver," he said, considerably surprising her by taking her hand and dropping to one knee, "will you do me the honor of becoming my wife?"

The next surprise was his. "Why la, sir!" she cried, her other hand fluttering to her heart as she opened her eyes wide. "This is so unexpected!"

"Dash it, Maggie—" he began, starting to rise. Hurriedly she put her hand on his shoulder to push him down again.

"Are you sure, Giles?" Her eyes searched his face, all hint of banter gone. "Because it isn't what either of us expected or wanted that day at Mrs. Murphy's inn—and my brother Charles assures me I am not an easy person to live with—"

The earl nodded sagely. "That, my dear, is very true. But—" he stopped her protest by turning her hand over and kissing her palm "—I have found that you are also impossible to live without!"

"Oh, Giles!" The capable Miss Tolliver was surprised to hear herself giggle. "What a romantic thing to say!"

Pleased with his success, his lordship continued to pour romantic sayings into her ears for a considerable amount of time until Miss Tolliver, her conscience recalling her reluctantly to duty, remembered that she really should go tell her aunt that there was no reason for Aunt Henrietta—or Lazaurus— to be sick anymore. Her aunt took the news in good part, saying that in that case she rather thought they—that is, Laz—would be better tomorrow, since she had received another book and a box of chocolates from the earl that seemed likely to keep her in bed the rest of the day.

Hiding a smile, her niece kissed her cheek and told her that she was very happy she would so soon be well. Her aunt nodded abstractedly, her eyes fixed on the printed page before her, and with a vague wave of her hand suggested that Margaret go away and entertain herself. Margaret promised to do so, and was almost out of the room when her aunt's soft voice recalled her, and she turned questioningly.

"I am very happy for you, Margaret," Aunt Henrietta said simply. "He is a good man. Lazaurus likes him."

If Aunt Henrietta was pleased with the news of her niece's *real* betrothal to the Earl of Manseford, Sir Charles was thrilled. Delighted. Ecstatic, even. In fact, Miss Tolliver told him with just the teeniest bit of pique that one would think it was Sir Charles himself who was getting married. And she asked, her tone dry, if it was his joy at her joy, or his joy at knowing he would now have continued access to the earl's well-stocked cellars, that made him so happy.

"No, no, Margaret," he assured her, pumping her hand

vigorously. "It is you I am thinking of—*your* happiness must of course be of the greatest moment to me. Twenty thousand pounds, Margaret! Think of it! The estates you'll have! The estates I'll visit! The jewels! The horses! The settlements—" Thought of the settlements made his face brighten further, and he vowed to seek the earl out immediately to discuss them.

"Because I am sure that he would not want to be backward in any attention, and neither would I, so we must discuss—"

"Charles," his sister said softly, and he paused in his perambulations to beam at her, assuming an air of great interest in anything she might have to say.

"Be careful in the settlements, Charles," she told him. "Because if I hear that you have done anything to embarrass me, arranged anything even the smallest bit uncalled for or pretentious, been anything but humble and unassuming in your requests, I promise you that when I am Countess of Manseford you will not be welcome in any of the earl's abodes."

"Here!" Visions of largess disappeared before his eyes, and Charles's brow darkened. "I say! Of all the scaly. . . That is no way to talk to the head of your family—"

Miss Tolliver smiled. "It is, however, the way I have found necessary to see that you are quite clear on my meaning."

He gave her to understand that she had wounded him deeply; that he had only her best interests at heart and he didn't know how she could think—could imagine for even one moment—that it was anything else. Then he somewhat spoiled the effect of his earnest declarations by adding that he didn't know why she expected him to do with a paltry amount when she would be living on the earl's twenty thousand pounds. A year.

Miss Tolliver told him quite pleasantly that she did not expect him to understand it, but the earl's money had nothing to do with her decision to wed. "There are some things more important than money, Charles."

"Well, yes—" He thought deeply, then objected. "But it takes money to buy those things!"

Miss Tolliver shook her head at him. "Charles, Charles, Charles. No matter what the situation, I can always depend on you to say something incredibly asinine."

"Now see here—" he said in a huff, but Miss Tolliver would not see.

"Just remember, Charles," she told him, walking from the room. "All things in moderation. *All* things. Even settlements."

It was a considerably crestfallen Sir Charles Tolliver who met with the Earl of Manseford later.

During the next two weeks Miss Tolliver learned that it was the dowager countess's grand plan to have a ball to announce their wedding, based on that lady's belief that once 200 of their nearest and dearest friends knew of the bridal plans, Miss Tolliver would hesitate even more to draw back. The invitations had been sent out without Miss Tolliver's knowledge to that end, but now that dear Margaret knew about the ball, why, that was all right, too. Now she could start earlier to help with the many details that accompany such an affair.

Miss Tolliver thanked the countess with becoming meekness for her graciousness in allowing Miss Tolliver to spend her days indoors soothing cook and housekeeper, while outside the sky was blue and the weather warm, and other people— just *some* other people, you understand—might have rather spent their time riding, driving, or walking in the garden. The countess, who held that all sunlight was injurious to the complexion, patted Margaret's hand and told her she was not one of those people.

"Posted and riposted," Miss Tolliver murmured, and asked just who comprised the guest list for the coming gala.

"Now you mustn't be thinking that none of your friends will be invited," the countess told her, patting her hand again, "for your aunt and brother supplied us with a great many names on your behalf. Such as—Cressida Fallsworth." At random the countess picked up a card of acceptance that had arrived that morning.

"Cressy Fallsworth!" Miss Tolliver sat bolt upright. "I detest Cressy Fallsworth!"

The countess gazed at her in surprise. "Lord Mortimer Raleigh?" she ventured, selecting another of the cards.

Miss Tolliver's consternation grew. "Mortimer Raleigh proposed to me the first year of my coming out, and I told him at that time that I would never—positively never—marry. And you invited him to my betrothal ball?" Worriedly she asked to see the list supplied by her family. The names that came from her brother were quite unexceptional—even if, she noticed in amusement, they were people much more acquainted with Charles than with herself—but her Aunt Henrietta's list was composed solely of persons Miss Tolliver always found it difficult to decide if she disliked more or less than visiting the toothdrawer.

When Henrietta was taxed about this, she gazed at her niece in surprise, and said it could not be so. After all, she told them, when the countess first approached her she had sat down and made two lists; one of the people Margaret most liked, and one of the people she most did not like. Then she had thrown the one list away.

"But why—" her niece started.

Aunt Henrietta's surprise deepened. "Why, so I wouldn't get confused, my dear!"

"But you did get confused!" the countess told her indignantly. "You gave me the wrong list!"

"I did?" Aunt Henrietta picked up Lazaurus and prepared to drift from the room. "I certainly didn't mean to! How extraordinary!"

Miss Tolliver's rueful eyes met the countess's indignant ones. "My dear countess, it promises to be a most—unusual—party!"

"But why would all these people come if you don't like them?" the countess almost wailed as she indicated a pile of acceptances.

Miss Tolliver smiled and said that an invitation to a ball at Willowdale must mend a lot of relationships. With a snort of disgust, her elderly companion hoped that being in costume would make it all all right, adding, "You must just try and guess who the most objectionable of the people are, my dear, and avoid them."

"But in dominoes and masks they'll all look alike!"

The countess shrugged philosophically, and suggested that Miss Tolliver avoid everybody. Privately Miss Tolliver thought that would be a trifle hard to do at her own engagement ball.

It *was* difficult. Miss Tolliver, in the soft blue domino she had draped around her so that the long, loose cloak covered her hair and gown, surveyed the crowd before her and sighed. His lordship, standing against the wall in his scarlet domino (his grandfather, his grandmama had assured him, wore just such a one at their engagement ball, a statement that effectively forestalled any further argument that he would rather wear black) engrossed in conversation with whom she guessed must be Chuffy Marletonthorpe, was easy to identify. The countess she could readily recognize by her size and the brisk way she moved, plus the fact that she was closely shadowed by two gray dominoes, Caroline and Cassandra having returned—despite their mother's vigorous objections—for the event with the pleasing news that Cousin Elizabeth was, upon Caroline's departure, becoming a keen lover of coffee, and upon Cassandra's leaving, about to fall into a great decline.

Aunt Henrietta was easy—she was the small pink domino carrying a rooster. And Charles, she believed, was the puce domino—how like Charles to choose puce!—making frequent forays into the supper room, where a rich supply of viands and the earl's best champagne flowed freely.

Gillian, she decided, was the tall man in dark green; his golden hair gave him away. Peter, she knew, had declined being present, the thought of 200 people he did not know enough to make him decide he would rather spend the evening in another wing. She had to guess at John, but thought him the slightly portly figure in charcoal gray tugging uncomfortably at his mask while he listened with painful duty to a most talkative feminine figure in gold. There was something about that figure that said "Cressy Fallsworth" to Miss Tolliver, and she turned to move the other way, knocking against a black domino as she did so, and offering a smile and a soft "excuse me."

"Ah, Margaret, Margaret, Margaret," said a melancholy voice, and her heart sank. She knew that voice.

"Why, Mortimer! How nice to see you!"

The figure in black shook his head from side to side, reminding her—as if she needed reminding—of how ponderous he had always been. "Margaret, Margaret, Margaret," he repeated.

"Excuse me, my dear," said a welcome voice to her left, "but I believe this is our dance."

Gratefully she looked up into the scarlet domino's face, and with an "Oh, yes—please, Mortimer, excuse me," she glided off on the earl's arm, answering "Later!" to Mortimer's astonished objection that he needed to talk to her.

As they moved through the steps of the dance, the earl smiled teasingly down at her. "Your past is coming back to haunt you, Miss Tolliver?"

"No such thing!" she answered primly. "Not the past— more of a strange nightmare!"

"I hope—" there was that teasing smile again "—that soon you will have reason for much sweeter dreams."

Movement in the dance parted them again, preventing Miss Tolliver from retort. It was just as well. She did not know what to say.

The next few hours were busy ones for Miss Tolliver. There were so many black dominoes at the ball that she could not avoid them all; and each time she turned around she seemed to walk straight into the one that contained Mortimer Raleigh. And each time he begged a word with her, only to find her spirited away by this partner or that, until his face and voice grew more melancholy with each meeting.

So when, about midnight, a note was delivered into Miss Tolliver's hand as she stood by one of the open windows fanning herself, waiting for his lordship to return with a glass of lemonade, she was not surprised to read it and find "The black domino urgently requests a few moments of your time this evening. Please meet me by the small pond in the gardens at 12:30 A.M. Please, dear Margaret, do not fail."

With a sigh she decided she owed him that—after all, Mortimer had tried for years, in his stuffy way, to please her, and although she had done her best to prevent his continuing to care, he had remained as faithful as a—the word dog sprang to mind, and she tried to banish it, only to find that an image of a large and sad-eyed St. Bernard so fit her would-be suitor that she could not help but giggle. But, mindful that the announcement of her engagement was to be made at 1 A.M., when all masks were removed, she determined to spare Mortimer no more than fifteen minutes of her time. Mortimer would understand that, she knew; he was a stickler for punctuality.

When the earl returned with her lemonade, Miss Tolliver chatted easily with him for several minutes and then, after inquiring the time and having him consult his large pocket watch, she excused herself, saying tranquilly that the lace on her gown had torn slightly while dancing, and she wanted to slip away to mend it before the tear grew bigger. The earl agreed and watched her go, only reminding her that they had an interesting announcement to make at 1 A.M., and he hoped she would return by then. She smiled and said she believed she could make it, and was almost out of the room when the earl, chancing to glance down, saw the small piece of paper Miss Tolliver had thought was safely tucked into the edge of her chair; apparently her movement had dislodged it.

He started to call to her, realized she was too far away, and, with a shrug, determined to give it to her later—and to tease her about it, too, he decided, after a quick glance at its contents. Like Miss Tolliver, the earl knew the note must come from Lord Mortimer Raleigh and, like Miss Tolliver, he felt he had nothing to fear there. The earl knew Lord Raleigh from his clubs in town and thought him a dull dog and a high stickler. Giles had watched in amusement Raleigh's efforts to confront Miss Tolliver all evening; and if she now chose to give him the opportunity—and to spare him embarrassment by meeting him in private—well, it was all right with the earl. As long, he would tell her with mock severity—oh, he could see her eyes spark now—as she did not plan to go on meeting strange men at odd hours after they were married.

And so the earl went pleasantly on, mingling with his

guests, gaining experience in why Miss Tolliver did not
favor Cressida Fallsworth and several of the others on her
aunt's list. He was standing by the refreshment table ex-
changing a jest with Gillian and John, both of whom had
repaired there for sustenance, and turned with a smile when
a hand touched his sleeve.

"Sir!" said a voice, and the earl's smile started to fade.
"If you please, where is Miss Tolliver?"

The earl's eyes narrowed. "Raleigh?"

"Yes, sir!" Lord Raleigh struck a pose of outraged
drama. "It is I! And I ask you again, *where* is Miss Tolliver?
I *must* speak with her."

"I thought," his lordship said slowly, setting his champagne glass down with a snap, "that she was in the garden,
meeting with you."

"In the garden—" Lord Raleigh's jaw worked several
times. He gave them to understand that if that was the earl's
idea of a jest, it was not his, for he would never do
something so improper as to meet a betrothed lady—or any
lady—in a dark garden at night. And further, he said, he
was aware of how insidiously the earl had kept Margaret
from him that evening, and he wanted—he wanted—

What he wanted was never known, for the earl, with a
grim "Follow me" to his brothers, was out the door. They,
after one swift glance of surprise, followed swiftly.

"But where are we going?" Gillian managed to ask as
they strode purposefully through the ballroom, attracting
considerable attention as they crossed the dance floor.

"To the garden," the earl said through clenched teeth.
"To the pond. If anything has happened—" Once out of the
ballroom he started to run, and his brothers ran with him.

Long before they reached the garden pond they heard
sounds that made it clear something had indeed happened.
Excited women's voices and the crowing of a rooster
intermingled with an oath or two, and John and Gillian
again exchanged glances as they forged ahead. When they
rounded the last hedge, it was to find Miss Tolliver standing
at the edge of the pond, one hand on her hip and a martial
gleam in her eye. With the other hand she held a large rake,

apparently left there by one of the gardeners. To her left was a sputtering Aunt Henrietta, and at her feet danced an indignant Lazarus, crowing and clucking in the most scolding way.

In the pond sat a thoroughly soaked Harry Marletonthorpe, his black domino wrapped around his legs in a manner that made it difficult for him to rise; an action made even more difficult by the fact that every time he tried it, Miss Tolliver used her weapon in hand to knock him down again.

At this sight the earl stopped suddenly, grinned, then moved forward with a leisurely stroll until he stood by his betrothed, gazing down at the seething Harry.

"Good evening, Marletonthorpe," he said, polishing his quizzing glass before raising it to peer at the man in the water. "That is, if you think it a good evening. Some people might find it a trifle—ah—damp."

He took the rake from Miss Tolliver with a pleasant "I don't think you'll be needing that anymore, my dear," and smiled at a bristling Aunt Henrietta who bustled up to him with a terrible frown to tell him severely that he had some very odd friends—very odd indeed—and that Lazarus was not used to such goings on, and never would be, and that if he didn't change his ways, well, she just couldn't answer, no, she couldn't—

The earl raised a hand in self-defense and with a smile for her alone, asked Miss Tolliver to tell them all what had transpired that evening.

It seemed, Miss Tolliver said, that Harry Marletonthorpe had sent her the message she believed came from Mortimer Raleigh—she paused, suddenly self-conscious, but the earl nodded and told her he knew all about it. She smiled in relief.

And when she had met Harry by the pond, it became clear that his motives were nefarious; having heard from his brother Chuffy that the earl and Miss Tolliver would be announcing their wedding at 1 A.M., he—Harry—had meant, by fair means or foul, to prevent Miss Tolliver's appearance at that hour.

"And all," Miss Tolliver said indignantly, "to embarrass you, Giles!"

There was something about the glint in the earl's eye that made Harry, about to rise, think better of the idea, and the earl nodded his approval of the other man's judgment before he begged his betrothed to continue.

"Well," Miss Tolliver told him, "you can imagine that I was not pleased! I told Mr. Marletonthorpe that he was a despicable toad—"

"—most true," the earl murmured, watching Harry.

"—and that I did not mean to stay talking with him one moment longer. Then he grabbed me—"

"*He what?*" Three voices interrupted her as the earl, John, and Gillian all stiffened.

"Well, yes," Miss Tolliver said, "it was most foolish of him, but he did grab me. And as I was struggling with him—"

"You struggled?" The earl's words were silky-soft, but Harry shifted uneasily in the water.

"I did," Miss Tolliver affirmed. "And just as I was doing so, Aunt Henrietta and Lazaurus came around the shrubbery (it seemed Lazaurus had grown tired of the festivities, and thought a nice walk and search for worms or beetles would be just the thing), and Lazaurus came at once to my rescue."

The earl looked down at the still-ruffled rooster. "Lazaurus?" he repeated.

"Yes." Miss Tolliver spoke with great fondness of how the bird had rushed forward to peck and scratch the back of Harry's legs and when that gentleman—no, she corrected herself, nobleman; there could be such a difference—was startled, and loosened his grip on the lady to ward off the angry rooster, she was able to push Mr. Marletonthorpe into the pond.

"Ah." The earl smiled. "The capable Miss Tolliver."

Her return of his smile was interrupted by the still-frowning Henrietta, who informed the earl that Lazaurus was seriously upset.

"Lazaurus," she told all and sundry, her head bobbing up and down to emphasize each word, "does not like bad men."

"No," the earl agreed, his gaze returning to the dripping

Harry. "I find I am not too fond of them myself. But I suppose one must do the gentlemanly thing . . ."

With a sigh, he reached down a hand to pull the wet Harry from the pond. Mr. Marletonthorpe, much relieved, grasped it and, with Giles's help, was able to rise, unwinding the cloak from his legs as he did so. John, Gillian, and Aunt Henrietta stared at the earl in disgust, while Miss Tolliver watched him in surprise.

"Now you are on your feet, Harry?" the earl questioned, and Marletonthorpe, running a wet hand across his even wetter nose, nodded.

"Good." With great satisfaction the earl aimed his famous right at that nose, knocking Mr. Marletonthorpe down again.

"Bravo!" John shouted.

"I knew you couldn't let him get away with it!" Gillian seconded. The earl silenced them with one motion.

"I probably should have done that long ago, Harry," he said to the man nursing his nose in the water. "It might have done us both some good. But now—well, I do not believe you were invited to this party, and we can certainly dispense with your presence from it."

And so saying, he turned with a bow to his affianced wife, offered her his arm, and proceeded to walk away, with Aunt Henrietta, John, and Gillian following.

"You know," Miss Tolliver said, smiling up at him as they strolled back to the house in the moonlight. "I think it is a very good thing that we are to wed."

"You do?" The earl's eyes were warm as he gazed down at her.

"Yes." Miss Tolliver smiled first at him, and then at the brown bird strutting self-importantly before them. "After all, Lazarus *likes* you!"

There was a pause, and the lady grinned. "Truth be told, so do I!"